Beyond the Storm

Beyond the Storm

E.V. THOMPSON

ROBERT HALE · LONDON

Hardback ISBN 978-0-7090-9088-5
Paperback C Format ISBN 978-0-7090-9180-6

Robert Hale Limited
Clerkenwell House
Clerkenwell Green
London EC1R 0HT

www.halebooks.com

2 4 6 8 10 9 7 5 3 1

Printed in Great Britain by the MPG Books Group,
Bodmin and King's Lynn

Book One

Chapter One

ALICE KILPECK'S FIRST glimpse of the Trethevy rectory that would be her home for the foreseeable future filled her with a dismay that came very close to despair.

The house was large, certainly, she estimated it must contain at least five bedrooms, but it was a jumble of a building that seemed intent upon offering the many angles of its sagging grey slate roof to all four points of the compass.

All this could be observed beyond a high granite stone wall as Alice and her brother David – the *Reverend* David – riding in a trap pulled by a willing little pony, approached the rectory along a pot-holed and neglected lane that followed the bleak cliff top of the north Cornish coast.

There was no more than a light breeze blowing today, but Alice could imagine that in a north westerly gale the exposed byway would be a very dangerous place for an unwary traveller.

'The rectory doesn't exactly look *inviting*,' she said, hesitantly.

The words did not reflect the true strength of her misgivings, but this was her newly-ordained brother's first appointment, albeit only as rector of a tiny parish, long-neglected and subordinate to the vicar of neighbouring Tintagel. She did not want to dampen the enthusiasm she knew he felt for his first real challenge as a cleric, but she realised she would need to try very hard if she was to keep the dismay she felt, to herself.

'We can hardly see more than the rooftop,' David pointed out, 'and it *is* a very old house. It is all very exciting, really …' Then, aware of her genuine misgivings, he added, 'It will probably be a whole lot better when we can see it properly.'

His optimism was to prove sadly misplaced.

In order to enter the rectory grounds David needed to guide the pony off the lane through what appeared to be – and smelled like – a farmyard, before turning right into a track that dropped steeply away in the direction of a heavily wooded valley through which a swiftly flowing stream tumbled over a rocky bed on its way to the sea. From here they performed another sharp turn into the rectory grounds – and Alice's spirits dropped even farther.

The garden was so overgrown it was difficult to make out where paths were, or where they had once been. Hidden behind undergrowth and overgrown shrubbery, what little could be seen of the rectory itself revealed dirty diamond-shaped panes of glass and peeling paintwork.

Even David's enthusiasm faltered at the forlorn appearance of their new home and he said, 'Dean Fitzjohn said the rectory had not been lived in for a long time but I don't think he could have realised quite how neglected it has become.'

Dean Fitzjohn, of Windsor, was a distant relative of Alice and David. He was also, by virtue of his office, patron of this remote Cornish sub-parish and responsible for offering the living of it to David.

Alice, who had kept house for her older brother since the death of their widowed mother soon after his ordination, had come along to take care of him here, in Cornwall.

The main church was in nearby Tintagel, but the vicar, Reverend Emmanuel Carter, himself appointed by the Dean, also held the lucrative post of headmaster at a school in Devon, many miles from his parish, and so spent little time attending to his pastoral duties.

Complaints had reached the ears of the Dean that parishioners were experiencing difficulties obtaining the rites of the established Church for christenings, marriages and funerals and he had decided to appoint a rector to take charge of the tiny church at Trethevy who might also take on some of the duties being neglected by the vicar of Tintagel.

Leaving the pony and trap outside the door with the trunks which held their belongings, it was with a heavy heart that Alice entered the near-derelict rectory behind her brother after he had unlocked the front door, trying to ignore the protests of hinges that had not been called upon to exercise their function for many years. Much to her relief, she observed that the property was furnished, although everything appeared to be old – and very, very dusty.

Aware that his sister was dismayed by the home to which he had brought her, David said, 'I'll go outside, unload the trap and find somewhere to stable the pony. While I'm doing that you can go upstairs and have first choice of a bedroom.'

Alice realised that David too was deeply disappointed with this, his first appointment within the Church of England. Hiding her own feelings, she said, 'It's been a long time since the house had anyone to love it, David, but we'll soon have it looking like a home, you'll see.'

Despite her words of encouragement, when David had gone outside Alice climbed the stairs with considerable trepidation, dreading what state of neglect and decay she was going to find.

Up here it smelled musty and she noticed patches of black mould around the windows, an indication that the house was damp. She initially looked into only two of the bedrooms, aware that her brother would no doubt prefer the larger of the two because it gave a view over the farmyard to the tiny low building that was obviously the church, even though it boasted no tower and weeds rose to half its height.

For herself she chose a smaller bedroom from which she could look out across fields to the sea. In spite of the presence of mould around the window frame and the air of neglect that was common to the whole of the house, she felt that in time it could be made into quite a pleasant room.

Alice realised it was the first positive thought she had entertained since seeing the rectory!

The whole house would need to be thoroughly cleaned, of course, and there was not a great deal of time in which to do it. A wagon was already on the road from their last home in Herefordshire with the bulk of their belongings, including a great many books for which they would need to find somewhere away from the dampness which was so much a feature of the house.

They would also need to employ a maid, preferably one who lived out, although – and this was a point to be seriously considered in view of their limited finances – it might prove cheaper to have a live-in maid who would share their food and so expect to receive less wages.

While such thoughts were running around in her mind Alice had been opening windows as she went around, hoping it would help dispel the damp odour that pervaded the whole house. It was not easy, dampness had also affected many of the hinges and windows were reluctant to open.

When she entered a small room tucked beneath the eaves of the house her nose wrinkled up in distaste, there was an even worse odour here than in the rest of the building. There appeared to be heaps of rags upon the floor, although it was difficult to see anything clearly because the window was so tiny and the diamond-shaped panes of glass almost hidden beneath what appeared to be a green, moss-like growth on the outside of the window but as she stepped over the rags to open the window they appeared to move beneath her feet!

Startled, she thought she must have imagined it and kicked the rags none-too-gently.

Immediately, a gruff and almost unintelligible voice rasped, 'Oi! What d'you think you're doing?' and, as Alice stepped back in alarm a face appeared from beneath the rags.

'Who…? Who are you?' Alice demanded when she had recovered from her surprise.

'I might well ask you the same question,' came the reply, 'but whoever you are you have no right to disturb a man when he's sleeping.'

The speaker struggled to sit up as he spoke and although he appeared to be unkempt and dirty Emma decided he posed no real threat and she pointed out, 'It's the middle of the afternoon and not a time when people sleep – and you should certainly not be sleeping here … this is the rectory.'

'It *was* the rectory, you mean. There's been no preacher here for as long as most folk can remember.'

'That might have been so in the past,' Alice said, gaining confidence, 'but there is a rector here now, so you will need to find somewhere else to sleep.'

'What are you talking about, I've got all my things here? Who are you, anyway?'

'I am the sister of the new rector, he's outside unloading our things from the trap. I think you had better be gone by the time he comes in to look for me.'

'Better be? I'm not going anywhere!'

'Then I will bring my brother in here to evict you, so I suggest that in my absence you gather up all these "things" you claim to have here.'

David had been unable to resist the urge to have a quick look inside his church before unloading their belongings from the trap and before Alice was able to tell him of *her* problem, he said, 'You should see the state of the church – *my* church. It … it's sacrilege! It looks as though someone's been keeping farm animals in there

– and in considerable numbers! There is straw and … and animal mess everywhere. It's absolutely appalling!'

Alice could sympathise with him over the state of the church, but she felt her problem took precedence – for the moment, anyway. However, when she tried to tell him, his mind was so full of the state in which he had found the church he could think of little else.

Brushing her revelation aside, he said dismissively, 'You must be mistaken, there's no one living in the house. No one has been living here for many months – years, probably, but the Dean could not have known about the state of the church.'

'I am *not* mistaken! Not only did this man speak to me, he virtually told me *I* had no right to be in the house and declared that he has no intention of moving out.'

Dragging his mind away from his preoccupation with the state of the church, David realised fully for the first time what Alice had been trying to tell him. 'What sort of man is he? No matter, I will speak to him myself. Whoever he is he has no right to be here.'

Alice was giving her brother a description of the intruder she had found in the bedroom when they met the man in question coming down the stairs.

Due to the state of the window panes visibility was not particularly good on the stairs but there was light enough for the uninvited guest to recognise the clergyman's attire worn by David. As a result, his reply to the question of what he was doing in the house was far more deferential than when he had spoken to Alice.

'I've been doing no harm, Your Reverence, I'm just a feeble old man without a home of my own, who's been seeing that no one got in to do damage to a house that belongs to the Church. Of course, now you've come to Trethevy I'll need to go, though where I'll be able to lay these old bones of mine I just don't know….'

'That should be no problem!' Stung by the old man's change in attitude now he was talking to her brother, Alice was less understanding than she might otherwise have been. 'I believe my brother and I saw a poorhouse when we came through the village down the road, you can go there.'

Recoiling at her words as though she had struck him, the old man said, 'Poorhouse … you're talking of the "workhouse"? Oh yes, there's a workhouse in Tintagel right enough – and I should know. It's where my poor, dear wife died no more than a year since – and me not allowed to go to her. She was left to die alone. Oh, I know all about the workhouse right enough.'

Alice immediately regretted the manner in which she had spoken to the ragged old man. 'I'm sorry … I didn't know.'

The old man shrugged, 'How could you – and why should you care even if you did, I'm nothing to you?'

It was David who spoke to the old man again now, 'Who are you, and what are you doing here, in the rectory?'

'I used to help in the garden here when I was no more than a boy. In those days my ma kept house for Parson Paddock and his daughter, who were living here. He'd sometimes take services in Tintagel too and when he came back I'd take his horse from him and see that it was fed and watered. Mind you, that would be long afore either of you was born. There hasn't been a service here for more than fifty years and the church has known more curses than blessings.'

When David looked puzzled the old man explained almost gleefully, 'That was on account of the church being rented out for some time to a farmer who was also a butcher. He'd slaughter pigs, sheep and an occasional heifer in there – and was none too expert at the job.'

Shuddering in sudden horror at the images his words conjured up, Alice said, 'What a horrible thing to do.'

'Why?' The old man responded, 'People need to eat.'

'I know, but to slaughter animals in a *church*? It's just too dreadful to think about.'

'I don't suppose it mattered very much to the animals where 'twas they were killed,' the old man responded, 'and after John Wesley came around these parts there weren't too many folk interested enough in the Church to care what happened to the old place.'

David thought it was time he brought this particular conversation to a halt. 'There will be no more animals slaughtered in St Piran's. If what you say is true I will have the church cleaned and re-consecrated and it will become God's house once more – but you still haven't told me your name, or what you were doing sleeping in the rectory.'

'My name's Percy … Percy Nankivell.' Adopting a crafty look, he added, 'I suppose you could say I was caretaking the old place. Not that I've ever asked payment for what I've been doing, 'though if Parson Paddock was still alive he'd have seen me right, I've no doubt about that.'

'Reverend Paddock is no longer with us,' David said firmly, 'and were the Church of England to be notified of your residence here they would no doubt demand rent for your unlawful occupation of the rectory. I am willing to forget to tell them but I expect something from you in return. You will, of course, no longer be permitted to live here, in the house, but if you feel you are capable of work I can offer you the employment you enjoyed as a boy, working on the garden here and around the church. It has all been sadly neglected, but perhaps it needs someone with more energy and less years than yourself.'

Indignantly, Percy replied, 'I can work as well as the next – be it man or boy.'

'That remains to be seen, and there is still the problem of your accommodation. Perhaps the poorhouse master will allow you to live there and come out during the day to work here?'

'I'm having nothing to do with the workhouse,' Percy declared fiercely, then in a more wheedling tone he said, 'Why not let me stay in the room I've been sleeping in upstairs? I'll be no trouble to anyone and I'll come and go same as I do now, by the back door. Why, you won't even know I'm around.' His statement was punctuated by noisy and deep throated sniffing as he drew the sleeve of his ragged jacket across his nose.

Before her brother could reply, Emma said firmly, 'No! My brother may take you on as a gardener but *I* will not have you living in the house. You'll need to go elsewhere.'

Aware that Alice was adamant about not having him in the house, Percy thought quickly. He was determined not to go to the poorhouse, or 'workhouse' as he preferred to call it. 'I tell you what, there's a couple of small rooms over the stable. I could tidy one of 'em up and move in there, and take care of your pony at the same time. I presume you have one?'

When Alice nodded cautiously, Percy said triumphantly, 'Well, there you are then. You'd do well to have someone around to keep an eye on things. You get a lot of no-good seamen coming off the ships at Falmouth and Padstow and making their way through Cornwall to Bristol, London and places like that. They'd kill a man for his horse – as they've done more than once in the past. Oh yes, you'll need someone to take care it don't happen to you.'

Wide-eyed, Alice was not certain how much truth there was in his words, but David was not only more gullible than his sister, he also felt guilty at the thought of turning this old man out to become a vagrant. Besides, he had obviously lived in the area for all his long life, it would be useful to have someone around to let him know what went on in this, his new and unfamiliar parish.

'All right, you may move in to a room over the stables but if you can't carry out your work, or make a nuisance of yourself, you will have to leave and find somewhere else. Is that understood?'

Gleefully, Percy said, 'You won't regret having me around, Your Reverence, and I thank you for your Christian charity towards an old man. Now, I suppose you wouldn't be lighting a fire and making a cup of tea, Miss…?'

Chapter Two

*F*OR FIVE DAYS, and many night hours, David and Alice, with spasmodic help from Percy, worked hard to thoroughly clean the Trethevy rectory and make it ready for the arrival of the bulk of their possessions from Herefordshire.

At the end of each working day brother and sister spent uncomfortable nights sleeping on hard beds in their respective rooms, having only a couple of blankets with which to cover themselves.

When their belongings eventually arrived and were placed in the spaces they were to occupy, and they had sufficient bedding to keep themselves warm, they awoke next morning with more optimism than they had been able to muster since their arrival in Cornwall.

Aware that the state in which they found their new home meant that David had needed to put off the work he was so eager to begin in this, his first parish, she said to him during breakfast, 'Didn't you have an invitation to visit Reverend Carter at his school in Devon any time this week? Why don't you go there today? It would do you good to talk to someone who is able to tell you things you need to know about the parish.'

The school where the Tintagel cleric taught, St Dominic's, was a small minor public school near Tavistock, some thirty-five miles away. In order to have a full day with him David would need to spend two nights there.

'According to Percy, Reverend Carter has not spent enough time in the parish to learn anything about Tintagel, he has probably never even heard of Trethevy, and it's hardly surprising. If Percy is to be believed no one has preached here for more than fifty years, at least.'

'You should not accept everything Percy tells you, David. He enjoys gossiping – especially passing on gossip of a depressive nature. I doubt if he has even met Reverend Carter. Anyway, once you've spoken to him you can come back and meet with the Tintagel churchwardens. They will no doubt be very pleased to know there is a clergyman resident in the parish once again.'

'You are probably right,' agreed her brother. 'They must find things difficult with Carter away from the parish for so much of the time. As for Percy, he *does* seem to delight in passing on depressing news. Earlier this morning he found ghoulish delight in telling me about the number of ships wrecked along this part of the coast and of the hundreds of sailors drowned. There are apparently some particularly dangerous rocks at the foot of cliffs not far from here.'

'Well, forget about such gloomy things for a couple of days. It will do you good to be out in the fresh air, speaking to someone other than me and a melancholy old man.'

When David had set off for Tavistock, Alice turned to Percy who had harnessed the pony to the trap for her brother. 'Ever since we arrived at Trethevy my brother has been working hard getting the house fit to live in. Now, while he is away, we will make a start on the thing that is closest to his heart – the church. Find a small ladder and bring a bucket of water, Percy. We will see how much we can get done before he returns.'

Alice's words and the briskness of her manner dismayed Percy. Having seen the parson off the premises he had intended finding a quiet corner of the garden, somewhere out of the wind in which to enjoy a pipe and contemplate a leisurely day, with the possibility of a visit to an ale house at the end of it.

'I don't know as I've got time to do that, there's things need doing in the garden!'

His protest was in vain. 'Whatever you have to do there is not going to go away, you can do it another day,' Alice declared, firmly. 'Having a church of his own has been my brother's dream for as long as I can remember. Instead, he has walked into a nightmare. I intend doing everything in my power to give him back his dream – and *you* are going to help me.'

Percy had not known Alice for very long, but it was time enough for him to recognise that she was strong-willed – far more so than her brother. He put aside any thought of enjoying an easy day in the parson's absence.

'What's a bloody woman doing messing around in my barn?'

The bellowed question, directed at Alice by the large, black-bearded man who occupied much of the space in the narrow doorway of St Piran's church so startled Alice that she dropped the bucket of water she was holding and almost lost the precarious balance she had on the fourth rung of the rustic ladder on which she was standing.

Descending to the slate-stone floor and stung by the angry stranger's rudeness, she responded heatedly in kind. 'This bloody woman would have been considerably bloodier had I lost my footing and fallen off the ladder! As to what I was doing … I was clearing up the mess in a house of God, made by some bloody farmer.'

Glaring at the man, she demanded, 'Would that be you?'

Taken aback by Alice's spirited reply, the man in the doorway opened and closed his mouth two or three times before replying, his tone somewhat less belligerent than before. 'This place hasn't been a church for as long as anyone can remember. I rent it for my animals.'

'I think I'm right in saying that the church has been in the family of a Mr Batten for a great many years and that you haven't paid a penny in rent since he inherited the estate from his father five years ago. Now he has given the building back to the Church and my brother has been appointed rector in charge of it. As it would seem it *is* you who are responsible for the disgusting state of the place you can take the bucket to fetch more water – and if you have nothing else to do you can help clean up in here.'

For some moments Alice thought she might have pushed the man too far as the face above the beard grew darker and his barrel-chest swelled until it seemed he was in danger of bursting the buttons of his waistcoat.

The anticipated explosion never occurred. Turning suddenly on his heel, the irate man left the doorway and strode stiffly away along the overgrown church path.

From a shadowed corner of the church interior, where he had been attacking the rust on a heavy iron latch removed from the stout entrance door, the noisy exhalation of breath from Percy was a combination of relief and admiration.

Breaking into a chuckle he said, 'I never thought I'd live to see the day when Eval Moyle was backed down – and by a woman! Miss Alice, you've done what no man hereabouts has ever been able to do, and there's never been a shortage of them as have wanted to.'

Still chuckling, he added, 'Not only that, for a moment or two I thought he might even have picked up the bucket and helped you clean up!'

'Are you telling me everyone is frightened of him? Why? He's nothing more than a blustering big bully.'

'Oh no, he's more than that, Missie! Eval Moyle was Cornwall's champion wrestler for nigh on ten years until men stopped challenging him after he left young Tristan Pethick crippled for life. He has a farm along the lane from here. It actually belongs to Eval and his brother, but neither are much good at farming and although they still live there together the brother has needed to find work on another farm so they have enough to live on. But you're right about him not paying rent on this place for years. It's because no one's dared ask him for it – not even the Battens, and they're as powerful a family as any hereabouts.'

'Well he doesn't frighten me,' Alice declared, but her bravado belied her innermost feelings. She was a positive young woman who was not afraid of speaking her mind, but she rarely quarrelled outright with anyone and could not remember when she had ever before been angry enough to speak to anyone as she had to Eval Moyle, using language that would have deeply shocked her brother.

With reaction beginning to set in, she said, 'I'm going to the rectory to make us a cup of tea. It's a pity Reverend Kilpeck is away today. He needs to be warned about Mr Moyle. While I'm gone will you refill my bucket please, Percy?'

Showing newly-found deference, Percy said, 'Of course, and I'll have a go at scrubbing that wall for 'ee too, it's not work the likes of you should be doing. But I don't think you'll need to say too much to the parson about Eval Moyle, he'll hear of him soon enough.'

'What do you mean?' Alice demanded.

'Well, Eval is preacher in a chapel in Tintagel that attracts more folks on a Sunday than the church ever has.'

'You surprise me, Percy. The very last thing I would have suspected Mr Moyle of being is a Christian preacher, even a dissenting preacher!'

'Well, Eval was brought up a Methodist but when he wanted to become a preacher they would have none of it, so he ups and leaves them and took up with the "Ranters".'

'Ranters?' Alice was puzzled.

'That's right. They call themselves Primitive Methodists, or some such, but them as don't belong call 'em "Ranters", on account of the shouting and hollering that goes on when they have one of their services – meetings that sometimes go on right through the night and keep anyone who lives nearby awake with their goings-on. There's no doubt at all *they'll* have enough of Eval before very long, but they seem to be suiting each other for the moment.'

'Thank you for telling me, Percy, that's something else I will have to tell my brother when he comes home. I can see there is going to be a whole lot more to living at Trethevy than just preaching to his parishioners!'

Chapter Three

*T*HE FOLLOWING MORNING was wet and blustery and Alice had been kept awake during the night by a storm more ferocious than anything she had ever experienced before. It rattled the windows of her bedroom so badly that she was forced to rise and jam a wedge of paper between window and frame. It solved the problem of the rattling, but left a gap through which the wind howled for the remainder of the night.

Despite the weather, she and Percy resumed work in the neglected little church immediately after breakfast but they were destined not to be allowed to continue it without interruption. They had been working for no more than half-an-hour when an ill-dressed, windswept man with a great deal of untidy facial hair and only marginally younger than Percy rushed into the church.

For a moment he seemed taken aback at the sight of Alice working inside, but he was far too excited to be distracted for long from sharing the news he bore. Inclining his head with a brief 'Ma'am,' in acknowledgement of her presence, he turned his attention to her companion.

'Come quick, Percy, a ship called the *Balladeer*'s struck the Lye rock and is breaking up fast. Word has it she was outward bound for America, so she'll be well provisioned. There'll be rich pickings to be had if we get there before the coast guards and revenue men. The workhouse master's sent every able-bodied man and boy down to the shore to bring back what they can.'

'What about those on board?' The unexpected question came from Alice. 'Have they been rescued?'

The visitor appeared momentarily puzzled before replying. 'I doubt it, there's not many survive being shipwrecked on this stretch of coast …' Then, as though dismissing her, he turned back to Percy, 'Are you coming? You'd best be quick or the whole of Tintagel will be there before us.'

When Percy looked at Alice uncertainly, she said, 'We'll *both* go to see what's happening. I don't know what the law says about gathering goods from a shipwreck, although it sounds as though it must be illegal if there's a need to beware of revenue men. Fortunately that need not trouble us, we will be looking to see if there are any poor souls in need of our help.'

Percy showed signs of embarrassment and the visitor looked at Alice in disbelief before saying, 'Of course we'll have a look for 'em, but it shouldn't put a stop to us picking up anything worth having. There's little enough comes the way of folk around these parts that doesn't need paying for in one way or another.'

As Alice, Percy and the old man – referred to by Percy as 'Henry' – made their way along a narrow path that led to the cliff-top they joined a horde of men, women and even small children heading in the same direction. It was apparent that word of the wreck had spread far and wide in the mysterious but efficient manner that news travelled in rural Cornwall.

Everyone was highly excited and Alice did not see a single face which appeared to show concern at the possibility of finding victims of the shipwreck in urgent need of help.

As they drew closer to the sea, the sound of waves crashing against the high cliffs grew frighteningly loud and such was their force Alice imagined the very ground beneath her feet to tremble.

The wind here on the edge of the cliffs was stronger than inland and when she and her two eager companions reached a steep wet path leading down to a small beach that was heavily studded with huge glistening rocks, she found herself looking at a sea that was a foam-flecked cauldron. Caught up in its fury she could see a dismasted ship, lying askew on rocks just beyond a small headland, some distance from the beach.

All around the ship an ever-expanding raft of broken timbers and flotsam rose and fell with the waves, as did the bulk of the stricken ship. Only the bow seemed immovably impaled upon jagged black rocks that reared above the turbulent water each time a wave retreated.

As she looked, horrified at the scene, a gigantic wave swept in from the sea and for many moments ship and rocks disappeared from view beneath hundred of tons of surging water.

All along the fluctuating shoreline hordes of excited sea-drenched foragers, too impatient to wait for the sea's bounty to be cast ashore, were plunging into the sea to seize something – any-thing – that might prove to be of value.

Some having rescued as much, or more, than could be carried were climbing back up the path from the beach, staggering dan-gerously under the weight of their booty and frequently shedding some along the way.

Then, as Alice and the others drew closer to the crowded beach she saw a small number of bodies stretched out in a line, well back from the water's edge. All were naked, or almost so. When Alice commented on their state it was Henry who replied. 'Some of their clothes will have been torn off by rocks and water, any-thing left will have gone to someone in need.'

Catching Alice's expression of disbelief, he added, 'Well, them as was wearing 'em have no more need of clothes, do they?'

'But … what will happen to the bodies now?'

Henry shrugged and the answer came from Percy, 'Depends. If

the coast guards get here in time they'll be buried in the sand. If the tide beats them to it they'll be taken back out to sea again.'

Alice was horrified, 'That's dreadful! Those bodies are of men – Christians, probably. They deserve to be treated with respect. They should be taken off, buried in consecrated ground and have prayers said over them, at the very least.'

They had reached the sloping sand of the beach now and, giving Alice a pitying look, Henry said, 'You pray if you want, I can see a firkin or two on their way in. They'll bring me more cheer than any prayer I've ever heard said.'

With this, Henry set off at a short-paced but speedy shuffle, heading for the water's edge.

Looking at Alice apologetically, Percy said, 'There's little to look forward to in the workhouse, even the smallest luxury is treasured by them as is lucky enough to benefit from it.'

'I don't begrudge them or anyone else the good things in life but they are still human beings and so were the men whose bodies are lying naked on the sand. They deserve the same respect that we would give to our own families.'

At that moment a hubbub on the small beach increased as one of a number of the small barrels being pitched around in the water came within the grasp of a number of men and women who, at risk of their lives, had waded into the sea in order to be first to lay hands on them – and a tussle had broken out.

It ended only when a large wave powered into the bay, sweeping the squabbling men off their feet and actually throwing the firkins over their heads, causing the scrabble for possession to shift to the mob onshore.

The same wave swept far up the beach and Alice retreated before it. Percy came with her reluctantly, casting a covetous glance in the direction of the heavily contested barrel, the contents of which had yet to be established.

Standing uncertainly at the edge of the excited crowd, wondering what action she should – or *could* – take in respect of the bodies of the shipwrecked sailors, Alice's attention was drawn to some children scrambling dangerously among the slippery rocks that stretched on either side of the small beach. The waves of an incoming tide thundered around them, drenching them with spray.

Suddenly Alice heard the voice of a young girl calling urgently from among the furthermost rocks. At first she thought the child was in trouble, but as a woman broke away from the mob around the barrels and began running towards the sound, Alice was able to make out what it was the child was shouting.

'Mama…! Mama…! Quick … I've found a body … it's a girl.'

Scrambling over slippery, sea-drenched rocks Alice was marginally beaten to the spot by the caller's mother, but she was in time to hear the woman demand, 'What are you so excited about? Look at her … her frock's been torn to bits by the rocks and she's got no shoes on – if she *ever* had any. She's not wearing any rings or jewellery, either. What'd you call me here for? Come on, back to the beach with me. There's things coming ashore we can make use of.'

Arriving at the spot where mother and daughter were, Alice looked past them to where the body of a girl of perhaps thirteen or fourteen was lying half in a shallow rock pool, her body rising and falling with the ebb and flow of the water. There was a length of rope tied about her waist, the other end of which was attached to a splintered spar that might once have been part of a vessel – although it must have been smaller than the ship being battered to pieces offshore.

Giving Alice only the briefest of glances, the woman took her daughter's hand and began scrambling back towards the crowded beach. Alice called after her angrily. 'You can't leave her here like this. Help me carry her to the beach.'

The woman looked at Alice for a second time, then, clutching her daughter's hand more tightly said contemptuously, 'She's as well here as anywhere else. You move her if you want to, I've got other things to do.'

With this she turned away and hurried off with her daughter.

Dropping down to the edge of the rock pool Alice looked at the near-naked girl and realised that only the lower half of her body was beneath the water swirling all around her, but another wave like the one that had thrown the barrels on to the beach could sweep over the rocks at any moment, taking the body with it when it retreated to the sea.

Percy, who had been slower than Alice at scrambling over the rocks now put in an appearance and Alice said, 'Give me a hand, Percy. While I try to pull her clear of the water see if you can untie the rope binding her to the piece of wood.'

Percy lowered himself into the rock pool and while he was fumbling with the wet rope Alice attempted to lift the upper part of the girl's body, using a hand to lift the girl's head when it fell back to hang into the water. Her fingers were on the girl's neck for a moment – and she felt a movement!

Startled, she moved her fingers over the neck until she found what she sought. Looking up at Percy excitedly, she said, 'She's not dead, Percy! The girl is still alive!'

Chapter Four

The Central Criminal Court, London, June 1840.

'*E*LIZA BROOKS, YOU have been found guilty of one of the most despicable of thefts, namely, stealing from your employer. Someone who not only rescued you from a useless and penurious existence in a poorhouse, but gave you work in a comfortable home and an opportunity to enjoy gainful employment which would carry you through life as a useful member of the society in which we live.'

Peering over the top of the tall and narrow dock in the high-ceilinged court-room, thirteen-year-old Eliza listened to the bewigged Judge's words with an impassiveness born out of a life-time of carrying blame for something or other and being told she was less than her fellow-beings.

She was aware that his words would be followed by punishment and that it came in many guises, most of which she had already experienced in her young life. She would take it unflinchingly, as she always did, by imagining it was happening to someone else. When it was over, her mind and body would return to the miserable existence that had been her lot for as long as she could remember.

Her only hope was that if it was a lashing it would not be too many strokes and not administered by someone who enjoyed his work too much ... but the judge had yet to deliver his sentence and he was still speaking.

'You, Eliza Brooks, were offered an opportunity that comes the way of few girls in your station of life. Unfortunately, avarice and dishonesty are so ingrained in your nature that you have chosen to throw it away. Your mistress, wife of the man from whom you stole money, has pleaded for leniency on your behalf, asking that you be given another chance and suggesting you are a basically honest person. She is a woman of some standing in the community and well-known for her charitable works....'

For a moment Eliza allowed her hopes to rise. If the judge thought so highly of Lady Calnan there was just a chance she might not be punished after all. Her optimism was short-lived.

'... However, my duty is to protect the community at large and not allow a convicted thief to walk free from my court in order that she may – and undoubtedly would – steal again. Eliza Brooks, you will be transported for a period of seven years – and think yourself fortunate. Not too many years ago I would have been able to order a whipping for you too, but the law no longer offers such a deterrent to your sex ... and more the pity! Take her away.'

As Eliza was led from the dock she looked up and caught a glimpse of the wife of the man who had brought the charges against her. Lady Calnan was in tears.

Eliza felt a moment's remorse – but only a moment. Lady Calnan had been kind to her, but she had refused to face up to the way her husband behaved towards their servants, the young females in particular, yet she must have known. Other servants in the household had told Eliza of the succession of young maids who had left the house, many in tears, some in more serious distress. Lady Calnan would have known that Eliza's conduct was directed at Sir Robert Calnan and not at the mistress of the house.

But it made no difference. She had told the constable who arrested her that she had taken the three guineas from Sir Robert's dressing-table because that was the amount owing to her in unpaid wages, and in order to escape from the house and his unwelcome attentions. The constable had been scornful, asking what else a workhouse waif could expect when she was taken into 'service', adding that she ought to have been grateful to be working in the house of a family of substance, with a roof over her head, good and regular food to eat and respectable clothes to wear.

Lady Calnan had tried to dampen the whole matter down, partly, as Eliza knew, because it was not the first time a servant-girl had tried to take some action against the amorous baronet, but the law had taken its course.

While awaiting trial Eliza had spent three weeks in the notorious Newgate prison, cast in among women whose only aims in life seemed to be to obtain alcohol and gain access to the male prisoners, neither ambition being particularly difficult to achieve. The experience was a nightmare, even to a young girl brought up to accept the rigours and corrupt practices of a London poorhouse.

It came as a relief after her conviction and sentencing to be taken from the gaol to a prison hulk moored in the River Thames, off Woolwich – but her relief was seriously misplaced.

The hulk was even worse than Newgate had been. Most of the women on board were awaiting transportation, although a few – some of whom should have been certified insane – were considered 'unsuitable' for transportation to the penal settlements of Australia and would serve out their sentences in chains on the Woolwich hulk, a danger to fellow prisoners, to their guards and to themselves. Three of their number succeeded in committing suicide during the two nightmare months Eliza spent on the hulk awaiting passage to Australia, their deaths going unreported for days in order that their rations could be claimed by the other convicts.

Eliza was beginning to wonder whether her sentence too

would be served on a prison hulk when, without any prior warning, early one morning she and twenty-nine other women were taken from the hold of the hulk and shepherded up various ladders to the upper deck. Here, with total disregard for a heavy summer downpour, the thirty women were shackled at wrists and ankles, then linked to each other by another chain.

None had been told anything and they were ordered not to talk among themselves. However, when it was Eliza's turn to be shackled she whispered to the sailor securing her, 'Where are we being taken?'

The sailor was about to tell her to 'Be quiet!' but when he looked up and saw how young she was, he took pity on her. 'You're lucky, my girl, there's a small ship going to Australia with supplies for the marines stationed there. The captain has said he can take thirty convicts, but has said they must be female and not likely to cause trouble because it's only a small ship and he doesn't carry enough crew to deal with it.'

Giving Eliza an appreciative wink, the sailor added, 'I think he might enjoy having you on board, I doubt you'll stay in irons for very long. Given a bath and some clean clothes you'll catch the eye of some young sailor. Who knows, by the time you get to Australia you could have someone looking after you and, if you're clever enough, it might even last!'

Eliza was about to retort that it was having someone wanting to 'look after her' that was responsible for the situation in which she now found herself, but she checked herself in time. The seaman had spoken the first kind words to her she had heard for a very long time, but even if he believed her – and there was no reason why he should, nobody else had – it would not matter to him. By the time he had secured a couple more shackles to convicts he would have forgotten he had ever spoken to her, yet his words made her think about the journey that lay ahead, and what it was likely to entail.

The sailor finished his task but before moving on, he said, 'Remember what I've said to you, girl. Take my advice and you could look back on this day as being the first in your new life.'

'I doubt it,' Eliza said scornfully, 'I don't even *know* what day it is.'

The sailor smiled, 'It's a Wednesday and it's the 14th June. Now you'll remember it.'

Eliza thought wryly that she was not likely to forget. Today was her fourteenth birthday.

Chapter Five

*T*HE WOMEN FROM the Woolwich prison hulk were taken upriver to Blackwall Reach where a four-masted barque, the *Cormorant* was moored. An almost new vessel, *Cormorant* was making its first journey to Australia under the command of Captain Arnold Leyland, a part owner of the vessel.

The hold where temporary accommodation had been prepared for the thirty women should have been filled with mining equipment for the copper mines of South Australia but the machinery was now lying in a sunken barge beneath the waters of the Thames estuary, lost in a collision between the barge and a man-o'-war.

The idea of converting the empty hold to accommodate women convicts had been the brainchild of Captain Leyland's wife, Agnes, who would be accompanying her husband on the voyage. She calculated that not only would it make up for the income lost from the sunken cargo, but could also provide her with an unpaid maid for the journey.

When the convicts clanked their awkward way up the gangway of the *Cormorant* the members of the ship's crew stopped work to eye them speculatively. Some of the sailors had served on convict ships before, while others had heard lurid stories of what was considered acceptable behaviour between crew and prisoners on a women's transport ship.

Captain Leyland's wife had heard similar tales and was determined there would be no such behaviour on board *Cormorant*, but the crew had not yet been made aware of her views and commented excitedly on the attributes, imagined or otherwise, of each woman convict as they made their ponderous way onboard.

The youngest of the convicts, Eliza created a particular stir but Agnes Leyland had seen her too – and she had her own plans for this particular convict.

When the women had been lodged in the hold that had been fitted out for them, the chains linking one to another were removed. However, the fetters on wrists and ankles were left in place despite the voluble protests of the women that the restricted movement afforded them made it almost impossible to carry out even the most basic hygiene.

'They'll come off only when the ship's underway and clear of land,' declared the *Cormorant's* mate, who was one of two men removing the convicts' chains.

He was unfastening the chain from Eliza when he made his statement and now she asked him, 'When will that be?'

'We'll be leaving on tonight's tide,' came the reply and he added, 'Mind you, it'll be a slow journey downriver, there are a great many ships on the move at the moment but by the time you wake in the morning you'll know by way the ship's behaving that you're at sea. Sometime the day after that you'll have left England behind – and I don't suppose any of you will ever see it again.'

'What do you mean?' Eliza demanded indignantly, 'I'm only being sent away for seven years. I'll be back by the time I've come of age.'

There was a chorus of derisory remarks from the other women and as Eliza looked about her defiantly, the mate said, 'They're right, young 'un. I've been on more than one ship transporting women to Australia, but I've never been on one that's brought any back again. From now on make the most of whatever comes your way and don't waste your time pining for whatever it is you've left behind, you need to accept that it's gone forever – talking of which, are you the youngest one here?'

'Yeah,' Eliza made the reply abstractedly, thinking of what the sailor had said. There had been nothing in her life so far that she would think of with any degree of fondness, but there *was* apprehension for what the future might hold. Despite the unhappy life which was all she had ever known, she felt uneasy at the thought of never again seeing the streets of East London – but the ship's mate was talking to her again.

'Captain Leyland's wife must have seen you coming on board. She wants me to take you to her, up in the captain's cabin.'

'Me? What for?'

'I don't know, but when the chains are off everybody else I'll take you up top and you can ask her yourself.'

Thirty minutes later Eliza climbed awkwardly up the ladder from the convicts' hold, helped through the hatchway by an eager sailor whose exploring hands went farther than gallantry decreed and earned him a sharp blow from the heavy fetter about her wrists.

The action was seen by a sharp-faced woman in her late forties who immediately snapped at her, 'I had you brought up here because I thought you might make a suitable maid-servant but if that's the way you behave...!'

'If you want a maid who's going to let every sailor on board do what he wants with her then you've chosen the wrong one,' Eliza said heatedly. Then, aware that she might have thrown away the only chance she had of escaping *Cormorant's* prison hold and all that would mean on the long journey to Australia, she added more meekly, 'It's because I wasn't willing to be treated like that that I'm on here.'

'You injured a man who attacked you?' The woman seemed shocked and Eliza realised that the reply she made now would be crucial for her. 'No, I never touched him, because he was master of the household, but I knew he'd try again when he'd had a few drinks, so I took three guineas from the top of his locker so I could get away from him.'

The woman looked speculatively at her for so long that Eliza was beginning to believe her honesty had been a mistake, when the woman said, 'What was your employment with the man?'

'It was his wife who took me on. I started work as a kitchen-maid, but Lady Calnan said I'd done so well that she made me a housemaid.'

There was another long pause while the captain's wife studied her thoughtfully before saying, 'If you maintain the same attitude towards *Cormorant's* crew and are able to keep your hands off things that aren't yours, you can have a far more pleasant voyage to Australia as my personal maid than any of your fellow con-victs. But you so much as put a foot out of line and you'll find yourself back in the hold. What's more, I'll see to it that you have a worse voyage than you could ever imagine. Is that understood?'

Eliza was so elated she attempted to curtsy but was unable to manage it because of her shackled ankles.

Aware of her problem, Agnes Leyland said, 'I'll have you unshackled first thing tomorrow morning when we've left the river behind. Until then you can go back to the hold, just to remind you of what you can expect if you don't suit me.'

'Yes, ma'am, thank you ma'am, but ...'

Agnes Leyland had turned away, now she turned back, an irri-table frown on her face, 'What is it, girl?'

'As your personal maid I'll need to look the part, ma'am. You wouldn't be happy to have me serving you dressed the way I am now. Then there's my sleeping quarters, ma'am. If I go back down to the hold to sleep with the other women they'd have my clothes off my back before the hatch cover was back on and I'd come back up top as lousy as they are. Once I get clean enough to suit you I'd need to stay that way ... ma'am.'

Eliza had made a shrewd summing-up of the wife of *Cormorant's* captain. She doubted whether Agnes Leyland had ever employed a personal maid before but wanted to exploit the opportunity that had come her way in order to make an impression upon the ship's officers and crew.

For a few moments Eliza thought she might have gone too far in setting out her needs. After all, she was a convict and possessed no rights whatsoever.

She breathed a silent sigh of relief when Agnes Leyland said, 'I see you are able to think for yourself, girl – but don't take it too far. I'll have one of the sailors go ashore and buy some maid's clothes before we sail and my husband has a small chart room attached to our cabin, you can sleep in there. Once we're at sea and you come up from the hold you can have a salt water bath and rinse your hair in vinegar to kill the lice. Then you can wash your convict clothes and keep them by you to remind you of what you are, in case you get any ideas above your station.'

'You'll have no cause to ever remind me of that – and thank you again, ma'am.'

Eliza had already taken a dislike to Agnes Leyland, but she was determined that her new 'mistress' would never know.

Chapter Six

*C*ORMORANT SET SAIL that evening with a pilot on board to guide the vessel on its way to the open sea and by the following morning the women convicts in the forward hold were made aware that the ship had left the shelter of the river banks behind when it heeled over and its movement increased significantly.

The vessel's unpredictable motion provoked a certain amount of feigned hilarity, and not a few bruises, before the novelty of the experience wore off.

When food was handed down to the women one of the sailors chatted to them but he left them with a warning. 'It won't be long before you have your irons removed. They'll be off for all the time we're at sea and you'll find Cap'n Leyland is a good skipper, but if you start misbehaving yourselves you'll have them put back on again and they'll be kept on until we reach Australia.'

'Now, what do you think this captain will consider to be "misbehaving"? I hope he's not against women who like to make men happy – particular sailors – like most of us here do.'

'I'm pleased to hear that,' grinned the sailor, 'and I don't doubt my mates will be too....'

The man's conversation was cut short by the ship's mate. A large, burly man he carried a great deal of authority on *Cormorant* and was treated with respect by the members of the crew.

'Have you fed the women?' he asked the seaman.

When he received an affirmative reply, he said, 'Then get back to your duties, there's work to be done.'

When the sailor had hurried away, the large man called into the hold, 'Where's Eliza, she's wanted up top?'

When Eliza showed herself at the foot of the ladder leading from the hold, the mate said, 'Get yourself up here, I have orders to take your shackles off and take you to the captain's wife.'

When he pulled her through the hatchway and she was standing unsteadily on the heaving deck, the burly man looked at her and, moved by her age and predicament, said, 'Agnes has agreed to take you on as her maid for the journey, young 'un, but she's not going to be an easy mistress. I don't think she'll ever be satisfied with anything you do, no matter how hard you try. I've yet to see her smile at anyone, or anything. But you must try your hardest because life with her will be a damned sight easier than living down in the hold with the other women. Anyway, let's get your shackles off, it won't do for you to keep her waiting.'

The ship was pitching and tossing more severely now and the mate grabbed her and pulled her into the lee of a deckhouse as a wave crashed against the ship's side, sending heavy spray sweeping across the deck.

Maintaining a hold on Eliza, the seaman asked, 'Have you ever been to sea before?'

'No.' Eliza was too busy trying to maintain her balance to say any more.

Keeping her in the shelter of the deckhouse, the sailor asked, 'Why are you being transported? What did you do?'

'I stole money from the husband of the woman I was working for?'

Another wave crashed against the ship's side and once more she would have lost her balance had the sailor not been keeping a tight grip on her.

'Why did you do it?'

'To get away from him, so he wouldn't do to me what most of the women back there in the hold can't wait to have done to them,' she replied, bitterly.

'Couldn't you have just run away and gone back to your family?'

'I've got no family. I'm a workhouse waif.'

The hand on her shoulder tightened in a brief gesture of sympathy, 'I know what it must have been for you, I was brought up in a poorhouse myself....'

Yet another wave crashed against *Cormorant's* side and, pulling her back into the shelter of the deck-house the sympathetic mate said, 'We have a beam sea right now and it's not comfortable but in an hour or two we'll be turning to run along the Channel, it will be better then. Now, let's get you to the captain's cabin and I'll hand you over to Agnes Leyland. My name's Jim Macleish and I'm the ship's mate. Remember the name if you have any problems, I can sort out most things on board *Cormorant*.'

Agnes Leyland was not a good sailor. When Eliza entered the captain's cabin the motion of the sea tore the door from her hand and it crashed noisily against the bulkhead. Agnes was lying on the bunk, her face grey. Looking up she said, 'I expected you an hour ago, what have you been doing?'

'I had to wait to have my shackles taken off ... ma'am. Now I'm here is there anything I can get for you?'

'Not until you've changed into some decent clothes. They're in there.' Agnes waved a limp arm in the direction of a brass handled door set in the corner of the cabin.

'Would you like me to fetch you some food – or perhaps something to drink?' Eliza was finding the movement of the *Cormorant* uncomfortable, but she was not suffering as this woman and many of the convicts were.

'Don't even *mention* food to me. Get changed and begin cleaning up the cabin … No! Fetch the bowl from over there – Quick!'

Eliza snatched up a bowl from a cabinet, the top of which was
fitted with wooden rails, to prevent items placed upon it from
falling off with the movement of the ship. Placing it on the bed
alongside the groaning and retching woman, she obeyed the
waved command to leave her.

From behind the closed door of what had been the captain's chart
room she could hear Agnes being sick. Eliza found satisfaction in the
knowledge that the captain's wife would not be looking to find fault
with her while she remained in such a wretched condition.

Emerging from the chart room she wrinkled her nose in distaste. Agnes had used the bowl and was now lying back in the
bunk, breathing heavily and moaning gently.

Removing the bowl and placing it upon the cabin floor, she
said, 'I'll take this away and empty it, but first I'll tuck you in and
make you comfortable. When I come back I'll bring some water
with me for you to keep by your side. I won't be away long.'

Her eyes tightly closed, Agnes nodded weakly and Eliza
realised her new mistress would cause her no trouble while the
rough weather lasted.

Outside the cabin she met with Captain Leyland who was
returning to see how his wife was.

'She's not very happy at the moment,' Eliza said, in answer to
his query, 'but I don't suppose anyone enjoys being on a ship in
this sort of weather.'

After asking Eliza her name and receiving her reply,
Cormorant's captain said, 'We'll meet up with far worse than this
before we reach Australia, this is merely uncomfortable, nothing
more. Anyway, we'll ride easier when we are heading west along
the Channel, although the barometer's dropping, so we can't
expect much of an improvement in the weather just yet, but you
don't seem too affected by it, have you spent time on the water?'

'The nearest I've come to it is falling off a barge I was playing on, into the canal. I must have been about five then, but this weather doesn't seem to bother me, not as much as it does Mrs Leyland.'

'She's never been a good sailor. I couldn't understand why she wanted to come on this voyage with me, but I suppose she believed life was beginning to pass her by and she wanted to see some of the world. Anyway, I won't go in and disturb her now. You look after her well on the voyage and I'll see that you're taken good care of when we get to Australia. There's plenty of scope there for a girl who wants to make something of herself – but only if she gets off to a good start.'

Thanking Captain Leyland, Eliza emptied the bowl over the side of the ship and, after cleaning it out, returned to the cabin where Agnes was still lying in the bunk, feeling sorry for herself – although she found the ability to ask Eliza why she had been away from the cabin for so long.

Eliza explained that she had met up with the captain who had been on his way to check up on his wife's well-being and she had been able to reassure him that although feeling very unwell, she was tucked up and warm and, as her maid, she would attend to her every need. Eliza added that the ship would be altering course soon and its movements would then be more comfortable to contend with.

Not fully placated, Agnes was able to find sufficient strength to tell Eliza she had been brought from the convict hold to assist *her* and not spend her time gossiping with others. She reminded her once again that the degree of freedom she would enjoy on the voyage depended upon carrying out duties to *her* in a satisfactory manner.

Little more than an hour later *Cormorant* turned into the English Channel and with the wind behind it conditions became a little easier for those on board.

Agnes fell into an exhausted sleep and Eliza busied herself about the cabin, at the same time wondering what life would hold for her onboard *Cormorant*. She had already decided she liked Captain Leyland a lot more than she did his acerbic wife.

Chapter Seven

*D*ESPITE THE FORECAST of the captain and mate of *Cormorant* the second day of the voyage was no smoother than the first had been. Agnes Leyland rose from her bunk and dressed but did not venture outside the cabin and seemed content to eat little more than dry bread and drink only water, supplemented at the end of the day with a couple of tots of brandy.

Nevertheless, she felt fit enough to criticise much of what Eliza did for her. Aware that his wife's criticism was unjustified, Captain Leyland took Eliza aside and assured her there was nothing wrong with her standard of work. He suggested it was the continuing bad weather that was the cause of his wife's irritability.

Eliza was grateful to him for at least troubling to make an attempt to explain away his wife's ingratitude for all that was being done for her. At the same time she realised that Agnes was by nature a difficult woman.

Although Eliza was relieved to be separated from the other convicts she believed that the voyage to Australia, which would take at the very least three months, might seem even longer.

Her only bright moment came when she was sent on an errand from the cabin and met up with Jim Macleish, the burly elderly mate who had befriended her from the beginning of the voyage. A fatherly figure, he had served with Captain Leyland for many years. Having known Agnes too for as long as she and the ship's captain had been married, he was well aware of her shortcomings.

Macleish told Eliza that *Cormorant* would be leaving the English Channel behind sometime during the next night and heading out into the Atlantic. He said the barometer was dropping, an indication of more bad weather to come, adding that it would probably result in Agnes Leyland being laid low once more.

Sure enough, when the ship cleared the English Channel after dark and turned on to a southerly course, those on board began to feel the effect of the powerful waves sweeping in from the vastness of the Atlantic Ocean.

Agnes showed little sign of acquiring 'sea legs' and after complaining bitterly about the instability of her husband's ship took to her bunk and soon fell into a sleep induced by a considerable amount of brandy.

Captain Leyland was seated at his desk writing up the ship's log, while at his suggestion Eliza was stowing away everything that could be dislodged if the weather deteriorated any more, when a rain and spray-soaked mate entered the cabin after only a cursory knock.

With water dripping from his oilskins on to the wooden decking Macleish glanced at the still figure in the bunk then, his voice lowered said, 'I thought I should tell you, Cap'n, the barometer's gone crazy and pressure has almost dropped off the scale. Something big is on the way and I'm worried about *Cormorant* being able to cope with it on our planned course. The swell is increasing too and if it gets any rougher we'll be in very real danger of rolling over.'

Walking to where a barometer was screwed to the bulkhead of the cabin, Captain Leyland tapped the instrument's glass with a forefinger and the pointer immediately dropped in an anti-clockwise direction.

'Damn! I should have remembered the pointer has a habit of sticking. You're right, Jim, it's fallen dramatically since I last checked it. We're in for a really bad storm. What do you think we ought to do, take in all sail, put out a sea anchor and ride it out?'

The concerned mate drew the back of his hand across his forehead to clear some of the water that was running down into his eyes, 'I think we need to do more than that, Cap'n, I've never seen such an alarming drop in the barometer in all my time at sea.'

Captain Leyland had known Jim Macleish for many years and was aware the mate was not a man prone to over-dramatising a situation. 'Are you suggesting we should turn and run for safety, Jim?'

'If we don't – and leave it any longer – it might be too late. We'd turn turtle. As it is we'll need to choose our moment very carefully.'

Convinced by the mate's words, Captain Leyland said, 'Right, Jim, call all hands on deck. We'll use the wind to help us turn, but too much sail and we'll go over anyway. God knows where we're likely to find shelter in this weather, but we need to try.'

'Falmouth would be the best bet,' Macleish said, 'but this wind and sea is likely to send us north of Land's End. That leaves only the *north* Cornish coast and I'd rather keep well clear of that in such weather.'

While the two men were having their discussion *Cormorant's* captain had been putting on his oilskins. Now he turned to Eliza, 'Secure anything that could possibly fall – then stay by Mrs Leyland and make sure she doesn't fall out of the bunk. *Cormorant* will be all over the place while we are changing course.'

Eliza had been listening wide-eyed to the conversation of the two men. It frightened her, and Macleish was aware of her fear. Speaking to her reassuringly, he said, 'Don't worry, Eliza, it's going to be very uncomfortable for a while but *Cormorant's* a fine ship, we'll make it ...'

At that moment another wave crashed down upon them and the ship rose slowly from beneath the many tons of sea water, shuddering alarmingly as it shook off the water in the manner of a wet and ageing terrier.

'I'd better get the men up on deck,' Macleish said.

'I'll come with you,' said the ship's captain. Pausing at the door he spoke to Eliza again. 'Remember what I said. Don't leave the cabin – and make certain Mrs Leyland remains here too.'

For the next few minutes Eliza worked feverishly to complete the task of securing moveable objects, jamming them wherever she could find space in cupboards or drawers. The erratic movements of *Cormorant* did not help her task and she lost count of the times she was thrown off balance and fell heavily against cabin furniture.

She thought her body would collect a great many bruises by the time the storm was over but fervently believed that if it suffered no more than bruises she would have reason to be grateful.

Eliza was amazed that Agnes Leyland was sleeping through the turbulence, but the bunk she was in had high sides to prevent her being pitched out and she had been exhausted by her long bout of sea sickness. This, coupled with the brandy she had drunk, had left her in a state of near unconsciousness.

It seemed a long time before there was any relief at all in the ship's movements, in fact, Eliza felt it was actually worsening. Meanwhile, on deck Macleish, with another seaman, had joined the coxswain at the ship's wheel, standing by to help when the rudder needed to be put hard over, fighting wind and sea for the 180 degree turn that would set the ship on a course towards the Cornish coast.

At last Captain Leyland discerned a momentary lull in the ferocity of the storm and gave the order to turn the ship about.

Every available man hauled desperately on ropes to change the configuration of the few sails that were set, while mate, coxswain and their helper heaved on the ship's wheel, which in turn moved the rudder to challenge the might of the sea.

For long moments it appeared their combined efforts would be in vain then, as the ship's bow rose on a wave, *Cormorant* suddenly heeled over, tilting so far the sailors on board feared it was about to capsize, but the ship successfully rode the wave, the stern slewing around as it slithered into a deep trough – and *Cormorant* righted itself.

The progress of the vessel was still influenced by the ceaseless motion of the sea combined with the fury of the wind but to those on board it felt less violent and, above the noise of the storm, Eliza thought she heard a cheer from the crew on the deck above the captain's cabin.

It was another half-an-hour before Captain Leyland returned to the cabin, water streaming from his oilskin and long sea-boots.

'Is everything all right now?' Eliza asked anxiously, 'Are we safe?'

'We can't congratulate ourselves yet,' Leyland replied, 'although we're running with the storm now, so things on board should be a little more comfortable for a while, but before dawn we're going to be dangerously close to the coast without knowing exactly where we are. Still, we'll tackle that problem when the need arises. Is everything all right down here?'

Eliza nodded, 'Mrs Leyland half-woke when the ship turned, but she didn't stay awake for very long. She's fast asleep again now.'

'Good girl. You go and try to get some sleep now and I'll do the same. I'll be woken and on deck before dawn and call you then, so that you're up and about when Mrs Leyland wakes.'

Chapter Eight

*I*T WAS STILL dark when Captain Leyland roughly woke Eliza and told her to hurry and get dressed. As she did so, Eliza was aware the ship was still pitching and tossing, but there was no sense of moving forward now, only an up and down movement, with an occasional fierce jerk, almost as though the ship had been tethered in the middle of the rough sea.

Dressing as quickly as she could, she opened the door to the Leyland's cabin and found Agnes struggling to dress, her husband with her. He looked gaunt and anxious and when Eliza asked what was happening, he replied, 'I don't know exactly where we are, but we are close to land – far too close. We can hear surf pounding against cliffs and have put two anchors out to keep us offshore. I hope they're going to hold, but in case they don't, we must prepare for the worst.'

With this stark warning he hurried from the cabin, leaving Eliza to help Agnes complete her dressing. When this had been accomplished, the captain's wife began gathering her jewellery, adorning neck, wrists and fingers with as much as was possible, fearing that the box in which they were kept would be lost if the ship foundered.

Before she finished a cry went up on deck that an anchor rope had parted and there were fears for the one remaining.

Eliza and Agnes remained in the cabin, uncertain of what they should do, when the door crashed open and a fraught Jim Macleish stumbled into the cabin.

In answer to Agnes's demand to know exactly what was happening, he replied, 'Exactly? I wish I knew. The only thing that's certain is that we've missed the Cornish coast. The storm has driven us up the Bristol Channel so we might well be in danger of being driven on to the *Welsh* coast, although I wouldn't have thought we'd gone quite that far. It's just possible it's Lundy island out there. If it is then God help us! Get up top as quick as you can, but beware of waves when you come out on deck. If we lose the second anchor I'll try to get you in a boat and clear the ship. It will be a desperate measure and our last resort, but there's nothing else that can be done to save anyone.'

A sudden thought struck Eliza and she asked, 'What about the women in the forward hold? How will they escape?'

'Just worry about yourself and Mrs Leyland, girl. We can't look for too many miracles.'

'But … they'll be given a chance, same as the rest of us?' Eliza persisted.

When the mate would not meet her gaze Eliza feared the worst and his reply confirmed her suspicions.

'Having a couple of dozen terrified convict women running amok on the ship at a time like this would risk the lives of everyone on board. They have as much chance of survival in the hold as anyone else.'

'You *have* had their irons taken off?'

Eliza was aware that if the women found themselves in the sea wearing their heavy fetters they would have no chance at all of survival.

'Right at this moment I have every sailor on board fighting to save *Cormorant*. I'll send someone to remove their irons as soon as a man can be spared – now hurry and get up on deck. We've got only one anchor holding us off the rocks now. When the rope breaks – and it will – we'll need to act fast to have any chance of survival. So move yourselves!'

As the trio emerged from the hatch on to the open deck they were almost washed overboard by a wave which crashed down on the stricken ship with all the force of an avalanche.

Agnes was emerging from the hatch ahead of Eliza when the wave struck and had it not been for Eliza's tight grip on her she would have been lost. As it was, they were both thoroughly soaked.

There was a great deal happening on the deck with men shouting and countermanding orders, voices vying – for the most part unsuccessfully – with the noise of the storm. The sailors' activities were illuminated intermittently by lightning, which also showed heaving waves thundering against high cliffs, perilously close to *Cormorant*.

At that moment the bow of the ship suddenly reared up, and when it crashed down again the movement was accompanied by the frightening sound of splintering wood. This was followed by a writhing motion that brought to Eliza's mind an incongruous memory of her early years, when, as a small child in the basement London room where she lived before being taken off to the work-house, she had witnessed the death throes of a rat, caught in a home-made snare.

The memory brought back the same feeling of terror she had experienced on that occasion. Then, above all the other sounds she heard women screaming and, knowing from whence the sounds came, and their implications, the horror she felt had a frightening immediacy – but at that moment someone blundered against her in the darkness.

Staggering off-balance, she was caught by strong hands and Macleish's voice demanded, 'Where's Agnes … Mrs Leyland?'

'She's here …' Agnes had fallen to the deck but Eliza could feel her gripping the hem of her skirt as the captain's wife struggled to regain her footing on the wet deck.

'Hold on to her. Don't lose her – and don't lose *me*. We're going to the boat.'

Eliza had noticed two boats on the deck at *Cormorant's* stern, one on either side and she asked, 'Which one?'

'There's only one … the other was washed overboard.'

Remembering the size of the boat compared with the giant waves battering *Cormorant* and the nearby cliffs, Eliza said fearfully, 'We can't trust our lives to a small boat like that in this sea!'

'It's our only chance, the ship is breaking up on the rocks and nothing can save it now … Hurry!'

As Eliza pulled Agnes to her feet, the captain's wife, half-hysterical with fear, cried, 'Where's my husband? Where's Arnold?'

Without slowing in his efforts to drag the two women along the wildly bucking deck towards the ship's stern, Macleish, head down against the wind and blinding rain shouted, 'He's ordered me to get you into the boat and pull away from the ship. He'll try to escape with the crew over the rocks to the shore. You couldn't make it that way.'

'I'm not going! I want to stay with Arnold….'

'He's busy trying to save his crew. Here we are – but be careful, the boat's swinging about like a mad thing.'

Macleish was fully aware that neither the captain nor any of the crew remaining on board stood any chance of survival. Agnes knew it too but before she could protest any further, the mate bundled her and Eliza into the wildly swinging boat and scrambled in after them.

There was a sudden, stomach-churning drop as the seamen holding the ropes attached to the davits released their grip, sending the boat crashing into the sea. It immediately began bouncing around in an alarming manner, at the mercy of the waves.

'Push away from the ship's side!'

Macleish bellowed the order to the eight or nine seamen who were in the boat, his voice only just discernible above the din about them. Using oars, the sailors levered the boat clear of the stricken *Cormorant*, snapping two oars in the process.

Eventually, to the relief – and disbelief – of everyone on board the small craft they cleared the ship's stern and suddenly the boat was in open water at the mercy of the sea and still far from safety.

'Get the oars in the rowlocks and pull together. We have to get clear of *Cormorant* – and the rocks. Pull as you never have before … *your lives depend on it*! Come on … put your backs into it. In … out … in … out…!'

The mate of the stricken *Cormorant* shouted the time for the oarsmen in a desperate effort to make them pull on the oars together and power the small boat clear of the mother ship.

It was not easy. The boat was rising and falling with the mountainous waves, the blades of the oars digging into water at one moment, flailing the air uselessly in the next – and not all the water stayed *outside* the boat. Eliza had been aware of water soaking her feet when she climbed inside and now she felt it swilling about her ankles.

Macleish was aware of it too. Struggling to hold the tiller with one hand, he felt beneath his seat in the stern of the boat and from a small locker pulled out two dish-shaped objects. Kicking them towards Eliza, he said, 'You and Agnes use these. Try to get rid of some of the water; we can't afford to ride any lower than we are now.'

Eliza handed one of the dishes to Agnes who, ill and terrified of all that was happening about her, only feebly followed the example of Eliza who began baling out water as fast as she could.

The task was not easy. The boat was pitching and rolling wildly and, despite all her efforts, Eliza felt that only half the water she was bailing out reached the side before spilling back into the boat but she urged the distressed wife of the *Cormorant's* captain to follow her example.

Suddenly, the movement of the boat changed perceptibly. It

was still highly mobile but now the waves seemed higher, the rise of the small boat greater than before and the drop into every trough even deeper, with a longer time between the two.

'We've left the lee of the land and are in open water,' Macleish shouted to the seamen in the boat. 'It's as I thought, *Cormorant* must have struck the rocks on Lundy. If we can raise the mast with not too much sail the wind should take us towards the Cornish coast.'

'The *north* coast,' one of the seamen growled, 'Most of that's as rocky as Lundy.'

'*Most* of it,' Macleish agreed, 'but there are harbours and beaches too. By the time we get there it should be light and we'll be able to choose where we go ashore. Let's get that mast up.'

The mast was raised and a modicum of sail set. Although the sail added to the boat's speed and made it easier for Mate Macleish to keep the boat on course, it did nothing to help Eliza and Agnes with the bailing. Half-an-hour after clearing the comparative shelter of Lundy Island the amount of water inside the *Cormorant*'s boat had reached alarming proportions. It hardly improved when Macleish made two of the sailors take the balers, telling Eliza and Agnes to do what they could with cupped hands in a feeble attempt to help.

It was evident they were fighting a losing battle and Eliza asked, 'How far are we from land?'

'Your guess is as good as mine,' the mate replied, 'And that's all I can make … a guess. It could be a mile – or it could be ten! What's far more certain is that unless we get there soon we'll be in serious trouble. We're so low in the water it's coming in faster than we can bail it out. I'll raise more sail and hope to reach the coast before we go under.'

'Is that wise?' The nearest oarsman put the question to the mate. 'The wind has strengthened and is likely to drive us straight into a large wave, instead of riding it.'

'We have no choice. The water in the boat is already so high we probably have no more than a few minutes afloat. If I raise more sail you can all stow the oars and bail as best you can – and pray while you're doing it.'

More sail was raised, but the oarsman was proved right. The wind had actually increased, making the boat far less manoeuvrable. Within minutes of the mate's last order – disaster struck.

The boat was riding the crest of a wave when a sound like a musket shot was heard above the noise of the storm – and the mast snapped. In doing so it carried the sail and jib with it, sweeping three of the boat's occupants into the sea.

One was Agnes Leyland, who had just straightened up to ease the pain in her back brought about by baling.

Eliza screamed as her late mistress disappeared over the side, but nobody was able to help those swept overboard now. The boat had become unmanageable. Nothing could save its occupants.

Suddenly, Eliza found the mate at her side, a knife in his hand. For a moment she cringed in terror, convinced he was about to kill her to save her from suffering in the water.

Instead, he shouted, 'I've cut the sail away and am tying you to the broken off mast. Keep your senses about you in the water and cling to the mast as tightly as you can. Don't let go of it, whatever else you do!'

With seamanlike efficiency he carried out his task, even as he was speaking. Moments later he uttered his last words as the boat sank from under the shipwrecked occupants, leaving them at the mercy of the raging sea.

'God bless you, girl! If you make it to safety say a prayer for me and the others.'

Then she was alone in the water, clinging to the broken mast, her cry of terror cut short by a mouthful of cold salt sea water....

Chapter Nine

*A*LICE HAD JUST dragged the unconscious girl to a patch of sand, farther away from the fluctuating water's edge, when a cry went up from the cliff top and was carried back down the line of weighed down pillagers toiling up the narrow cliff path with their booty. Coast guard officers had been seen hurrying towards the scene of the wrecked vessel.

There was an immediate flurry of activity on the beach. Those who had already gathered goods from the wrecked ship were eager to carry it to the cliff top and escape before the coast guards arrived upon the scene.

There had been a time when such officials were sympathetic towards Cornish coastal dwellers, most of whose lives were spent in abject poverty, but this had changed in the last decade, since the Admiralty in London had won the right to appoint Royal Naval officers and some ratings to the coast guard service.

In most cases the officers were men from outside Cornwall and, in the wake of rumours, not always exaggerated, of shipwrecked seafarers being murdered for their possessions, they showed little sympathy for those who felt they had a time-honoured right to anything that came ashore as a result of shipwreck.

A number of bitter battles had been fought along the Cornish coastline in recent years, resulting in casualties and fatalities on both sides. As a result the coast guards were hated by those who had once profited by smuggling and the pilfering of wrecks – but they had earned a healthy respect for themselves and their Service.

There was a mad scramble to evade the coast guards now, but a number of less agile scavengers had not made it to the top of the cliff by the time the uniformed men appeared at the top of the path.

Those still toiling to the cliff-top hastily jettisoned their booty, causing consternation and occasional injury to those still on the sand of the cove.

Most of this activity was lost upon Alice who, with Percy, was struggling to lift the rescued girl clear of the rocks and away from the incoming tide. They reached a spot that Alice considered safe, at the base of the cliffs and close to where the path met the beach, just as the first of the coast guards arrived there.

Those few hopeful looters who remained on the beach were mostly older men and women, standing close to the water's edge, hoping to create the impression that they were concerned only with what was happening to the stricken ship, and had no interest whatsoever in the items being washed ashore around them.

Because Alice and Percy appeared to be the only two on the now near-deserted beach who were doing anything, they attracted the immediate attention of the uniformed arrivals.

One of two officers who hurried to them addressed Alice's companion, saying, 'Hello, Percy, I would have taken a wager that I would find you here, but I never expected there to be a young woman helping you, and by the look of that body you've carried here you're not likely to get much of value from it.'

Alice realised that, soaking wet as she was, with lank hair hanging out of a waterproof hat belonging to her brother hiding much of her face, she must have looked no different to the dozens of other women the man had passed hurrying away from the scene ... but she was not prepared to waste time explaining herself to him.

'If you've come here to be helpful you and your friends can get the girl up the cliff and take her to the rectory at Trethevy as quickly as you can. She's still alive but appears to be seriously hurt. While you're doing that some of your companions might want to check those laid out further along the beach. It is quite possible some of those are still alive too.'

The coast guard who had addressed Percy was startled. He had previously merely glanced at Alice. Plastered with sand and wet and bedraggled, he had dismissed her as a local village girl, but her manner of speech was not that of a village girl and now he looked closer he could see her clothes were not home-made.

Addressing his companion, he said, 'Stay here with them, I'll go and have a word with Lieutenant Kendall.'

'I have no intention of waiting here while you go off for a discussion with your friends. This girl needs urgent medical attention if she's to survive and I mean to ensure she receives it.'

Her raised voice pursued the coast guard as he hurried away heading for a group of uniformed men standing on the beach, looking out to where the vessel on the offshore rocks was being unmercifully pounded to pieces by the relentless sea.

There were no visible signs of life on board the wrecked vessel and as the coast guard approached the group of fellow officers, two of them waded into the sea to retrieve the body of a man floating face down in the water, arms outstretched to his sides, being washed in with the tide.

The coast guard who had been with Alice and Percy spoke to a young man wearing the uniform of a lieutenant of the Royal Navy, pointing back the way he had come. Heads turned to look in the direction of Alice and the lieutenant, accompanied by two coast guards, began hurrying towards her.

When he arrived, the lieutenant looked at the wet and dishevelled girl kneeling beside the prostrate survivor and was no more impressed with her than the other man had been.

Addressing her, he said, 'Coast Guard Pascoe says the young girl is a survivor from the wrecked vessel and he found you and your companion searching her....'

'Then Coast Guard Pascoe has a vivid imagination,' Alice retorted. 'The state of the girl's clothing makes a search unnecessary. The sea and rocks have not left her with enough to even satisfy decency. Percy and I found her among rocks at the far end of the beach, she is still alive – but only just. If she is not seen by a doctor very soon she'll no longer be a survivor and will join the line of bodies farther along the beach.'

As had the coastguard who had been first to reach her, the Royal Navy lieutenant realised that Alice was not just another local young woman intent upon plunder and he reacted immediately. Turning to the coastguard with him, he said, 'Pascoe, collect a few men and something to support the girl then carry her to the top of the cliff.'

Turning back to Alice, he said, 'I am Lieutenant Jory Kendall, the officer in charge of the North Cornwall coast guard. Where do you want the girl taken? I'll have a doctor sent for but he can't treat her out here in this weather.'

'Have her carried to the rectory at Trethevy. I'll go with her and settle her in a spare room.'

'The rectory? I was not aware of a church at Trethevy.'

'It has been unused for many years, at least, as a place of worship, but my brother has been appointed rector there and it will soon be serving its original purpose once more.'

Her reply satisfied a number of the naval lieutenant's unasked questions, but he had more. 'Why are you here and not your brother? This is hardly the place for a woman – a woman like you – in such circumstances.'

'My brother needed to go to Tavistock yesterday and will not be back until tomorrow. Had he realised what would be happening he would never have gone, not that it would have made any difference. I would still have been on the beach with him. But we are wasting time, this girl needs help – and quickly.'

Stung by his implication that she, as a woman, had no place at the scene of a shipwreck, she added, 'Had I not been here I doubt whether the young girl would have had any chance of survival – but what exactly do you and your men hope to achieve now you *are* here?'

'We came in the hope of rescuing crewmen from the stranded ship if at all possible – but there doesn't appear to be anything we can do. There is very little of the ship left, it has taken such a pounding from the storm. It is also part of my duty to ensure that anything coming ashore is saved for the vessel's rightful owners and is not stolen.'

'You have arrived too late to save *everything*,' Alice commented, 'but what about the bodies over there. There are five or six of them. Will you recover them before the tide is fully in?'

Lieutenant Kendall shook his head, 'By the look of them any means of identification has either been stolen or lost. As they are unknown and their bodies unlikely to be claimed by anyone, they might as well be buried here on the beach as anywhere else.'

'That is appalling!' Alice was distressed by the lieutenant's casual attitude towards the bodies laid out on the beach. 'The men who have drowned will have wives, children or mothers – there might even be women among the bodies too. They deserve more than a shallow grave in the sand. They are entitled to a Christian burial with someone to say a prayer for their souls.'

'I wouldn't argue with that,' he agreed. 'It's what every man who goes to sea would hope for should he be unfortunate enough to be victim of a shipwreck, but a Christian burial requires payment for a parson and gravediggers, as well as an undertaker, coffins and bearers. Who would pay the costs? They would not come from a parish where the dead men are total strangers.'

Alice realised she had given no thought to the practicalities of giving a proper burial to all the shipwreck victims laid out on the tiny beach, but she was determined not to admit it to this naval lieutenant who she felt was being particularly smug at pointing out the lack of thought she had given to arranging a decent burial for the bodies recovered from the wrecked ship.

But now the coast guards had arrived to carry the unconscious survivor to the rectory and she said defiantly, 'I don't think cost should be the first consideration when a disaster such as this occurs. If you and your men have nothing else to do once the girl is taken to the rectory, they can carry the bodies up to Trethevy church. My brother will ensure they are given a proper burial.'

Chapter Ten

*T*HE FIERCE STORM that had brought destruction and death to ships and their passengers and crews in the Western approaches to the British Isles blew itself out during the following night, leaving an uneasy calm along the coastline that had suffered such a battering.

Returning to the Trethevy rectory the next day, Reverend David Kilpeck strode into the kitchen where Alice was seated eating a light lunch. Beaming at his sister and before she had a chance to say anything to him, he said, 'What a delightful drive I have had from Tavistock, Alice, one could almost feel the storm had washed the sins of the world away and brought new life to everyone. What is more, I had a most successful meeting with Reverend Carter and … oh, I have so much to tell you! But first I will have something to eat. The drive in the fresh air has made me quite hungry. I trust you had a peaceful time in my absence and that the storm did not affect Trethevy too badly?'

Alice thought of all that had happened during the two days and nights of his absence and of the four able-bodied men from the Tintagel poorhouse who were at this very moment digging a mass grave in the small piece of enclosed ground behind Trethevy's tiny church. She felt guilty that she was about to destroy the sense of well-being with which her brother had returned to the rectory.

'I have rather a lot to tell you, David. I think you should sit down before I begin.'

David looked surprised, but did as she suggested then listened with increasing shock and dismay to what Alice had to tell him about the storm, its impact upon the people of his parish and of the now semi-conscious girl lying in the spare bedroom upstairs in the rectory. Finally and with some hesitation now there had been time to reflect on her actions, she told him of the bodies washed up in the small cove below Trethevy and which were now lying in the church. *His* church!

When she came to an end, David looked at her with an expression of disbelief on his face. Struggling to find words to express his feelings, he eventually said, in a strangled voice, 'You mean there are bodies ... *dead* people laid out in my church?'

'That's right, six men and a woman, all victims of a shipwreck. It is very, very sad.'

Seemingly still in a state of shock, David asked, 'What on earth were you thinking about, Alice? Quite apart from any other considerations at this moment the church is not fit to keep animals in, let alone lay out bodies – and what am I supposed to do with them now?'

'Give them a Christian burial,' Alice said firmly, with renewed conviction that her actions were justified, 'In the plot of land behind the church that looks as though it might once have been a burial ground.'

'We can't be certain it *was* ever a burial ground, or that it was consecrated. We could be breaking any number of ecclesiastical laws by burying them there, Alice.'

'Possibly,' agreed Alice, defiantly, 'but would you rather they had been buried in shallow graves in the sand down at the cove – or the tide allowed to take them back out to sea again, because that is what was going to happen had I taken no action? This way they will be laid to rest with your blessing and our prayers.'

'There are also a great number of practical issues to be taken into consideration,' David persisted. 'Expenses for coffins, pall bearers and grave-diggers … why, there is not enough money in the church coffers to pay for a flagon of Communion wine, let alone a number of funerals!'

'That has all been taken care of,' Alice said triumphantly, refusing to concede a single point to her brother's arguments, 'The poorhouse master has produced the gravediggers – they are digging a mass grave at this very moment – and the coffins have been provided from the poorhouse store, paid for in a Christian gesture by the Royal Navy lieutenant in charge of the local coast guard. His men have also offered their services as bearers, free of charge.'

David realised that Alice had thought the matter of the burial of the shipwreck's victims through thoroughly, but he was not used to making snap decisions on matters likely to result in controversy.

'This is all most irregular, Alice. I do wish you had waited to consult me before making decisions that were not yours to make.'

'You were not available when they needed to be made,' Alice replied decisively, aware that she had won the argument, 'and a decision needed to be reached immediately if the victims were to be given a Christian burial.'

Knowing his sister as he did, David was aware that nothing he could say would make her change her mind. He had no alternative but to accept the arrangements she had made for the interment of the shipwreck victims.

'Were any survivors able to identify those who are to be buried?' He asked. Resignedly.

Alice shook her head, 'There is only one survivor, a girl named Eliza. It seems she was taken on at the last minute as a maid to one of the very few passengers on board the vessel. She apparently knew none of the crew, or indeed any of her fellow passengers and with all that has happened to her she is thoroughly confused. She is upstairs now, in one of the spare rooms. Eliza suffered a nasty injury and was unconscious for a great many hours. Nevertheless, she is a very lucky girl. Lieutenant Kendall, the officer in charge of the coast guards, says as many as seven ships were wrecked on the Cornish coast alone during the storm – and he has heard of another on Lundy Island. It seems it was the worst storm in living memory hereabouts.'

Determined to rid himself of the unchristian relief he felt that more of the storm's victims had not been washed ashore in his parish, David said, 'Well, as you have made the burial of these unfortunate people a *fait accompli* for me, I had better find out how soon the gravediggers will complete their task and make the necessary arrangements for a simple graveside burial service to be held. When I return to the rectory I will go upstairs to meet your rescued girl – and tell you *my* news. That too is going to involve considerable extra work, but it will bring in extra money for us and so is *good* news.'

'I am sorry, David, so much has been going on here that I haven't even *asked* how your visit to Reverend Carter went. I'll come with you to the church and on the way you can tell me all about it.'

Even though he knew he was being entirely unreasonable, David was unable to entirely hide the disappointment he felt that his own news had been overshadowed by all that had been going on here during his absence.

'It is quite all right, Alice, I feel you have coped incredibly well on your own during what must have been an appalling and traumatic experience and you are needed here to take care of your patient. My news will keep for a quiet moment, when I will tell you all about my meeting with Emmanuel Carter. All I will say for now is that he has asked me to stand in for him as curate of Tintagel, with a salary that, while small, will enable you to take on a housemaid and help us both enjoy a less frugal lifestyle.'

Chapter Eleven

'I RATHER LIKE that coast guard officer of yours, Alice. He was most generous with his donation towards the funeral of the poor unfortunates from the shipwreck. Apparently he comes from a good Cornish family, too. One of the Tintagel churchwardens attending the ceremony says his family own land in South Cornwall.'

'Lieutenant Kendall is not *my* coast guard officer,' Alice replied indignantly. 'He is a naval officer who felt that dead sailors are as entitled to a respectful burial as anyone living on land – and if he comes from a well-to-do family I need not feel so guilty about the money he has spent on something that was my suggestion.'

'I doubt if he will be able to call on his family to pay for his philanthropic whims. Unless he has an allowance the money will come from his naval officer's salary. It is a thoroughly Christian gesture and as such is most praiseworthy.'

Taken by surprise by her defensive response to his remark, David thought it was probably because she really *was* concerned because a suggestion from her had resulted in the young naval officer spending money.

'After the service, Lieutenant Kendall mentioned that he would like to speak to Eliza. He has to submit reports to the Coast Guard headquarters in London about the shipwrecks that occurred along the North Cornwall coast during the great storm. There were very few survivors and it would seem Eliza is the only one from the *Balladeer*.'

It had been confirmed from the wreckage washed ashore that *Balladeer* was the vessel wrecked upon the Lye rock.

'He is not likely to learn much from Eliza, she is terribly vague about everything that happened,' Alice said. 'It is hardly surprising, she is little more than a child and it must have been a terrifying ordeal for her.'

'We must hope she regains her memory in due course, we need to notify someone of her whereabouts.'

'There is no one,' Alice replied. 'She is a poorhouse girl and as a child was put into service with an old lady. Sadly, her employer became senile and was taken to live with a daughter, somewhere in the north of England. They had no need of Eliza and she might have been returned to the poorhouse had she not been taken into service by a lady travelling on the vessel to join her family, only hours before the *Balladeer* sailed. It seems this lady's own maid changed her mind about going aboard at the very last minute. It all happened so suddenly that Eliza knew her mistress only as "Miss Jenny". She had been told her surname, but Eliza said it was very long and foreign-sounding and there was no time to familiarise herself with it.'

David frowned, 'That is all very well, but what will happen to her now, she cannot stay here.'

'But she *can*, David, don't you see? When you returned from Tavistock with the news that you were to act as Reverend Carter's curate at Tintage, you said we could now afford to take on a housemaid. Well, providence has presented us with one!'

Taken aback, David said, 'But I was thinking of employing a local girl, someone who would know all the people in the area and be known by them. We know nothing about Eliza and if all she says is true we have no means of obtaining references.'

'She is a fourteen year-old girl, David. If she has shortcomings as a housemaid she is young enough to learn new ways. I think this was meant to be – and I *want* her for our housemaid.'

It was apparent that Alice had made up her mind and David was aware that further argument would be futile. Sighing in resignation, he said, 'Very well, but she will begin work on the understanding that she is on a month's trial. If she proves unsatisfactory during that time she must go.'

'I believe she is exactly what we are looking for, David, but thank you. Had you not persuaded Reverend Carter to take you on as his curate we would never have been able to afford a housemaid at all. You are a very clever brother.'

David was aware his sister was only flattering him because she had got her own way, but he did not mind. Alice had always worked hard on his behalf and he was pleased to be able to do something to make *her* happy.

When Alice put the suggestion to Eliza, the young girl could hardly believe her luck. Since recovering consciousness and being told where she was, she had feared her rescuers would be bound to learn *why* she had been on the shipwrecked vessel in the first place.

Fortunately, for some days after her rescue she had difficulty in speaking, the doctor attending her declaring it was the result of swallowing large amounts of sea water. He ordered her *not* to talk until the effects wore off.

As a result, Eliza *listened* to the conversations of those who frequented the sick room where she lay and by so doing learned that they believed she was the sole survivor of the *Balladeer*, a ship which had foundered on Lye rock, close to where she had been washed ashore, victim of the ferocious storm which had wrecked so many other ships in the Bristol Channel.

By listening and not talking, Eliza had been able to mentally build up a new identity for herself – including a new name. She would still be Eliza, but it would now be Eliza *Smith* and not Brooks, a girl whose working life would follow closely upon the life she had known, but leaving out her conviction and sentence of transportation and bypassing those incidents in her life which might lead anyone with an inquiring mind to learn of her true past.

She was also deliberately vague about the actualities of her survival, an attitude supported by the doctor attending her. He declared her to be suffering from the trauma of her recent experience, advising Alice that she should not be questioned on the subject. It was, he said, something with which she would come to terms 'in the fullness of time'.

Eliza was less reticent about the duties she had performed as a housemaid when Alice tentatively suggested she might like to work at the rectory. She was desperately eager to be taken into the household of Reverend David Kilpeck and his sister.

Should the authorities discover that Eliza Brooks was alive and free, she would be taken back into custody and the sentence of the London judge carried out. On the other hand, Eliza *Smith* could lead a comfortable enough life here in Cornwall, far from those who had once known her. At least, until she had grown old enough for her appearance to have changed sufficiently to fool anyone who might have know the *other* Eliza well enough to be able to identify her.

Chapter Twelve

'*D*O YOU THINK Eliza is well enough now to answer a few questions about the shipwreck?'

It was almost a fortnight after the storms that had caused havoc to shipping in the Western Approaches and Lieutenant Jory Kendall was paying a visit to the Trethevy rectory. In response to his report on the ships wrecked along the North Cornwall coast on that eventful night he had received a letter from the Admiralty, requesting more details in respect of the loss of the *Balladeer*.

'She is *physically* well enough,' Alice replied, 'but she becomes quite upset if the shipwreck is mentioned and there are great gaps in her memory of all that happened to her on that night.'

'It's hardly surprising,' the coast guard officer said, sympathetically. 'She is only a young girl and it was a horrific and terrifying experience for her. She is very, very lucky to have survived at all, only a handful of people were rescued from the ships lost that night. Three went down with the loss of everyone on board. I wouldn't be asking her any questions at all but the master of *Balladeer* was related to a senior officer at the Admiralty who wants to know whether it is possible one of the bodies found might possibly be that of his relative. I don't know whether Eliza saw any of them?'

Alice shook her head. 'She was terribly confused and far too ill to attend the funeral … but I saw the bodies and the men were all young, far too young to be master of a ship. Is that all you wish to speak to Eliza about?'

'Yes ... well no, actually, but it is nothing important. For some reason, probably purely because of the interest someone in the Admiralty has in the ship, they have sent me a list of passengers and crew. The name of Eliza Smith isn't among them – although I have to admit there is nothing particularly unusual in that. The passenger lists of most ships are notoriously inaccurate, mostly through sheer inefficiency on the part of those making them, although sometimes it is because someone has taken the fare and kept it for himself. However, I thought I might mention it.'

'You may, if you wish, she is sitting out in the sunshine at the back garden, but I believe I can give you an answer. A lady booked passage on the *Balladeer* for herself and a maid. At the very last moment the maid decided she did not want to leave England and the woman found Eliza to take her place shortly before the ship set sail for America. She probably did not even think about changing the name on the passenger list for a servant travelling with her. I have spoken to Eliza about the ship itself and she is very vague about it, but that is hardly surprising either. She went on board in the dark and the vessel set sail the same night, running into such bad weather when it left the Thames that she and her employer never left their cabin before the ship ran into trouble. At some stage when the ship was in distress she and her mistress were put into a boat in a vain attempt to reach safety. I think we both know what happened afterwards.'

Jory Kendall nodded sympathetically. 'I have experienced a great many storms at sea, some can be thoroughly alarming, even for a sailor. I can only imagine how Eliza must have felt. The poor girl would have been terrified. I don't need to trouble her right now, if at all, but what is going to happen to her when she is well? Will she return to London and her parents?'

'She is a poorhouse girl with no parents but as she has experience of being in service David and I thought we would take her on trial as a housemaid. If she proves satisfactory – as I am convinced she will – she will remain at Trethevy with us.'

'That would be a very acceptable arrangement for everyone. I hope the girl will be duly grateful to you....'

Before he could say any more there was the sound of hurried footsteps along the passageway from the front door and a moment later Percy burst into the room, his face above the greying beard ruddier than normal.

Before Alice could reprove him for not knocking at the door, the old man asked breathlessly, 'Where's the Reverend? I just went up to the church to fetch a rake I'd left there yesterday and there's a whole lot of young bullocks been turned loose in the churchyard. They're trampling over everything! It's Eval Moyle's work, no doubt about it.'

'Reverend Kilpeck went to Tintagel earlier this morning. He walked there because it's such a fine day.'

'Are you talking of Moyle the Ranter preacher?' The question came from Jory Kendall.

'You know him?' Alice queried.

'We've met,' Jory said, tight-lipped, 'He had shares in a fishing-boat we caught smuggling. The boat was ordered to be broken up and Moyle kicked up a rumpus about it. He is inclined to believe the laws of the land don't apply to him. But how do *you* know him, I wouldn't have thought he had much time for anyone associated with the Church of England.'

'Before David and I arrived at Trethevy Moyle had been using the churchyard, indeed, the church itself, as somewhere to keep his animals. He had not paid rent to the previous owner for years but was very annoyed to learn the property had been given back to the Church. I had better go there to make quite sure the cattle do not go inside the church itself now that it has been cleaned, but I can't think of anything else that can be done until my brother returns from Tintagel.'

'I can,' declared the young naval lieutenant, firmly, 'We'll simply turn his cattle out of the churchyard.'

'But then they might go anywhere!'

'No doubt they will, but that will be Moyle's problem, not yours. Come on, Percy, you can help me.'

'You two go ahead,' Alice said, 'I will follow as soon as I have told Eliza where we are going. She might panic if she comes into the rectory and finds no one here.'

When Alice went to the back garden and found Eliza, the young girl asked immediately, 'Is there anything I can do to help?'

Alice had become quite attached to the young prospective housemaid during the brief time she had spent recuperating at the rectory and she smiled at the question. 'I suppose you could come up to the churchyard and frighten Eval Moyle away should he return. You are so pale he might imagine you are a ghost, coming to haunt him for his sins. No, Eliza, stay here and let the sun put some colour into your cheeks. I will put the kettle on the fire before I go. If we are not back soon perhaps you could pop into the rectory kitchen and move it to the hob. Lieutenant Kendall will be with us. He is here to have a brief chat with you about the shipwreck.'

Her words alarmed Eliza but, unaware of the true reason for the young girl's fearful expression, Alice placed a reassuring hand on her shoulder. 'Don't think about it too much, Eliza, it's purely routine. It seems he has received a letter from a relative of the captain of the *Balladeer*, asking if you could say whether any of the bodies we buried in the churchyard might have been him. I told Lieutenant Kendall you had not seen the bodies but I had and they were all far too young to be a ship's master.'

'I wouldn't have known him anyway,' Eliza said uneasily, 'I

don't think I ever saw him during the short time I was on board. If I did, I certainly can't remember what he looked like … but the weather was so bad I never left the cabin.'

She was genuinely fearful at the thought of being interrogated and caught out by the lieutenant's questions, but Alice said, 'There is no need to look so worried, I have already told Lieutenant Kendall you are unable to remember very much about the ordeal you have been through and he is a very understanding man. But now I must go to the churchyard and learn what is happening there. Only deal with the kettle if you feel up to it – and don't worry about anything.'

When Alice had left the garden Eliza *did* worry. She realised the tragic consequences of the storm had given her an unexpected opportunity to build a new life in a manner she could never have believed possible – and such a chance was not likely to come her way again.

Despite her conviction in a London criminal court, Eliza was a basically honest girl and given such kindly employers as Alice Kilpeck and her brother she felt confident she would be able to put the unhappy past behind her and serve them both loyally and happily.

Eliza had no ambitions beyond her present station in life. Work as a servant in a stable household was all she wished for. All she had ever wanted. Fate would be cruel were this to be taken from her by the questions of Lieutenant Kendall, however kindly and well-meaning he might be.

In her mind Eliza went over the story she had told to Alice and her brother, determined not to give Lieutenant Kendall the slightest reason for doubting it was the truth.

Chapter Thirteen

*H*URRYING ALONG THE lane from the rectory, Alice had covered no more than half the distance to Trethevy church when she was suddenly confronted by a small but lively herd of young bovines and forced to dash back the way she had come, losing one of her shoes in the process.

She found safety before reaching the rectory by scrambling inelegantly over a five-barred gate into an adjacent field as the wild-eyed, jostling bullocks cavorted past, filling the narrow lane from hedgerow to hedgerow.

Following on behind was a concerned Jory Kendall, who had seen Alice's wild dash for safety. Struggling to untie the rope securing the gate, his relief to see her standing in the field, apparently unharmed, was quite evident.

'You had me very worried, Alice. I was in the churchyard when I saw you coming along the lane just as Percy was opening the gate to let the bullocks out. I shouted for him to close it again, but I was too late and when I ran out into the lane you had disappeared. I feared you might have been trampled!'

'For a few moments I thought I was going to be, but by running faster than at any time since I was a young girl I succeeded in beating them to the gate.'

The length of rope securing the gate had been rendered stiff and hard to manipulate by long exposure to extremes of weather and, finally admitting defeat, Jory helped her to climb over it once more, lifting her to the ground in the lane with ease, surprised at how light she was.

Smiling up at him, Alice said, 'That was far more ladylike than the manner in which I went over the gate when Moyle's cattle were in close pursuit.'

'I am sorry, Alice, I would never have allowed Percy to let them out of the churchyard had I realised you were in the lane.'

'It was my fault, not yours. You and Percy did what you had gone there to do – and judging by the speed at which they were running, they will be miles away by the time Eval Moyle comes looking for them.'

'Yes, but he certainly *will* come,' Jory said, suddenly serious. 'I believe he put the animals in the churchyard with the deliberate intention of provoking your brother. The decision to bury dead sailors there has gained much support from the parishioners, many of whom have family or friends earning a living from the sea. Having a parish priest who cares enough to ensure that unknown sea-going men are given a Christian burial, even though there is no profit to be made from it, has impressed them greatly. One of the reasons the established Church has lost so many followers to non-conformist groups is because of the perceived view that Church of England priests are appointed not so much for the salvation of ordinary people, but to take as much money from them as possible in order to benefit both Church and priest – and not necessarily in that order!'

'That is a very cynical observation,' Alice protested indignantly, 'it is certainly not the way David feels about his work here.'

'I know,' Jory agreed. 'That is exactly why he will find himself a target for Eval Moyle. The last thing Moyle wants is to have a popular Church of England cleric in the area. A great deal of his support comes from God-fearing people who are desperate to have someone lead them in their worship, someone they feel able to turn to in troubled times, providing reassurance and the promise of a better life to come. Eval Moyle is certainly not the right man for the job, but he is better than nothing! Reverend Carter rarely visits the parish and people have been unable to marry, have their children baptised, or even call upon a qualified priest to bury their loved ones. Despite this, the Church is swift to act if the tithes it demands are not forthcoming. The resentment this has built up against the established Church plays right into the hands of men like Moyle. The last thing he wants is to have someone like your brother appointed to the parish. You can be quite certain he will do everything in his power to drive him out, and Moyle is a dangerous and primitive man, both in his thinking and his adopted form of worship.'

Aware that he had been somewhat carried away in his fierce condemnation of Eval Moyle, Jory said, less heatedly, 'Anyway, I think I should stay around for a while, at least until your brother returns, just in case Moyle puts in an appearance. He is going to be very angry about having his cattle turned loose.'

'Thank you. I doubt whether Eval Moyle would physically attack me but he *is* a very volatile man and most unpleasant. When I have found my missing shoe we will return to the rectory and I shall make some tea for us.'

Alice recovered her shoe and although it had been trampled upon by the lively bullocks it was wearable and when they reached the rectory she decided they should have their tea in the garden. Leading Jory to where Eliza was seated beside a table in the shade of a gnarled and ancient apple tree she suggested he should remain with Eliza and chat to her while tea was being made.

Much to their surprise, Eliza declared that *she* would make it for Alice and the coast guard officer.

Concerned, Alice asked, 'Do you think you are well enough yet, Eliza? You have been very ill, you know?'

'I am feeling much better, thanks to you ma'am and if I'm to be your housemaid it's high time I showed what I can do about the house. I probably won't be able to manage *everything* right away, but you've been both patient and very kind towards me. Now I'd like to make a start on doing things for *you*.'

'Well, if that is how you feel, I am very happy, but do not do too much right away.'

Eliza made her way to the kitchen, aware she had made a favourable impression upon her employer, but the truth was that she was relieved to have found a way to avoid being questioned by Lieutenant Kendall about the events leading up to the ship-wreck.

At the moment there was no reason why anyone should doubt her story about being a passenger on the *Balladeer*. The ship had been wrecked on the rocks just beyond the nearby cliffs and she had been washed ashore in the cove, together with the bodies of those who had died on that vessel, but if she said something that did not ring true and it was suspected that her story was false…!

She would need to remain on her guard for a long time and, if at all possible, avoid any lengthy conversations about the ship on which she had been sailing, especially when talking to the coast guard officer.

It might prove difficult unless she made it clear from the begin-ning that she was a servant, a housemaid, and as such was expected to keep out of the way of her employers and their friends as much as was possible in a house the size of the rectory.

Chapter Fourteen

WHEN ELIZA LEFT the garden, Jory said, 'She is very eager to please you, Alice – and rightly so. You saved her life and have taken her into your household, but in truth you know very little about her background. Don't you think you should carry out some enquiries?'

'Why? I know she survived a shipwreck, is lucky to be alive and I will soon learn whether she is telling the truth about having been in service. What else do I need to learn?'

'I don't know, but she does seem very reluctant to talk about the shipwreck itself.'

'Is that so surprising? She is a young girl who has been through a thoroughly terrifying experience. The mind tends to blot out memories of such things – and it is perhaps just as well. Besides, in the short time I have known her I have come to like her and believe I am going to be very happy to have her working for me.'

Jory realised that any further suggestion from him that Eliza might possibly be hiding something about her background would be resented by Alice, and it was something he was anxious to avoid. He wanted to come to know the Trethevy cleric's sister better.

'I am pleased … for both of you. I must confess I know very little about poorhouses, but I *am* aware they are very unhappy places. Besides, as her recent experiences fade with time I have no doubt you will learn a great deal more about her.'

'If she carries out her work to my satisfaction she can tell me as much, or as little, as she pleases. For now I am happy just to have been able to save her from the sea.'

Eliza made the tea and carried it to the garden table and was assuring her solicitous employer that she had encountered no problems in performing her first duty as the rectory housemaid, when a furious Eval Moyle stormed into the garden.

Jory was absent at that moment, having gone to the stable to ask Percy to water his horse as he was remaining at the rectory longer than he had anticipated.

When Moyle looked around and located Alice, he advanced towards her menacingly, declaring angrily, 'I want words with you!'

Trying very hard to appear calm and self-assured, Alice replied, 'And good morning to you too, Mr Moyle. May I perhaps offer you a cup of tea?'

'Don't try making a fool of me, young woman, I'm not one of your soft-living English churchmen. Now you're in Cornwall you'll need to learn how a woman's expected to behave, before someone takes a mind to put you firmly in your place.'

'That someone is certainly not going to be *you*, Mr Moyle, so if this is not a social call, I suggest you go on your way and attend to your business.'

'I'll go when I'm good and ready and not before – but I haven't come to bandy words with *you*, any business I have right now is with your brother. Where is he?'

'Reverend Kilpeck went to Tintagel early this morning. You'll either find him in the church, or with the churchwardens.'

Looking at Alice speculatively, Moyle said, 'If your brother's been in Tintagel since this morning then it wouldn't be him who turned my cattle out on the road, they was where I put 'em only an hour ago. Was it you? If it was...!' He took a step closer, clenching his fists.

'No, it wasn't Miss Kilpeck, Moyle, it was me.'

Jory had come from the stables, unseen behind Moyle and now the burly preacher swung around to face him.

'You? What business is it of yours what I do with my animals? Ain't it enough that you had my fishing-boat broken up with your interfering? Are you out to ruin me, and all the men like me, here-abouts?'

'Lieutenant Kendall was helping me by removing cattle which had been deliberately turned out to graze on consecrated ground, Mr Moyle. Had he not done so *I* should have reported the matter and you would be facing a hefty fine.'

Returning his attention to Alice, Moyle said angrily, 'I told you just now to remember your place, girl, you have far too much to say for yourself. That might be alright for them mamby-pamby preachers you're used to, but I'm not one of 'em. If I have any more of your lip you'll feel the back of my hand.'

'That's quite enough of such talk, Moyle. You'd do well to set off after your cattle or they will be halfway to Devon.'

'If they are it'll be *your* doing.' Stepping towards Jory, Moyle said angrily, 'You and me have a score to settle and you're not on duty now. Even if you were, turning my cattle loose into the countryside has nothing to do with coast guard business. I think it's time to see what you're made of without a dozen or more men backing you up.'

Jory realised how vulnerable he was in the confrontation with this man. He was not carrying a weapon and the man facing him was not only a brutal and experienced fighter but also far more heavily built than himself. However, he could not back down now. All he could do was issue a warning, fully aware it would be disregarded.

'If you attack me you'll not convince a court it wasn't to take revenge for what's happened between us in the past, Moyle. You'll go to prison for it.'

Shaking his head, the preacher said, 'I'll not be convicted by any *Cornish* court. Not for breaking the bones of a coast guard in a fair fight, I won't.'

'But you will certainly go to prison for sacrilege – and I doubt whether even a Methodist ministry will want anything to do with a preacher convicted of such a crime.' Aware of the very real danger Moyle posed to Jory, Alice made a last-ditch attempt to head off violence.

At that moment Eliza provided an unexpected diversion. She had disappeared soon after Moyle arrived and now, hurrying to where the two men stood facing each other, she addressed Moyle. 'Excuse me, sir, do you have a pony, a small, brown, shaggy one?'

Taken by surprise, Moyle scowled, 'What's it to you, girl? But yes, it's tied up outside the gate.'

'Not any more. You couldn't have tied it up properly. I've just seen it wandering off along the lane with its reins dragging on the ground.'

His anger flaring-up once more, Moyle glowered at Eliza, 'There was nothing wrong with the way I tied the pony. Have you turned it loose? If you have ...'

'I haven't been out of the house,' Eliza lied, adding with assumed indignation, 'I saw it through the window. 'Sides, I'm scared of horses, I wouldn't go near one.'

This too was a lie, in London she had never been able to pass by a tethered pony without stopping to stroke its muzzle, but Moyle was unaware of this and Eliza continued ...

'I think I should tell you, sir, there's a dog from one of the places along the lane that barks whenever it sees a horse. If it barks at your pony it could run a mile or more in fright and might well hurt itself if its leg got caught in the reins and trips it over.'

Eval Moyle was far from satisfied with Eliza's reply but at that moment there was the sound of a dog barking in the distance. Seizing the opportunity it offered, Eliza said, 'Listen! That sounds like the dog. I hope your pony hasn't reached that far yet, sir, or you'll never find it again.'

Her words succeeded where Jory's threats of jail had not.

'I haven't finished with you by a long way,' Moyle threw the words at Jory, but it was a parting threat as he hurried from the rectory garden, leaving Alice, Eliza and Jory greatly relieved.

It was Alice who was the first to speak. 'That was a very timely intervention, Eliza, but did Moyle's pony really break free of its own accord?'

'Well, it wasn't really *tied* to the rail,' Eliza admitted. 'The reins were just wrapped around it a couple of times. It wouldn't have taken much for the pony to do it by itself.'

'But no doubt the process was accelerated with a little help from you?' Jory suggested, adding, 'You are a very resourceful young lady, Eliza, and I am in your debt. I am not unused to violence and can hold my own with most men, but I don't think I would have lasted long against Eval Moyle without suffering a severe beating.'

Pleased with the coast guard officer's comments, Eliza was clearing the tea things away when Jory began talking to Alice.

'I have received a letter from the coast guard headquarters in London, the storm we suffered here, in the South West, was even worse than we realised at the time. Of all the ships wrecked around our coasts there were only a handful of survivors. Perhaps one of the most tragic was the foundering of a ship named *Cormorant* on Lundy Island, in the Bristol Channel. It had a number of female convicts on board, being carried to Australia. They were all drowned and some of their shackled bodies are still being washed up on the island …'

The crash as tea things fell to the ground from the tray Eliza was holding interrupted what Jory was saying and, seeing the distressed expression on Eliza's face, he hastened to apologise, 'I am so sorry, Eliza, it was quite unforgivable of me to talk about such things in front of you.'

'It … it's all right,' Eliza said, the tears that had sprung to her eyes giving the lie to her words, 'It's just … I'm sorry about the tea things.'

Once again she faltered and Alice came to her aid. 'Don't worry about them, Eliza, I'll pick them up and take them in. It is going to take you a long time to get over your horrible experience. You go to your room now and rest for a while, you are looking very tired.'

Giving the young girl a wry but warm smile, she added, 'Your first working day has been rather more eventful than I trust your normal duties will be. You will not be expected to deal with bullying dissenting preachers as an everyday occurrence.'

'I apologise once again, Eliza, and I trust Miss Kilpeck is right – but I think you should keep out of Eval Moyle's way for a while.'

Alone in her room, Eliza found she was shaking, but her distress had nothing to do with the visit to the rectory by the Primitive Methodist preacher. Her mind was filled with thoughts of the women with whom she had travelled from the prison hulk moored at Woolwich to the *Cormorant* and who had remained shackled in the forward hold of the ship during the storm.

She had thought of them at the time when the storm was raging, but only in passing. Now the sheer horror hit home of what they must have experienced, shackled and helpless as they were, when *Cormorant* was breaking up on the rocks of Lundy Island. Imagining their plight, memories of her own ordeal flooded back.

Flinging herself face down on to her bed, she began sobbing into the pillow.

Chapter Fifteen

*T*HE DISSENTING PREACHER did not return to the Trethevy rectory and Alice and Jory spent a pleasant time together, taking full advantage of the opportunity to discover more about each other.

Jory learned that Alice and David came from an ecclesiastical family, their late father having been Dean of an East Anglian cathedral before his untimely demise while Alice was still young. His death seriously affected their mother's health for the rest of her life and she eventually died too, having been nursed by Alice for many years.

Since their mother's death Alice had kept house for her brother in various parts of the country, while he waited for an appointment to a parish. It eventually came through the nepotic influence of their uncle, also a Dean.

Unlike Alice, both of Jory's parents were still alive and his family owned a large house and estate on Cornwall's South coast, close to the ancient town of Lostwithiel.

Much to Alice's surprise, she learned that Jory's father was *Lord* Kendall, a family ancestor having been raised to the peerage as a Baron during the English Civil War.

'Does that mean you are in fact Lieutenant the *Honourable* Jory Kendall?' she queried.

'A quite meaningless accolade,' Jory admitted. 'It's not as

though I will ever inherit the title. I am the third of five brothers and the wife of the first of them is expecting what the family hopes will be a future heir to the title and estate.'

'Does it trouble you to know you are unlikely to inherit the title?' Alice was puzzled by Jory's apparent indifference to the situation.

'Not at all. It means I have none of the responsibilities that come with the inheritance and I was able to leave home and pursue a naval career without the distractions that come with being heir to a large estate. At least, I could before hurting my leg.' Patting his thigh to emphasise his remark, he added, 'Actually, it seems to have confounded the prognosis of the surgeons by mending itself.'

Alice had observed that Jory had a slight limp, but had never thought it might be anything serious. Now she asked, almost casually, 'What did you do to it?'

Giving her a wry smile, he said, 'I did nothing, it was a Malayan pirate's large-bore musket ball that did the damage. It made such a mess that the ship's surgeon wanted to amputate the leg, but at the time I believed it looked far worse than it really was and refused to allow him to operate. He wasn't terribly concerned by my refusal, saying I was probably going to die anyway! Fortunately, I was right and he was wrong, but it put me ashore and set back any chance of promotion for a while. However, I anticipate returning to sea-going duties again before too long.'

Shuddering at the thought of an operation that would have removed Jory's leg, Alice said, 'I am glad your leg was not lost, of course, but surely the work you are doing is important enough to keep you in Cornwall?'

'We are at war with China and need to put more ships to sea. With my seniority I might possibly be given a command, even though it would certainly be of something small, like a brig, or perhaps a schooner.'

The thought of returning to sea was quite obviously pleasing to Jory Kendall, but Alice hoped his departure would not happen *too* soon.

When David returned home that evening he was told of the incident involving Eval Moyle's cattle and the threatening attitude the Primitive Methodist minister had adopted towards Alice and Jory Kendall.

The Trethevy rector was furious and his first thought was to seek out Moyle and take him to task for his actions but he was dissuaded from such a course by Alice and Jory. Both were aware that David was not a violent man – and Moyle most definitely was!

David accepted, albeit reluctantly, that discretion was preferable to foolish valour on this occasion but he said, 'Whatever course of action is taken, Moyle cannot be allowed to flaunt the laws of the Established Church in such a manner. He must be warned of his conduct by a letter from the archdeacon, or perhaps from the bishop.'

'Think very carefully before you do anything, David,' Alice said. 'If you bring the Bishop into the matter he might decide to take Moyle to court. That would really stir him up, and possibly alienate some of your parishioners. Think about the possible consequences before you take any action against him.'

Grudgingly, David saw the wisdom of Alice's advice. He was still a newcomer to the parish and although Moyle preached in a dissenting Church he was a local man – and in Cornwall that counted for a great deal.

When Jory concurred with what Alice had said, David agreed he would do nothing without first discussing it with Alice, and perhaps consulting Jory too.

Aware her argument had won the day, Alice made an effort to move her brother's thoughts away from the difficult dissenting minister. 'You have said nothing about your visit to the church-wardens at Tintagel, how was your day?'

Her ploy worked immediately. His face lighting up, David said, 'It was most successful. The churchwardens were delighted to hear I will be taking on Reverend Carter's duties. It seems they have a waiting list for christenings and weddings – especially weddings. There are at least two prospective brides who are likely to give birth out of wedlock if not married very soon. There are also a number of mothers asking for churching, to give thanks for the safe delivery of a child. So it looks as though I will be kept busy and able to add a little to our income.'

The problem of Eval Moyle forgotten for the moment, David beamed at his two listeners. 'One of the churchwardens is Henry Yates, master of the poorhouse and the meeting gave me an opportunity to thank him for his help and generosity in helping to bury the unfortunate victims of the shipwreck. He was delighted to have his contribution acknowledged and I feel he is basically a good man. He has promised to bring many of the poor-house inmates along to my first service in Tintagel church. I doubt if they will boost the collection at all but they will certainly add to the congregation numbers and that should impress the bishop's office – and Reverend Carter. Yates was helpful in other ways too. I happened to mention that I am going to find it diffi-cult to keep the churchyard and rectory garden tidy here at Trethevy and he says he has a very suitable candidate to take on the task. It would seem this young man lived with his grand-mother and took excellent care of her and when she died applied to join the army. He was accepted, but before he actually signed the papers he was injured in an accident whilst working tem-porarily in a local quarry. He badly broke a leg and as a result ended up in the poorhouse. Yates assured me the leg has healed now, but has left him with a bad limp. He can work as well as any other man and is pleasant, honest and strong, but these are not the easiest of times and there would seem to be no employment for anyone with even the hint of a disability – especially a poorhouse lad. I have said I am willing to give him a trial.'

The poorhouse master's reported praise for the out-of-work young resident of his establishment failed to impress Alice. 'Having someone from the poorhouse working here at Trethevy might be satisfactory in summer, but in winter, or when there are storms about such as the one we have experienced recently, even a fully able man could not be expected to walk to and from Tintagel on a dark morning or night. For someone with a disability it would be positively dangerous!'

Jory had been listening to the conversation and now he spoke for the first time. 'I know the lad in question and have gone into his background very thoroughly. His name is Tristram Rowe and if you were to take him on I think you would find him as dependable as anyone you are likely to wish to employ at the rectory. A couple of months ago he applied to me for work and he was willing to do anything I was able to offer him. Unfortunately, I could not take him on as a coast guard but I felt sorry for him because of my own experience of a serious leg injury and found a few odd jobs for him around the coastguard station. He did them well, completing all that I gave him to do much more quickly than I expected. He is a very likeable young man and had I been able to take him on permanently, I would certainly have done so. I told him I would be happy to recommend him to any potential employer. So there you are, I have now done exactly that!'

'Thank you,' said David, then, turning to Alice once more and appearing slightly embarrassed, he said, 'Er … Yates and I discussed the problem of the distance between the poorhouse and Trethevy and I told him we could probably put young Rowe up here, at the rectory.'

Forestalling Alice's predictable objection to this latest proposal, he added hastily, 'Not in the rectory itself, of course, but there are the rooms over the stable, Percy only occupies one of them. Rowe could have one of the others. I have no doubt he would make far more of tidying it up than Percy has.'

'Give him a room of his own and he would be in absolute heaven,' Jory said, enthusiastically. 'He feels the ignominy of living in a poorhouse very strongly.'

Shifting her gaze from one man to the other, Alice shrugged her shoulders in a gesture of resignation before addressing her brother. 'I can see that whatever I feel about the matter will make no difference and it is you who will be paying for him. When is he coming?'

After throwing a brief but grateful glance in Jory's direction, David replied, 'I told Yates I would speak to you this evening and if you were in agreement with the arrangement I would ride to the poorhouse tomorrow and meet with Rowe.'

'You will like him,' Jory commented, positively, 'you too, Alice.'

'Whether I like him or not is quite immaterial,' Alice replied, 'he will be working outside and not here, in the house. In fact, it will make life easier for me. Now we are to have *two* outside workers, he and Percy can come to a mutual arrangement for feeding *themselves*.'

Alice was aware she was behaving in a peevish and probably unreasonable manner. It did not help when realisation came that she was more upset because Jory had sided with David against her than by the fact her brother wanted to take on another employee, when it was not at all certain they could really afford the additional expense.

Chapter Sixteen

*D*AVID WAS AT the back door of the rectory, instructing Percy on his day's work, before leaving to carry out his own parochial duties on foot, when Alice called from the kitchen. 'David, tell Percy to have the pony and trap made ready. I am coming out with you.'

Taken by surprise, David asked, 'Why? I am only going to the poorhouse to interview the young man recommended to us by Henry Yates. There is really no need for you to come along.'

'If he is to be employed around the rectory grounds I want to form an opinion of him too. Besides, I would like to see what conditions are like in the poorhouse, especially for the women and girls accommodated there. If you had a wife she would be expected to take an interest in such things. As your sister, I am the next best thing.'

David had to admit to himself that she was right. A parish priest's wife was expected to involve herself in a great many aspects of parish life. He was secretly delighted that she wished to involve herself in his work … but was also aware she was basically opposed to taking on another employee. Her presence at the poorhouse could lead to Tristram Rowe being deemed 'unsuitable' to work at the rectory.

Nevertheless, he knew it would be futile to argue the point with her. 'I will tell Percy – but bring a coat. There is a chill wind blowing from the sea.'

*

Alice enjoyed the drive to Tintagel. She had only rarely left the Trethevy rectory since she and her brother arrived there, but with Eliza now fit enough to take on many of the household chores she intended being less tied to the house.

As though reading her thoughts, David asked, 'Do you feel quite confident about leaving Eliza in charge of the rectory in your absence?'

'Perfectly confident. After witnessing her resourcefulness in dealing with Moyle yesterday I would entrust her with any task.'

Less assured than his sister, David said, 'Yet we really know so little about her, and she has no references.'

'In view of the manner of her arrival at Trethevy that is hardly surprising,' Alice retorted, 'and we both know that many servant references are exaggerated simply because the employer is anxious to be rid of them. I like to think I am a good judge of character, indeed, you have said so yourself, on many occasions.'

At that moment the pony and trap rounded a bend in the narrow lane and were immediately in the midst of a small flock of sheep being driven by a diminutive, bow-legged farmer who had a weather-beaten face that must have witnessed the seasons of more than three-quarters of a century.

Allowing his sheep to enjoy the grass that was plentiful on the lane's verges, the farmer doffed his stained and misshapen hat to the young rector and for almost half-an-hour regaled the sister and brother with tales of past parish priests, and the current gossip of the area.

By the time the conversation came to an end sheep were scattered the length of the lane for farther than could be seen and, with a series of unintelligible commands, the old man sent his patient sheep-dog off to round up the flock and bring them back to their garrulous shepherd.

Resuming their journey, David and Alice discussed what the old farmer had told them about the area and, long before the subject had been exhausted, they arrived at the poorhouse.

The building was not as large as Alice had imagined it would be, but David explained that this was merely a *parish* poorhouse and soon to be superseded. A law had been passed by the parliament in London, ordering adjoining parishes to amalgamate into 'Unions', with a view to saving money by having a single poorhouse – or 'workhouse' as they were becoming increasingly known – to serve a much wider area. A far more rigorous routine would be enforced in these establishments, with the intention of discouraging those it was felt were *able* to work, from claiming aid.

The new law failed to take into account the dearth of work in many rural areas and the new poorhouses would also be required to provide accommodation for the aged and infirm, as well as an asylum for those of unsound mind. In addition, there was the problem of foundlings, orphans, vagabonds and destitute mothers-to-be to be taken into consideration.

Although the law was now on the statute books, in this part of Cornwall, as in many other areas of the country, the buildings that would provide the necessary facilities had yet to be built and most of the needy were still housed in parish poorhouses.

The Tintagel building was spotlessly clean – a tribute to Henry Yates, the poorhouse master – but Alice felt it lacked 'soul'. The men and women she saw as she and David were being escorted to Yates's office seemed to be no more than the empty shells of human beings. There was little life force discernible within them and it made her feel uncomfortable.

She felt even worse when she and David passed through a room where children sat in an unnatural silence on either side of a central aisle, boys on one side copying words from books, girls on the other, heads bent over various forms of needlework. There was not a smile or a hint of curiosity from them about the visitors and Alice found their lack of inquisitiveness unnerving.

In contrast to the inmates of the establishment he supervised, Henry Yates was a jovial, roly-poly man with an ingratiating manner. Welcoming them to his office, he sat them down and sent one of his female assistants off to fetch tea for them all.

The tea was duly produced and consumed and when David declined an offer by Yates to be shown around the establishment, Tristram Rowe was sent for. Alice had formed no opinion of what the young man would be like, nevertheless his appearance came as a surprise.

The majority of Cornishmen she had met with were dark-haired, brown-eyed men, but Tristram, who was able to claim Cornish descent through countless generations, was proof if any was needed that roving Viking adventurers had reached the Cornish shores and left behind enduring evidence of their visitation. The young man who limped into the poorhouse master's office was tall, fair-haired and blue-eyed.

There was also a restless energy within him that many months in the Tintagel poorhouse had failed to quench and, unlike the other residents Alice had seen, he had a ready smile that was never very far away.

'Reverend and Miss Kilpeck, this is Tristram Rowe, the young man I told you about, Reverend.'

Smiling briefly at Alice, Tristram turned his attention to David, and it was to him he spoke now, 'Mr Yates said you're looking for someone to work at the Trethevy rectory and in and around the old church there, Reverend. For as long as I can remember I've thought what a pity it is that such a lovely little church building has been allowed to get into such a state. Old Percy – Mr Nankivell – tells me you've almost got it ready to have services there ... and that you've done more than your share of the work, Miss ...' this directed briefly at Alice. 'My grandmother once lived close to

Trethevy and she told me that many of her family were buried in the churchyard up there in times gone by. Old … Mr Nankivell, says it's being used to bury folk again and I would love to feel that I'd had a part in putting things there to rights again.'

David's expression had become one of excitement while Tristram was talking and now he said to his sister, 'Do you hear that, Alice? It *is* consecrated ground! We were quite within our rights to bury bodies from the *Balladeer* there.'

'I never doubted it,' Alice said, refraining from reminding her brother that it was her idea to bury the shipwreck victims there in the first place, then turning to Tristram she said, 'So you know Percy?'

'Yes, Miss, he used to visit my grandmother sometimes, usually when he was particularly hungry. They knew each other when they were both children and enjoyed talking together about the "good old days".'

'It's good that you and Percy get along with each other,' David said. 'If you come to work at Trethevy you'll both have rooms above the stables at the rectory and will need to make joint arrangements for eating.'

'That will not be necessary,' Alice interjected. Avoiding her brother's surprised glance she explained, 'If you come to work at Trethevy, you and Percy will be fed from the rectory, although such an arrangement will be reflected in your salary, of course.'

Only now did she meet her brother's puzzled gaze, explaining, 'Eliza has said she will help with the cooking. Apparently it is something she enjoys and would often help the cook in her last employment. I allowed her to cook your breakfast this morning – under my supervision, of course – but as you did not complain I imagine it must have met with your approval?'

'It was excellent,' he agreed. 'Had you not told me I would never have known it was not *your* cooking.'

Turning back to Tristram, he said, 'Mr Yates has told me about your accident, do you think you can cope with working at Trethevy, where you would be gardener, horse-keeper and general handyman?'

'I will be able to do all that's asked of me, Your Reverence, and do it well.'

Tristram spoke eagerly and Alice realised he was desperate to be given a chance. She glanced at her brother and, correctly reading her expression, he said to the anxiously waiting young man, 'Very well, I will take you on trial for a month at six shillings a week. If you prove satisfactory, it will be raised to seven shillings, inclusive of accommodation and food. If that is suitable, when can you start work?'

'There's nothing to keep me here, and my belongings will fit into a single bag. I could start right away. Today!'

'Very well, you can travel to Trethevy with my sister and I in the trap.'

Finding it difficult to hide his delight, Tristram said, 'Thank you, Your Reverence, you will have no complaints about my work, I promise you, and if we are going in a pony and trap I'll drive, just to prove I can handle it as well as anyone, then I'll set to work as soon as we arrive at the rectory.'

He was so eager to show his worth that Alice found it almost painful, and she said, kindly, 'You can drive the pony and trap by all means, but when we reach Trethevy you will need to spend the rest of the day making your room over the stables fit to live in. You can begin your duties tomorrow. Percy can help you to settle in if you think you will need any help. He will be delighted to have someone to share his work at Trethevy.'

Alice thought that Percy would undoubtedly unload most of his work on to this fit and eager young man, but she doubted whether it would be resented.

As an afterthought, she wondered what Eliza would make of such a presentable young man.

*

Percy's enthusiasm for having a youthful helper to take on much of his workload was not shared by Eliza. Whilst genuinely enjoying the opportunity to spend time in the rectory kitchen, she was decidedly cool towards Tristram Rowe and seemed determined to have as little to do with him as was possible within the small Trethevy household.

It was decided that Tristram would collect meals for himself and Percy from the kitchen and the two men would eat them in the rooms they occupied above the stables, Eliza eating alone in the kitchen, after everyone else.

The arrangement suited Eliza well. It meant she would not have to worry about fielding any of the awkward questions about her past that inevitably crop up during conversations over meals between people who are not familiar with each other.

There was another reason she preferred eating alone. During her young life – especially within the confines of the workhouse – Eliza had met with few men. Those she *had* come into contact with had done nothing to earn her trust, the husband of her late employer and Eval Moyle not helping to enhance her opinion of men.

She regarded old Percy as a kindly, if crafty figure but he had shortcomings in respect of personal hygiene, and David Kilpeck … well, he was a *Reverend*. Tristram Rowe was different. She found him somehow disturbing and decided she would be wary of him.

For his part, Tristram always behaved with the utmost propriety towards her, never anything but polite yet remaining aloof, his opinion of *her* known only to himself.

This state of affairs continued for some months after his arrival at the Trethevy rectory until a change in their relationship was unexpectedly brought about by none other than Eval Moyle.

Chapter Seventeen

*F*IFTY MILES FROM Trethevy, in the town of Truro, events that were destined to have a lasting effect upon the future of the servants of the North Cornwall rectory were already unfolding in a manner that would end in violence.

In Truro, as in other parishes throughout the land, a tax was levied on householders and businesses for the benefit of the parish church, symbol of the Established Church of England. This tax was bitterly resented by Nonconformists and they would occasionally refuse to pay what they regarded as an unjust tax.

It so happened that this is what had occurred in Truro, one of the largest towns in Cornwall, as a result of which three dissenting shopkeepers were taken to court and a distress warrant issued by the magistrate, ordering the town's constables to seize goods from the three men and have them auctioned in order to raise the unpaid tax.

The items were duly gathered and, in accordance with the court's instructions it was arranged for them to be auctioned and the monies from their sale paid to the churchwardens.

News of the actions taken by the magistrate and town constables quickly circulated throughout Cornwall, helped by Nonconformist preachers who broadcast details of the proceedings from the pulpits of their own churches.

As a result, on the day of the auction many Dissenters

descended upon Truro, led by work-hardened tin-miners who had a reputation of physically fighting for anything they perceived to be their 'rights'.

Eval Moyle was among the crowd gathered outside the auction rooms and his voice rose above all others, urging the increasingly volatile crowd to disrupt the proceedings of the forthcoming auction.

It was unfortunate for the auctioneer that he arrived upon the scene when Moyle's oratory was in full flow. A dapper little man of middle-age, he was immaculately dressed in a dark grey frock coat, striped waistcoat, Oxford blue cravat and white doe-skin trousers. His outfit was topped by a tall beaver hat perched upon an impressive head of dark brown hair which curled over his ears.

In such clothes he stood out from all those in the crowd and his arrival was greeted with noisy derision. When Eval Moyle caught sight of him he announced, 'Here's the man who's hand-in-glove with Church and magistrates! He'll make certain the treasured possessions of hard-working and God-fearing Christians are sold for a pittance, the money going to them as pay no more than lip-service to the Lord while living off the fat of the land in His name.'

The auctioneer was a mild-mannered man but, although frightened to find himself surrounded by such a noisy and angry mob, he had a task to perform and was determined to carry it out.

Addressing those closest to him, he said, 'All the goods that come under my hammer will be fairly sold to the highest bidder....'

The statement was greeted with howls of derision, but the auctioneer refused to be prevented from saying his piece. '... Any money received over and above that ordered to be paid to the churchwardens will be handed over to the persons from whom the goods were seized.'

'They don't want any leftover offerings from the likes of you.' Once again the loud voice of Eval Moyle rose above the hubbub from the crowd. 'They want the return of the goods the Church has stole from 'em – and we're here to see that's what they get!'

The auctioneer would have been wise to accept that the mob were intent upon disrupting the business of the auction house for that day, at least, and turn away leaving them to celebrate what would have been a meaningless and purely temporary victory. But he was neither wise, nor lacking in courage.

'I sympathise with those who have had their goods seized, of course I do, but theirs are not the only items in the auction and I have my duty to perform, so if you will excuse me.'

While he was talking, Eval Moyle, determined that the unruly mob would accept him as their leader, pushed his way through the throng of volatile demonstrators and confronted the auction-eer. 'You'll do no business today with selling other men's goods, so I suggest you turn around and go home.'

'I can't do that.'

Trying to hide the very real fear he was feeling inside at being confronted by Moyle, the auctioneer tried to move forward, by-passing him, but a leg was thrust out from the crowd and he tripped, cannoning into the Primitive Methodist preacher and losing his beaver hat. Reaching out to retrieve it, he was foiled by the heavy boot of a miner which stamped upon the expensive headgear.

When the unfortunate man tried to rise to his feet Moyle kneed him and he fell to the ground once more. A cheer went up from the crowd and they closed in upon the fallen auctioneer.

A small group of hopelessly outnumbered town constables had been watching what was going on from the comparative safety of a nearby narrow alleyway but, aware of the very real danger posed to the auctioneer, they bravely chose to come to his rescue.

It was a grave mistake. They were instantly set upon by a mob eager to vent its pent up anger and frustration on anyone in authority.

With attention turned away from him, the original object of the crowd's fury was able to crawl to the auction rooms, but he had not escaped unscathed. Bruised and beaten and minus his hat, frock coat and cravat, his waistcoat had been torn beyond repair and he had also been dispossessed of his fine head of hair, which proved to be no more than an expensive wig that had disappeared in the mêlée to reveal a balding pate, adding some ten years to his appearance.

Despite his battered and dishevelled state, minutes later the brave auctioneer appeared at an upstairs window of the auction rooms and endeavoured to conduct an auction from here.

It was an impossible feat. The crowd of Dissenters and miners were now battling among themselves, as well as fighting the constables who had been reinforced by reserves hurriedly called in to help deal with the brawling crowd.

It was not long before a magistrate arrived on the scene and called upon the brawling mob to cease their unruly behaviour. When his orders were ignored he proceeded to read out the Riot Act, at the same time sending off a messenger to call out the militia to quell what was now a riot in law, as well as in essence.

Missiles were being hurled about, many aimed at the auction rooms and the plucky auctioneer was finally forced to bring his attempts to conduct business to a close when glass from the window above his head began showering about him.

When the riot in the street was at its height, a well-respected Cornish nobleman appeared upon the scene. His title had been bestowed upon him for great gallantry at the Battle of Waterloo, in 1815, and he had interests in a number of the mines where the rioting miners worked.

Standing on the steps of a nearby house he repeatedly called upon the men to stop their fighting before the militia put in an appearance and began taking action against them.

At first it seemed he would be ignored but, as he was recognised by more and more of the rioters, the fighting in the battle-strewn street gradually died down.

The riot was over and the fighting on the streets of Truro had come to an end before the arrival of the militiamen. The objective of the rioters had been achieved inasmuch as there would be no auction of chapel-goers' property in the auction room on this day and, after raising three hearty cheers for the veteran Cornish peer, the rioters dispersed.

The Dissenters and their allies had won the day, but retribution would pursue them throughout the county. The names of many of those involved were known to the constables and the magistrate who had been present throughout the disorders and arrest warrants were made out for a large number of them.

Foremost among those singled out to pay the penalty for their actions at the riot scene was Eval Moyle.

Aware that he was known to the constables who had been attacked during the rioting, Moyle knew he would be among the first they would come seeking, and a magistrate sympathetic to the Established Church would have no hesitation in committing him for trial to a higher court, where he would undoubtedly receive a harsh sentence.

Moyle realised that if he was to avoid retribution he would need to leave Cornwall – to leave the country, perhaps, but before he did so he had a few scores to settle.

Chapter Eighteen

'EVAL MOYLE HAS put his cows in the churchyard again – but this time there's a bull in with 'em!'

The dramatic news was shouted to Tristram by a breathless Percy as he reached the hay loft where the younger man was forking hay from a wagon. 'I'll go on up to the rectory to tell Reverend Kilpeck.'

Tristram was alarmed. Stopping what he was doing, he said, 'Eliza's just gone along to the church with some new covers Miss Alice has been making for the hassocks!' With more hope than conviction, he added, 'but she's bound to see the bull and not go in there.'

'Eliza wouldn't know the difference between a bull and a cow if she was sent along to milk 'em!' Equally alarmed, Percy added, 'But she won't see 'em, even when she gets to the churchyard. They're grazing behind the church, out of sight of the lane. I only saw 'em myself because I decided to take a short cut back here through Ted Spargo's field, at the side of the church.'

Spargo was a farmer who owned a number of fields close to the church and rectory and Percy had been to a copse some distance beyond them, cutting up a fallen tree to provide wood for the rectory fires.

Throwing the pitchfork he was holding to the ground, Tristram climbed down from the hay-loft after it, shouting to Percy, 'While you're telling Reverend Kilpeck what's happening I'll go and find Eliza….'

Retrieving the pitchfork, Tristram headed for the church at a speed that paid little heed to his injured leg. Arriving at the churchyard gate he was dismayed to see the grazing cattle had moved from the back of the church to the side. Among them was the bull, a large shorthorn-cross animal that appeared to have something of its owner's make-up in its temperament.

When it became aware of Tristram's presence at the lych-gate the animal raised its heavy head to look at him warily through bloodshot eyes, making Tristram uncomfortably aware that the ancient warped gate that stood between him and the one ton weight of the bull was only the flimsiest of barriers.

He would have liked to open the lych-gate and enter the church in order to warn Eliza of the danger she was in, instructing her to remain inside the building until the cattle could be removed from the churchyard, but he realised it would be impossible to reach the church in safety.

He was still pondering on what could be done when David Kilpeck arrived from the rectory, closely followed by Alice, with a breathless Percy trailing a long way behind.

'Have you seen Eliza?' The deeply concerned cleric put the question to Tristram.

'She must still be inside the church and probably has no idea that there's a bull in the churchyard, and I can think of no way to let her know. If we call to her she'll come out of the church and that's the very last thing we want to happen.'

Arriving in time to hear most of Tristram's statement, Alice said, 'Can't we do what we did before, turn them loose and let Eval Moyle worry about finding them again?'

'No,' Tristram said firmly. 'Percy told me all about what happened then, but they were young animals, with no harm in them. We've got a bull here, and it's one with a bad reputation. Turn him out in the lane and he'll likely kill anyone he meets up with. He's best where he is for now but we've somehow got to stop Eliza from coming out of the church.'

'But how?' Alice asked, deeply distressed by the danger Eliza was in.

Tristram countered her question with another. 'How long is what Eliza's doing in the church likely to keep her occupied?'

'Probably no more than another fifteen minutes. Why?'

'We can't risk having her come out while the bull is still this close.' Turning to the still breathless Percy who had just arrived on the scene, he said, 'I want you to go back to the hay wagon as quickly as you can and bring back as much hay as you can carry – the more the better. Carry it high alongside the wall so that the cattle can see it and they'll hopefully follow you. When you reach the far corner of the churchyard – as far from the lych-gate as you can possibly go – throw it over the wall to them then go back for some more.'

'How will that help?' This time the question came from David.

'If Eliza comes out she won't be expecting the cows – and the bull – to be in the churchyard and if the bull sees her and charges it will take her completely by surprise, but if Percy can draw the cows away from the church door the bull will follow. It will give me a chance to get to the church and warn her.'

'What if the bull sees you?' Alice queried. 'You have a bad leg and could not possibly outrun it.'

'I can if I choose my moment. It's sweet, new hay and I'm counting on the bull being just as eager to get at it as the cows. Once its head down among them I should be halfway to the church before it sees me, and inside with the door closed before it can get there.'

'How will that help?' Alice asked. 'All it means is that we'll have two of you trapped inside instead of one.'

'There are quite a few cows in there and it won't take them long to eat the first lot of hay. When it's gone and they start drifting away Percy can carry the second lot along there and let them see him doing it. There's that tiny slit window up by the altar in the church, from there I'll be able to see what's going on. When the bull's fully occupied once more Eliza and me'll come running out of the church – fast! One of you will need to be ready to open the gate for us and then close it again quickly once we're safe.'

'What about your bad leg?' Alice was still doubtful. 'From all I have heard a bull has a surprising turn of speed when it charges.'

'Don't worry about me,' Tristram spoke with more confidence than he was feeling, 'I'll be all right, I'm not unused to dealing with bulls. It's Eliza we have to think about. She has no experience with country animals and is too fearless for her own good. She'll probably think she can just shoo it away like most other animals.'

Alice went cold at the scenario Tristram's words conjured up, but it was David who replied to him.

'You are quite right, Tristram. I'll go with Percy and help with the second load of hay while you carry on with your plan but be careful, be *very* careful – and may God be with you.'

The first part of Tristram's plan worked better than could have been anticipated. It seemed an interminable time before Percy returned with the first load of hay, but as he walked slowly along the lane beside the churchyard with his load in plain view of the cows, they trotted to the wall, following his progress from inside.

Percy threw the hay into the corner of the churchyard and the cows crowded it, the bull among them. Hurriedly opening the lych-gate, Tristram ran for the church door as fast as his injured leg would allow. For all his earlier bravado, he was aware that if the bull saw him early enough it was doubtful if he would be able to outrun the powerful animal.

As it happened, the dash to the church door was without incident, the bull remained head down among the cows, mouthing the sweet-smelling hay, and did not even see him.

Rushing through the door and slamming it shut behind him, Tristram was confronted by a startled Eliza. Looking up at him in alarm from the cover she was stitching into place around a hassock, she demanded, 'What's the matter? Why did you come in like that?'

Greatly relieved to have reached the safety of the tiny church, Tristram realised he was grinning like a half-wit. 'I've come to warn you. Moyle has put his cows in the churchyard again, but there's a bull with them this time. They must have been behind the church when you came in, so you wouldn't have seen them.'

Unaware of the full significance of his words, Eliza said scornfully, 'I'm not frightened of a few old cows. They sometimes come up to the wall behind the kitchen garden and I give them a cabbage leaf or two. They may be big, but they're gentle enough.'

'The cows might be but the bull *certainly* isn't. He's big, mean and dangerous. We've got to get you safely out of here, then see what can be done to get the bull out of the churchyard.'

'I haven't finished fitting the new covers on these hassocks yet.'

'They can wait,' Tristram said firmly. 'The most important thing right now is to get you out of here. Miss Alice is waiting by the lych-gate and Reverend Kilpeck and Percy should be there soon.'

Leaving Eliza, he hurried to the window at the rear of the church. Looking out, he saw that the cattle had already eaten most of the hay brought by Percy on his first journey from the hay wagon and there was as yet no sign of him or David Kilpeck returning with more.

He told Eliza of the plan they had formulated for getting her to safety and although he spoke of it as matter-of-factly as he was able, Eliza began to realise just how serious was her predicament and what might have happened had not Tristram come to warn her.

'Are all bulls as dangerous as you are making them out to be?' She asked.

'Only a fool would trust one,' Tristram replied. 'Almost all the deaths on farms are the result of someone thinking a bull they might have known for years can be trusted. It can't – and Eval Moyle's bull is as bad-tempered as its owner. Reverend Kilpeck won't let Moyle get away with this and neither will a magistrate. Moyle will be in big trouble, and deservedly so.'

Eliza had been giving Tristram an increasingly wide-eyed look as he spoke and now she said, 'But … if this bull is so dangerous, didn't you take a big risk by coming through the churchyard to warn me about him? Especially with that bad leg of yours?'

'Somebody needed to do it.' Tristram was discomfited by Eliza's intimation that he had done something particularly courageous on her behalf. 'Anyway, bad leg or not, I can outrun Percy – and can you imagine Reverend Kilpeck running anywhere, for *whatever* reason?'

David Kilpeck was not a man given to moving anywhere very fast and was prone to stop and think before doing anything out of the ordinary.

Glancing through the slit window again, Tristram said, 'Ah! Here's Percy now. Go to the church door and, when I shout open it and run for the lych-gate as though the Devil himself is after you … No, leave the hassock covers in the church, just take yourself.'

'But what about you?'

'Eliza! Just do as I say, but leave the door open when you run out, I'll be right behind you.'

There was such urgency in his voice that Eliza questioned him no further. No sooner had she reached the church door than Tristram said, 'Percy and Reverend Kilpeck are walking slowly along the lane and the cows are following. I can't see the bull … yes I can! He's following the cows. Get ready, but don't go until I say so, we want him to be right among them before we make a move.'

Waiting with her hand on the iron ring of the door latch, the full danger of the situation hit home to Eliza. She had never knowingly seen a bull and had no idea just how powerfully-built they were, but she had seen cows in the fields around the rectory. Although seemingly docile they *were* large and she could imagine them being dangerous if they were angry. She suddenly felt fear for the first time.

She was startled out of her thoughts by the shout from Tristram, 'Now! Go … go … GO!'

The time for thinking was over. Eliza flung open the door and ran. Looking straight ahead at the lych-gate she resisted the urge to glance to where she knew the cattle were feeding upon the hay.

Because of this she was unaware that Eval Moyle's bull had raised its huge head at the very moment she lifted the latch of the church door and began her desperate run. Moving with remarkable speed for such a large and heavy animal, the bull set off across the turf of the churchyard after her.

Coming out from the church, Tristram was horrified by what he saw. Realising the bull was gathering speed and would catch Eliza before she reached safety and without pausing to think of the possible consequences of his actions he set off after Eliza at the same time shouting, '*Faster*, Eliza … *run faster*!'

He began waving his arms wildly in a frenzied attempt to distract the bull and his tactics succeeded only too well.

The bull's attention switched from the fleeing girl to what it perceived as a more immediate threat to its well-being. Hardly slackening speed it veered away from Eliza and headed for Tristram!

It was the sheer speed of the aggressive animal that saved Tristram in this first charge. Instinctively jumping to one side when the bull was almost upon him, he succeeded in dodging it as it thundered past.

Wasting no time in dwelling upon his good fortune, Tristram

resumed his limping run towards the gate and safety, observing as he did so that it was being held open to let Eliza through.

The aggressive bull, failing to run down its intended victim in its initial charge tried to turn too quickly and slipped on the churchyard grass, its front legs buckling beneath it, allowing Tristram to increase the distance between them.

Nevertheless, in spite of frantic vocal encouragement from those watching his flight from the safety of the lane, Tristram's lameness handicapped him in his attempt to outrun the pursuing animal and, aware at the very last moment that the animal was upon him once more, he leapt to one side yet again – but this time fortune was not with him.

He successfully avoided being knocked down and trampled by the aggressive animal but a swing of the bull's great head struck him and sent him tumbling head-over-heels across the grass to crash heavily against the stone wall, tantalisingly close to the safety of the gate.

This time the bull slid to a halt and turned without losing its balance and, head down, came back at his victim.

Tristram was lying parallel with the wall and tight to its base and it was this that saved him from the bull's determined attempt to gore him as its horns clashed against the stonework.

Then, letting out a sudden snort of pain, the bull swung around, away from Tristram as the prongs of a pitchfork, wielded over the wall by a fearful but determined Eliza, sank into its haunches.

Quick to seize the unexpected reprieve from the bull's attentions, Tristram managed to scramble to the safety of the lych-gate, where he was hurriedly hauled to safety by Alice and her brother and the gate slammed shut behind him.

'Are you alright?' The anxious question came from a concerned Alice.

'I am now.' Seated on the ground outside the lych-gate,

Tristram rubbed his upper arm which had struck the wall when he was thrown against it by the bull. 'I am going to have a fair bruise there, but nothing worse … thanks to Eliza.'

He nodded to where she stood shaking but triumphant, still clutching the pitchfork.

'Lieutenant Kendall once said she was a very resourceful girl,' Alice declared, 'and she has proved it once again. Your actions were very brave too, Tristram, you undoubtedly saved Eliza's life.'

Looking at her brother who seemed bewildered by the events of the last couple of minutes, she added, 'We are most fortunate to have two such young people in our employ, David. Now I think we should all return to the rectory and have a strong cup of tea, then find the constable. He can deal with Mr Moyle and have his animals removed from the churchyard.'

The cattle were removed from the churchyard the following day but not by Eval Moyle. A neighbouring farmer and his grown-up son eventually succeeded in leading the bull away with the aid of a rope passed through the ring in its nose, and they subsequently purchased a number of the cows when they were sold off after being impounded and not claimed within the requisite time.

Of Eval Moyle there was no sign. As a result, he could not be brought to account for turning his animals loose in the church-yard, but if he had run away as a result of the warrant that was issued for his arrest in respect of the riot that took place in Truro, he had left the area unnecessarily.

When those who *had* been arrested came to court, the case was dismissed, a clever defence lawyer pointing out that the wording of the Riot Act stated that if those involved dispersed within an hour of the Act being read out by a magistrate, it was no longer a riot – and that is what had happened.

As a result, all those involved in the Truro disturbance went free, it being impossible to prove who among them was actually involved in the assault of the constables, and it not being considered worthwhile pursuing the matter any further.

Soon afterwards rumours began to circulate that Moyle had gone to America where it was believed Primitive Methodism was gaining a strong following. No doubt Moyle would be accepted there, for a while, at least.

Meanwhile, his land was being farmed by his long-suffering younger brother who had always been a partner in the farm left to them by their father but had been overshadowed by his domineering brother. Alone on the farm, he was at pains to remain at peace with his neighbours.

For now it was enough that Cornwall was rid of Eval Moyle.

Book Two

Chapter One

1843

*T*HREE YEARS HAD elapsed since Eliza's rescue from the rocks at the sea's edge below the Cornish cliffs. Three happy and settled years, which had passed quickly at Trethevy.

Although it would never be possible for her to forget the manner of her arrival in the Kilpeck household, the memory of life before that time had receded to such an extent that it was almost as though all that had gone before had happened to someone else.

Eliza Brooks was no more. She had died with the other women convicts on board the doomed *Cormorant*.

There was also more in her life than work now. The incident involving Eval Moyle's bull, when Eliza and Tristram were each instrumental in saving the life of the other, had forged a bond between them which had slowly but steadily grown stronger with the passage of time.

Reverend David Kilpeck, in particular, ensured that their relationship remained within the bounds of 'propriety', but recently he had raised no objections to them walking out together on a Sunday afternoon, when both were freed from their duties to the rector and his sister, and had dutifully attended morning service in the Trethevy church.

*

It was the young couple who were the subject of Alice and David's conversation now, as brother and sister travelled by pony and trap to Tintagel Church, where David was to conduct evensong.

Along the way they overtook Eliza and Tristram, who were also on their way to the same church to witness the baptism of a workhouse baby when the service was over.

After waves were exchanged, David, always anxious to be seen to be 'doing the right thing', asked Alice anxiously, 'Do you think I should have offered them a ride to church? It seems rather mean to leave them walking when we have room in the trap for them.'

'They would not thank you for such a suggestion and were holding hands before they heard us coming along behind them,' Alice replied. 'They enjoy each other's company and I give them little opportunity to spend time with each other at the rectory.'

'As is right and proper,' David declared, pompously. 'There is far too much immorality in the parish. I don't think I have married one girl in the past year who has not been *enceinte* when she walks down the aisle. It is quite scandalous. I expect our staff at Trethevy to set an example.'

Smiling to herself at her brother's reluctance to use the word 'pregnant' when describing the brides being married in his church, Alice said, 'I have spoken to Eliza on the subject and am confident she will not let you down, David. Tristram too is an honourable young man, we have been extremely fortunate in our choice of servants, but that reminds me, there is a fair at Camelford next month and Tristram has asked for permission to take Eliza there. I have said he might, subject to your consent, of course.'

'Do you think that wise, Alice? It is a long way to Camelford, five miles or more and they will be returning home in the dark! I share your trust in them but they are both young and healthy and are obviously very fond of each other. It would be foolish to put unnecessary temptation in their way.'

Aware of her brother's strong and somewhat puritanical views about the morals of young people, Alice said, 'I think we might be able to find an answer to that problem, David. In the last letter I received from Jory he mentioned the fair. In addition to all the entertainments there, it is a well-known hiring-fair and he intends being present to recruit young men for both the Coast Guard and the Royal Navy. The letter was sent some time ago and his plans might have changed, but if they have not I thought it would be a nice idea to invite him to stay with us at the rectory after the fair and ask him to bring Tristram and Eliza home with him.'

David did not reply to her suggestion immediately. Aware that Alice had a very deep affection for Jory Kendall, he believed the naval officer would one day ask her to marry him. It would be an excellent marriage for her, of course, one of which their late parents would have heartily approved, but it would pose a great many problems for *him*.

He could not possibly continue to have only a young maid living in the rectory with him. He would need to take on a housekeeper, an elderly lady, and quite apart from the extra cost involved, they would need to learn each other's ways. It would cause disruption to what was at present a very pleasant way of life.

Nevertheless, to refuse to allow Jory Kendall to spend a night at the rectory would not only be churlish but deeply upsetting for Alice.

'Have you already made mention of this to Jory?'

'Not yet. I wanted to speak to you about it first.'

After thinking it over for a little longer, David nodded his approval. 'It would be a very hospitable thing to do, but I feel it might be more appropriate for such an offer to come from me. Remind me when we return to the rectory tonight and I will write and extend an invitation to him.'

Giving her brother's arm an affectionate squeeze, Alice said, 'You *are* a generous brother, David, but I know you enjoy Jory's company too. Oh, I forgot to mention, in his letter Jory mentioned that an uncle, the Bishop of Winchester, will be paying a visit to the Kendalls' family home soon. He says that while the bishop is there he will arrange for you to meet with him.'

Alice had *not* forgotten to mention this piece of information to her brother, but had been keeping it in reserve should David prove difficult about allowing Jory to stay at the Trethevy rectory on the night of the Camelford fair.

David was an ambitious cleric and although he thoroughly enjoyed his work in North Cornwall he had said on more than one occasion that Trethevy was very much a backwater where he was unlikely ever to meet with anyone able to further his career in the Church.

The Bishop of Winchester was a very influential figure in the Church of England hierarchy and able to do a great deal to help David if he was so inclined.

Alice also had hopes that Jory Kendall might one day ask her to marry him and by consenting to the marriage, as she certainly would, she realised the problems it would pose for both David and herself. She felt it her duty to take care of her brother, and had promised her dying mother she would do so. The most satisfactory solution would be for *him* to find a wife but since coming to Cornwall they had met with no one even remotely suitable.

However, she was trying to find solutions to problems that had not yet arisen. Although she had known Jory for some three years she had never met with any of his family – and they might not approve of her.

Indeed, for some time she had not seen as much of Jory as she would have liked. Although still a coast guard officer he had succeeded in achieving his wish for command of a ship. He was now the commanding officer of a coast guard cutter, the *Vixen*, patrolling the whole of the Cornish coast, both north and south.

On a couple of occasions *Vixen* had anchored in the cove where Jory and Alice had first met and he had climbed up the steep cliff path to pay a surprise visit to the rectory. However, his visits were few and far between and as a consequence their relationship had not progressed as rapidly as she had hoped it might.

Alice was aware she was in love with Jory, but there had been none of the excitement she had always expected to accompany such a depth of feeling for the man she wanted to marry.

Her thoughts were interrupted by David. As they were passing through a tiny hamlet with houses scattered on both sides of the lane on which they were travelling, he said, 'I would like to stop here for a few minutes, Alice. I wish to call in on a veteran of the Peninsular wars. He and his wife live here with their increasingly demented daughter and I fear for their safety. I want to check they are alright.'

'Would you like me to come in with you?'

'No, the daughter becomes very agitated at meeting strangers, it has taken me a long time to gain her confidence and persuade her to pray with me. The old soldier says my prayers are better than anything the doctor gives her and she is quiet for a couple of days afterwards. Sadly she will need to go into an asylum soon because the parents are becoming too old to take care of her and they are dreading it. Life is very difficult for them but they love the girl deeply. Indeed, their whole life is centred about her.'

'All right, go in and see her now but tell the girl's parents I would like to call on them sometime to see if I might do anything to help them. The girl might come to accept me in time.'

'That would be very nice. There is nowhere to tie the pony, but I will leave the reins over the rail where you can reach them if she decides to wander off. I won't be long.'

When David had gone Alice sat in the four-wheeled trap, thinking her own thoughts and looking at the cottages of the tiny hamlet. Some were thatched, others had slate roofing but all were old and shabby, the one David was visiting particularly so, its thatch ragged and stained with patches of variable coloured moss and mould, and there were a number of small panes of glass missing from the leaded windows.

The gardens were better cared for than the cottages, a few having roses growing around doorways and windows, distracting attention from peeling paint and rotting woodwork.

The condition of the cottages in this particular hamlet was not unusual, here in North Cornwall. The parish served by Reverend David Kilpeck was in an area where poverty was an ever-present problem and it was hardly surprising that those who lived here should turn to non-conformist religions that promised them better things in after-life.

All these things were going through Alice's mind and as a result she was only vaguely aware of a horse trotting along the lane behind the stationary pony and trap.

Suddenly, a large dog emerged from the garden of the cottage next to the one David was visiting and, dashed at the horse and rider, barking furiously. The sound startled Alice – but it alarmed the Kilpecks' pony more. Throwing up its head with a snort of fright the animal bolted, and Alice was catapulted backwards to land inelegantly, legs in air, in the rear of the four-wheeled vehicle.

Scrambling to her knees with difficulty in the bouncing and lurching vehicle, she looked for the reins. To her dismay they were no longer hanging over the front rail but were trailing in the dust of the lane, beneath the careering vehicle.

Alice realised she was in grave danger. The pony was galloping out of control with the light trap bouncing along on the uneven lane behind it and likely to overturn at any moment. She was also aware that not far ahead there was a sharp bend at the end of a short downhill stretch of lane. If the pony maintained its present speed the trap would certain overturn – but there was nothing at all she could do about it!

At that moment a horse and rider overtook the trap, the horse travelling at a reckless gallop, its rider crouching low on its back, outstretched arms gripping the rein. Bringing his horse alongside the runaway pony, the rider reached out and took a firm grip on the pony's bridle, then, using sheer physical strength, pulled the pony's head down to one side, at the same time slowing his own mount.

For a few terrifying moments Alice feared his actions would cause pony, trap, horse and rider to veer off the lane but the unknown rider proved to be a very skilled horseman. Gradually the pony slowed and was eventually brought to a halt, to stand, glistening with sweat, its sides heaving and shivering with fright in consequence of its recent experience.

'Are you alright?' The rider put the question to Alice as he gathered up the long reins trailing from the pony and handed them up to her as she climbed back into the trap's driving seat.

'I will be when I have time to catch my breath – thanks entirely to you. Had you not been at hand to show such presence of mind I fear I might well have lost my life when we reached the bend ahead.'

'I am glad I was able to be of help. It was the fault of that stupid hound back there.' The rider spoke with a cultured voice and, suddenly smiling, he added, 'I must say, it is the most excitement I have had since returning from cavalry duty in India!'

When he smiled at her, Alice realised he was an extremely handsome man. She also knew intuitively it was something of which he was very much aware – but he *had* undoubtedly saved her life.

There was a shout from farther back along the lane they had just traversed so dramatically and they both turned to see David running towards them, wide-brimmed hat clutched in his hand.

'Your little escapade would appear to have given your husband something of a fright,' Alice's rescuer commented.

'He is my brother, not my husband. Reverend Kilpeck is rector of Trethevy and curate at Tintagel, where he is due to take a service this evening. We stopped for only a few minutes in order that he might visit a needy parishioner.'

'He has an impressive turn of speed for a man of the cloth,' the horseman said, dryly, 'but then, there can be few parish priests who have such an attractive sister to be concerned about.' Giving Alice a bold look, he added, 'I am Hugo Trevelyan, by the way, *Captain* Hugo Trevelyan. You are…?'

'Alice Kilpeck, and my brother is David.'

Alice was aware that Captain Trevelyan had gone beyond the bounds of etiquette by his remark about her 'attractiveness', and perhaps she should have been offended, but she was not. Alice had never before met a man quite like Hugo Trevelyn and she found him both attractive and exciting.

David had witnessed the pony bolt with Alice in the trap and when he reached them he was fulsome in his breathless gratitude to the dashing young army officer.

Captain Hugo Trevelyan rode alongside the pony and trap for the remainder of the journey to Tintagel and left with a promise that he would call in at the Trethevy rectory when he returned from his visit to Padstow in a few days time.

Chapter Two

ALICE FOUND HERSELF thinking about the young army officer with a disturbing frequency during the next few days, although she never really expected to meet with him again. On the journey to Tintagel he had mentioned that he had only chanced to be on the coastal road through Trethevy because of a wish to visit the ruins of the ancient castle situated on the headland at Tintagel. Hugo Trevelyan had said he would call in on his way home from Padstow, but she was doubtful whether he would pass that way again.

However, exactly a week after the incident with the pony and trap, Alice's rescuer rode up to the rectory to be greeted at the garden gate with great enthusiasm by David. From the church where he passed much of his time he had seen the visitor and ran to meet him as he dismounted from his horse.

Clasping the cavalry captain's hand, he declared, 'I am *so* glad you have called in. I confess to being so shaken by what had happened to Alice that I feel I never thanked you fulsomely enough for your brave actions in saving her from what would have been a dreadful accident. I shall always be deeply indebted to you. Alice too will be delighted to see you, do come in and join us for lunch, at least.'

Now Hugo Trevelyan was here, Alice was less certain about him. Not only was he a type of man she never met with before and a handsome man of the world, he also possessed a devil-may-care attitude that was in sharp contrast to her brother's careful and cautious approach to life.

Despite the excitement Captain Trevelyan undoubtedly engendered in her, Alice could not rid herself of the slight unease she felt about the familiarity he showed towards her, even though she told herself the problem lay entirely with her. He was a man who had travelled extensively and was at his ease with all that life had to offer, while she had been brought up within the narrow confines of an East Anglian deanery. Before coming to Cornwall she had never ventured outside of the restrictive lifestyle imposed upon her by such an environment and very little had happened here to widen her experience of life.

Over lunch David insisted that Hugo Trevelyan should stay for dinner and remain at the rectory overnight and, when the midday meal was over, he insisted upon taking Captain Trevelyan to visit his church.

In the churchyard the two men paused at the wooden cross marking the mass grave in which the victims of the shipwreck three years before were buried and Hugo Trevelyan read the inscription …

'7 *unknown passengers and crew of the ship Balladeer wrecked on Lye Rock during the night of 16/17 June 1840 during a violent storm. God Rest their souls*'.

'Having been at sea in violent storms during my voyages to and from India, I feel for them,' said David's companion.

'Yes, Eliza was the only survivor and she too had been given up for dead. Had it not been for the efforts of Alice and Lieutenant Kendall she would have been buried here with the others.'

Showing immediate interest, Captain Trevelyan queried, 'Are you speaking of Lieutenant Kendall from Lostwithiel?'

'Yes, you know him?'

'I certainly know *of* him, but we have never met. Is he a particular friend of yours?'

'He visits the rectory whenever possible, but he comes to see Alice, rather than me.'

'Is there an "understanding" between them?'

'Nothing official. They seem to enjoy each other's company, although his duties have kept him away from Trethevy of late, but Alice will tell you more, I am sure. Now, here we are at my little church, it was derelict for very many years before my appointment and Alice has worked wonders in renovating the interior, let me show you....'

While the two men were absent Alice helped Eliza in the kitchen, clearing up after the meal and preparing dinner for that evening. The relationship between Alice and Eliza was quite unlike that of mistress and servant in a large household, or even that which might have been expected in a city environment.

Trethevy was a very remote rural parish with no large houses or wealthy families and, as a result, there was a total absence of social activity in the immediate area and Alice and Eliza seldom met other women with whom to talk. As a result, they had come to value each other's company.

As they worked together Alice was enthusing about their house guest. 'He is such an *interesting* man,' she said. 'Over lunch he was telling us about life in India, it must be terribly exciting there, dangerous too for officers in the army. They need to be very brave and ready for anything that happens. It is hardly surprising that he reacted so swiftly when the pony bolted with me.'

Eliza did not share Alice's enthusiasm for the army officer. She felt that Jory Kendall was a much more pleasant man in every way.

'Lieutenant Kendall would have behaved in exactly the same way had it been him there and not Captain Trevelyan.'

'Perhaps, but Lieutenant Kendall was *not* there, and has not visited the rectory for many months.'

'That's not his fault. He's in command of a coast guard ship now and because most of the navy ships are still out in China, or some such place, he has to spend far more time at sea. He's come to see you whenever he could, and sometimes even brought his ship into Bossiney Cove especially to pay you a quick visit. He'd probably have got into a lot of trouble if news of *that* got about.'

When Alice failed to reply, Eliza asked, hesitantly, 'Do you like Captain Trevelyan better than Lieutenant Kendall?'

If she was being honest with herself, Alice knew she was not absolutely certain at this very moment, but only because Hugo Trevelyan was *here* and Jory was not. As a result she replied sharply, 'Of course not! Although I have known Lieutenant Kendall for three years now and we are still hardly more than just good friends. I had thought ... well, never mind what I thought. The truth is that I am not getting any younger and he has never suggested that our relationship is anything more than just a casual friendship.'

'Have *you* ever hinted that you'd like to be more than friends with *him*?'

'Of course not, that would be most improper. Anyway, we are talking nonsense, I could not possibly leave my brother to fend for himself.'

'If Reverend David found someone *he* wanted to marry, *you'd* be left to fend for yourself.'

'David is unlikely to find anyone while he has a parish like Trethevy, but this is a foolish conversation, Eliza. David and I are grateful to Captain Trevelyan for his prompt and brave action in saving me when the pony bolted and there is nothing more to it than that. The very least we can do is offer him our hospitality and enjoy his company while we can. When he leaves tomorrow I doubt whether we will ever see him again. That reminds me, will you ensure that the sheets on the bed in the spare room are properly aired? This is a damp house, we do not want him catching a chill.'

Eliza hoped Alice's assessment of their guest's future movements would prove accurate and that he would leave the rectory the next day never to be seen by its occupants again. Mistrusting the too-handsome captain and his over-familiarity with Alice, she had also felt uncomfortable on the couple of occasions she had found herself alone in his company.

She tried to tell herself that her dislike of him was unreasonable, stemming as it did from the fact that he reminded her of Sir Robert Calnan, the man whose actions had led to her appearance at the London criminal court in what she now looked upon as her 'other' life.

Hugo Trevelyan did *not* depart from Trethevy the next day – or the day after and Eliza was dismayed to realise his charm offensive aimed at her employer was beginning to have some success.

The Army captain was still a guest at the rectory when, five days after his arrival Jory Kendall made one of his rare and unexpected visits to Trethevy. Having anchored his ship, *Vixen*, in the nearby cove he climbed the steep cliff path to reach the rectory and arrived bearing a gift of two very large sea bass, part of a number received from a fishing crew to whom he had given aid when their vessel broke a spar some miles out at sea.

Unfortunately, neither Alice nor David Kilpeck were at home when Jory arrived and it was left to Eliza to explain that they had both gone to visit the ruins of Tintagel Castle, with Hugo Trevelyan.

Finding it difficult to hide his disappointment, Jory handed over the fish to Eliza and accepted her offer of a cup of tea, at the same time asking, 'Is this Captain Trevelyan someone Reverend Kilpeck has met through his ministry?'

'He is an army man home on leave from somewhere – India, I think. Fortunately, he was near at hand when the pony bolted with the trap and Miss Alice in it.' She went on to give Jory details of the dramatic rescue.

Thoroughly concerned, Jory said, 'What a terrifying experience for Miss Alice, was she injured?'

'No, Captain Trevelyan managed to stop the pony just before it reached the sharp bend at the bottom of the lane between here and Tintagel. If he hadn't...?'

Eliza left the possible outcome unsaid and after a few moments of silence between them, Jory asked, 'When did this happen?'

'Almost a fortnight ago.'

'I see. I suppose Captain Trevelyan came here today to check that Miss Alice was fully recovered from her experience?'

'No, he was on his way to Padstow when all this happened. He called in here on his way back and Reverend Kilpeck invited him to stay. That was five days ago.'

Clearly disturbed by Eliza's news, Jory said, 'I have a feeling I have heard something about this Trevelyan, Eliza, but I can't be certain. What sort of a man is he? Young? Old? Personable? He is obviously quick-thinking.'

Secretly pleased that Jory was concerned about the man who had recently come into her employer's life, Eliza replied, 'I suppose he must be about your own age, sir. He is good-looking, *very* good-looking, and seems to have led an adventurous life as a cavalry officer in other countries.'

After mulling over what he had been told, Jory said, 'I wish he had been here so I could have met him, Eliza. Would you know whether he has a home in Cornwall?'

'Yes, sir, it's somewhere on the edge of Bodmin Moor, near a place called North Hill, I believe.'

'Ah! Then it probably *is* the man I have heard about. We all have reason to be grateful to him for what he did in stopping the runaway pony, but I don't think it would be advisable for Miss Alice to spend too much time in his company. Are you expecting them to return to the rectory soon?'

Intrigued by his words, Eliza replied, 'Not until this evening, sir. Miss Alice had me make up a picnic for them all, but is there something I should tell Miss Alice about Captain Trevelyan, sir?'

Seemingly ignoring her question, Jory said, 'I can't remain here that long, *Vixen* needs to rendezvous at sea with another Coast Guard ship before nightfall.'

'I'm sorry about that, sir, me and Miss Alice were talking about you only the other day and she was saying you must have forgotten about her, it being so long since you last called here.'

'I have written to her, although, I must confess, not as often as I might have wished, but Miss Alice knows I could not forget her, even if I wanted to – and I certainly do not.'

'Perhaps she might like to hear that from you, sir,' Eliza said, aware she was saying far more than a loyal servant should. 'Trethevy can be a very lonely place. One where it's easy to believe you've been forgotten by the rest of the world. I think that's what Miss Alice feels sometimes, and she knows no one of your family she could turn to for news of you.'

Aware that Eliza was trying to tell him something, Jory said, 'You are quite the little sage, Eliza, and I am aware you really care for Miss Alice, as indeed I do. You are quite right, of course, I *should* have made time to visit Trethevy more often and to write more than the occasional letter, but life has been very busy for me. With so many of the Royal Navy's ships in the Far East because of the war with China I have needed to perform both Naval and Coast Guard duties. Fortunately, those days are coming to an end. The war is over and when more of our ships have returned I will be employed solely on Coast Guard duties once more. That is part of the news I came here hoping to impart to Miss Alice today. My ship is long overdue for a refit. As soon as a suitable Royal Navy vessel is available to take its place I and my crew will be paid off and I shall return to a shore base. I am hoping it will be Padstow, from where I will be able to spend far more time on matters close to my heart – and Miss Alice comes top of that list.'

Arriving at a decision, he added, 'Perhaps you could find me a pen and ink and some notepaper. I will write a note telling her about it.'

'I'll do that with great pleasure, sir. It makes me very happy to hear your news. I know Miss Alice is going to feel the same too.' Then, hesitantly, because she realised she was acting far beyond her duties as a servant, she added, 'Perhaps *you* will say some-thing to warn her about Captain Trevelyan, sir. To be perfectly honest *I* don't like him, but it's not my place to say what I think about a family guest.'

Hastily hurrying off to find the writing materials for which Jory had asked, Eliza wondered whether she might have said too much, but she decided she could have done no less. Jory's news and confirmation of his feelings for Alice gladdened Eliza's heart, but she was worried about the influence of the personable young army captain upon her employer.

She hoped that Jory's long overdue display of affection and interest for Alice had not come too late.

Chapter Three

WHEN ALICE RETURNED to Trethevy that evening her face was flushed and warm, in sharp contrast to her brother's unnatural pallor and haunted expression.

When Eliza brought cool water and toiletries to her mistress's room, she learned the reason why.

'Captain Trevelyan is an absolute madcap!' Alice said, laughing merrily, 'He took the reins of the pony for the journey back from Tintagel and drove home at a breakneck speed that had me clinging to the seat like a leech for much of the time. I don't think the pony has ever galloped so fast – not even when she bolted with me.'

Aware that this was not the moment to mention Lieutenant Kendall's warning about the charismatic captain, Eliza said, 'You are lucky the poor animal didn't drop dead, it's not used to going at such a speed twice in a couple of weeks. By the look of Reverend David's face when he came in through the door he never enjoyed it very much, either.'

'He actually called upon Captain Trevelyan to stop, but it only made him drive even faster and poor David seemed to lose his voice! Mind you, I am not saying I actually *enjoyed* it, but it *was* very exciting and I never doubted that the Captain was in control the whole time. After all, he is a cavalryman.'

Eliza kept her opinion of Captain Trevelyan to herself. She realised he had been showing off in order to impress Alice, and it would seem he had succeeded, but she did not argue with her employer. Instead, she said, 'You missed a very special visitor while you were out. Lieutenant Kendall brought his ship into the cove and came up here with a present of two huge sea bass for you. I've gutted them and put them in the dairy. He also wrote a letter for you, I have it in my apron pocket. I thought you would prefer me to give it to you here, in your room.'

Taking the letter from her pocket she handed it to Alice.

The letter comprised of two sheets of Reverend Kilpeck's writing paper and had been sealed with red wax on which the crest of the Kendall family had been impressed by Jory's signet ring.

Eliza was relieved at the disappointment displayed by Alice at not being at the rectory when Jory Kendall called. She had been concerned that her mistress might have become so infatuated with the army Captain that he had replaced the naval lieutenant in her affections.

Alice began reading the letter eagerly but her expression gradually changed and when she reached the end of the second page she looked up and said angrily, 'How *dare* he tell me how I should behave and with whom! What right does he have?'

Gaining control of herself, Alice said, 'I have seen almost nothing of him for absolutely ages, and now he writes to me as though he *owns* me.'

Trying hard to hide her dismay, Eliza said, 'Lieutenant Kendall was very disappointed you weren't at home, Miss Alice. He said he will soon be based on shore once more and hopes to be able to see far more of you. He also mentioned that he'd like to take you to meet his family.'

'Yes, he says as much in his letter, but that excuses nothing.'

Folding the letter, Alice added, 'For three years I have been clos-eted in Trethevy leading an almost nun-like existence, now, in the course of a few hours I have two men wanting to take me off to meet their families.'

'*Two* men?' Eliza asked the question although she had no doubt about the identity of the second man.

'Yes, Captain Trevelyan has invited me to spend a few days at his father's manor on the edge of Bodmin Moor. He invited Reverend David too, of course, but David has to officiate at a wedding this weekend, and has his services to attend to, so will be unable to come.'

'So you won't be going,' Eliza said with some relief, 'You can't go with him on your own.'

'Of course not, although I have no doubt he would behave with the utmost propriety should I do so, but I fully intend going – more than ever after reading Lieutenant Kendall's letter – and *you* will be coming with me, Eliza, as both companion and personal maid. Captain Trevelyan has offered to take us in our own pony and trap, tying his horse behind the trap.'

'When will we be going?'

Eliza was not at all certain she *wanted* to visit the home of Captain Trevelyan but she was relieved her employer had not considered travelling on her own with the dashing East India Company cavalry officer. She did not have the same faith as Alice in his gentlemanly behaviour.

'Captain Trevelyan will be leaving on Saturday, Eliza, that gives us two days to make ready to go with him. It will only be a weekend visit so we need not take too much, but we will discuss it at more length in the morning. In the meantime we must prepare dinner. We will use the fish brought by Lieutenant Kendall, if there is sufficient to feed us all....'

*

Lying in her bed that night, Alice thought about the events of the day and tried to analyse her feelings about the two invitations she had received.

She had always found it rather hurtful that Jory had never invited her to his home, or asked her to meet any members of his large family. She had sometimes felt it might be because his was one of the great families of Cornwall, while she was a newcomer to the county and sister of a rector who held the living of what must be one of the smallest parishes in the whole of the diocese. In other words, that she would not be considered 'suitable', either for Jory, or as a guest in the Kendall home.

Alice had tried to tell herself many times that this was not the way Jory thought of her and the letter she had received from him today should have put her mind at rest on the matter, but his warning about becoming too friendly with Hugo Trevelyan had angered her, perhaps far more than was reasonable.

She believed the warning was the result of jealousy, although even that did not excuse him from writing to her as though he had a *right* to tell her how she should behave, or be perceived to be behaving.

At the same time, she was sufficiently intelligent to realise that she probably *wanted* to be angry with Jory. Angry enough to give her all the excuse she needed to justify going off to spend a weekend with the dashing captain and his father. Hugo Trevelyan had already explained that his father lived alone, Hugo's mother having died many years before.

Had she received invitations from both men for the same weekend, she had no real doubts about which one she would accept. She had wanted to meet the Kendall family for a long time and until very recently had even nursed a hope that one day she might become a part of it.

Nevertheless, the thought of travelling to the manor of the dashing cavalry officer and staying at *his* home, excited her. She had led a very sheltered and humdrum life until now. She believed it was time she did something that might not necessarily meet with the approval of everyone who knew her.

Chapter Four

ALICE, ELIZA AND Hugo Trevelyan set off for the Cornishman's home after lunch on Saturday. The handsome cavalry officer was in a jocular mood, urging the pony to a speed that had his two passengers clinging to their seats, but on this occasion Alice did not encourage him in his recklessness.

She told him firmly that he had given the pony more than enough exercise on their last outing and warned him that unless he drove in a more sedate manner *she* would take the reins and he could continue the remainder of the journey in the saddle of his horse, which was already showing signs of rebelling against the unaccustomed manner in which it was travelling behind the pony and trap.

Much to Eliza's surprise Captain Trevelyan meekly accepted Alice's ultimatum and slowed the pony's pace to one that was far more comfortable for the two women. Somehow, his meek capitulation made Eliza even more uneasy than if he had disputed Alice's warning.

It proved to be a lengthy journey, along lanes and roads that were, at best, indifferent, especially when their route took them across the bleakness of Bodmin Moor, where there was a wind that Hugo said was present for much of the year, day and night, his statement verified by the branches of the few trees that existed here bowing low in an acute angle, in deference to the power of the moorland wind.

Alice had never ventured this far from Trethevy during all the time she had been living there and she knew little of the moor, but she found the feeling of lonely space here awesome. 'Is it as bleak as this where you have your house?' she asked Hugo, somewhat nervously.

'Good Lord, no! Helynn Manor is in a beautiful valley beside the River Lynher and well sheltered from the wind. There has been a manor house there for almost eight hundred years. Those who built it knew exactly what they were doing and studied the elements well before building something as substantial as a manor house.'

'Is it a very large house?' Alice queried.

'Large enough,' Hugo replied, ambiguously. 'Far too large for my father to be living in on his own, especially since my sister is no longer around to look after him.'

'You have a sister?' Alice had never thought of Hugo as having brothers or sisters. His behaviour had led her to believe he was an only child, used to having his own way since boyhood. 'Where is she now?'

'Sadly she died while I was in India.'

'Oh, I am so sorry! What was the cause of her death?'

'According to my father she died of a broken heart, badly let down by a young naval officer from a good family near Lostwithiel.'

Apparently concentrating on guiding the pony through a flock of sheep grazing on either side of the narrow moorland track, Hugo spoke without turning his head to look at Alice, but Eliza believed he was fully aware that he had her employer's immediate interest.

After a few moments silence Alice asked, hesitantly, 'This naval officer … What is his name?'

Still not looking at her, Hugo replied, 'Kendall. Lieutenant Kendall.'

'Not Lieutenant *Jory* Kendall?'

'Why yes, I'm sure that's his name.' Appearing surprised, he added, 'Do you know him?'

'Yes. At least, David and I – and Eliza – know a Lieutenant Jory Kendall, he is a naval man but was with the Coast Guard service when we first met with him.'

'That must be him, he certainly spent a great deal of time on land for a naval man. Long enough to court poor Isabella and lead her to believe he would marry her, only to change his mind and forsake her in a most heartless manner. My sister's death had a serious effect on my father, which is partly why I returned from India. I am his only son and am most concerned for him.'

Alice was only half-listening to what he was saying about his family affairs. She found it difficult to equate what Hugo Trevelyan had said with the Jory she knew, but Jory *did* come from Lostwithiel and, although she was aware he had four brothers, he had once told her in conversation that he was the only one of the brothers to leave home and join the navy.

'Are you alright, Alice?' Hugo was looking at her in apparent concern.

'Yes.' She made a great effort to pull herself together, she did not want to let him know she was upset, or that it was because of what he had said about Jory. Changing the subject abruptly, she asked, 'How far are we from your home now? It feels as though there might be rain in the air and it would be nice to reach the house before it becomes any worse.'

Seated behind Captain Trevelyan and Alice in the trap, Eliza had listened to their conversation with utter disbelief. Of all the men she had ever met, Jory Kendall was the one she most trusted and respected. She refused to believe he was guilty of deceiving any girl to the extent that she would die of 'a broken heart'.

She remained quiet for the remainder of the journey, thinking of what had been said.

*

Helynn Manor was not what either Alice or Eliza had been antic-ipating. It was large, certainly, but there was an air of neglect about the house and gardens that both women found disconcert-ing. It looked as though nobody cared about the house any more and, hemmed in by hills and tall trees, it seemed as if it was trying to hide from the world.

The manor was older than Alice had imagined it would be, much of the present building dating from the fifteenth or six-teenth centuries. The architectural style, coupled with the close proximity of surrounding trees gave the house a gloomy, over-shadowed feel.

The interior did nothing to dispel this image. Dim light enter-ing the house through small diamond-paned windows disclosed heavy, ageing furniture that echoed the neglect of the house as a whole.

Hugo Trevelyan entered the house ahead of the women and, walking behind with Alice, Eliza whispered, 'It's creepy!'

Alice was of the same opinion but in a bid to bolster her own sinking feelings as well as Eliza's she replied, in an equally low voice, 'It is *old*, Eliza. It must be one of the oldest manor houses in Cornwall, but I am surprised that Captain Trevelyan's father has not come out to greet us.'

'And where are the servants? Eliza questioned.

Entering the hall, her question was partially answered when a grey-haired and frail woman dressed in sombre black appeared from one of the doorways set around the large, irregularly shaped entrance hallway.

A stern glance taking in the new arrivals, she addressed Captain Trevelyan, 'We expected you home a week ago, and who are these…?' She indicated Alice and Eliza with a movement of her head without looking at them.

Extending a hand towards Alice, Hugo said, 'This is Miss Kilpeck, sister of the rector of Trethevy and her maid, Eliza. Alice, meet Miss Grimm, she has been housekeeper at Helynn since before I was born.'

Eliza thought the housekeeper's name was most apt, but the housekeeper was talking to her. 'It's a good job you're here, girl, we don't pay servants unnecessarily at Helynn and with only Mr Trevelyan in the house I can do all that's needed but with Captain Trevelyan and an uninvited guest in the house you will be earning your keep. The sooner you get out of those fancy clothes of yours and go into the kitchen, the better, although what you are going to feed to everyone I don't know.'

Hardly able to believe the attitude of the gaunt housekeeper, Alice said sharply, 'Eliza is here as my personal maid and companion, she is not here to take on a house servant's duties at Helynn!'

Aware that Alice was still upset at what Hugo Trevelyan had said about Jory Kendall and anxious that her employer should not become embroiled in an argument with the rude and eccentric Miss Grimm, Eliza said hastily, 'I don't mind helping out in the kitchen if they are short-staffed, Miss Alice.'

'It sounds more as though there *are* no other servants, Eliza, and you will tend to my needs before considering any other duties.'

Turning to Hugo who had listened to the exchange in silence, she said, 'Perhaps you will be kind enough to show me to my room, Hugo, while Miss Grimm shows Eliza where she can obtain some water. I would like to freshen up after the journey. While I am doing that with Eliza's help you might like to sort out whether we should stay, or return to Trethevy.'

Leaving the tight-lipped housekeeper standing in the hall, Hugo led the way upstairs and on the way said, 'I must apologise for Miss Grimm. She has been here so long she feels she is in a position to dictate everything that goes on at Helynn – as she actually does! My father is in his dotage and has always left her to run the household. He has frugal tastes and Miss Grimm has always kept a tight grip on the purse strings. There is a butler somewhere about, but he is much the same age as my father. There *are* servants who come in to clean and carry out household duties, but it is Miss Grimm who dictates *when* they work and she obviously felt they were not needed today – but here is your room. Settle yourself in. I will find the butler and have *him* fetch water, while I sort out Miss Grimm and have her show Eliza to her room.'

It was not the butler but Eliza who brought water to Alice's room and, as toiletries were being laid out on a marble-topped table in a corner of the bedroom, Alice sat on the edge of the bed and with a gesture of despair, said, 'What sort of an establishment have we come to, Eliza? It started off as such a happy day, but first there was what Captain Hugo said on the way here about Lieutenant Jory, and now this!'

For the first time in the three years she had been working for Alice, Eliza saw tears well up in her eyes. It made her very unhappy and she said vehemently, 'I don't believe what Captain Trevelyan said. Lieutenant Jory just isn't that sort of man – and I know how much he thinks of you. He made that very clear to me when he called at the rectory and wrote you a letter while he was there.'

For a moment Alice's spirits rose, but then she said despondently, 'No, Eliza, Captain Trevelyan had no reason to lie to me, he was not even aware that Lieutenant Jory is known to me. It must be true.'

'Something might have been said about who it was brought the fish you had for dinner the other night,' Eliza persisted.

Alice shook her head unhappily, 'It wasn't even mentioned. Had it been Captain Trevelyan would no doubt have commented on the name then. I am as sceptical as you, Eliza, possibly more so, but I fear it must be true, even though it is painful to think about.'

Eliza knew better than to continue to argue with her mistress, but she did not trust Hugo Trevelyan – and she refused to believe ill of Lieutenant Jory Kendall. Either the Indian army cavalry officer was deliberately lying, or there was an explanation for what Jory Kendall was supposed to have done.

'Your room isn't too bad but I dread to think what mine will be like. Miss Grimm said it needed to be got ready and she'd call me when it was done, but I don't suppose she'll be in any hurry to do anything.'

'Whatever the room is like make no comment on it, you'll not be sleeping there. As soon as she has shown it to you and gone away bring your things down here. We'll make up a bed for you on the chaise-longue. I doubt if either of us will sleep very soundly but I would rather not be alone in this house at night.'

Eliza was tidying her employer's toiletries and as she worked, Alice said, 'I wonder what Captain Trevelyan's father is like? It's strange that he hasn't appeared to greet a house guest.'

'Perhaps he's taking an afternoon nap and nobody likes to wake him,' Eliza remarked. 'There doesn't seem as though there's very much to stay awake for around this place. We haven't seen anything of the butler, either. I hope he'll prove a bit more helpful than Miss Grimm.'

Just then both women could hear the sound of slow footsteps on the stairs and Eliza commented, 'Perhaps this is him coming up the stairs now.'

It *was* the butler and he introduced himself to Alice as 'Jenkins'. Not only was he probably older than Miss Grimm, but he was also profoundly deaf. When Alice asked him where his master was he gave a toothless grin and replied, 'I haven't been out today, so it could be raining, but you needn't worry about it, the roof doesn't leak on this side of the house.'

Having imparted this piece of information, he said, 'When your maid has finished here she can use the servants' stairs at the far end of the passageway to go up to her room, it is the first on the left. I'll go up there now and check for myself that she has everything she is likely to need. It's a duty that is usually carried out by Miss Grimm, but the stairs are steep and she has trouble with her knees. I hope you will enjoy your stay at Helynn manor, Miss, it is a long time since we last had a visitor.'

Giving Alice just the hint of a bow, Jenkins turned and left the room.

Seating herself heavily on the bed, Alice said, 'So much for finding the butler more helpful than Miss Grimm. He is as deaf as a post! What do you make of the situation we have found ourselves in, Eliza?'

Assuming the round-shouldered posture of the aged butler, Eliza replied, 'I haven't been out today, Miss Alice, so it might be raining, but the roof doesn't leak in this part of the house.'

After a few moments of surprised silence, Alice began to giggle and the tension and foreboding that had taken charge of both women since their arrival at Helynn Manor began to crumble – but the respite would be short-lived.

Chapter Five

*T*HE EVENING MEAL was prepared by Eliza and an ever-grumbling Miss Grimm from a goose, owned, killed and plucked by a neighbouring farmer. It would be accompanied by a mixture of vegetables collected by the equally disgruntled butler from a walled garden belonging to the house and apparently tended by a part-time gardener who was not paid for his services but allowed to use the plot to supply his own large family.

The cooking utensils in the kitchen were old and in a bad state and there was a dire shortage of such things as spices, cooking fats and even butter. When Eliza asked for salt for the potatoes she was given a jar with only a thin sprinkling of the condiment in the bottom.

In sheer exasperation, Eliza said, 'Surely the Trevelyan family isn't so poor that it can't afford salt? Even the poorest household in the land would have more than this!'

'The wealth, or otherwise, of the Trevelyan family is none of your business, my girl. You get on with what you need to do and hope they leave enough left over to keep you from going to bed with an empty belly.'

'If I thought they were going to eat it all I'd have mine first and tell 'em we'd been given a one legged bird!' Eliza made the comment in a jocular manner, but Mrs Grimm had no sense of humour.

'You'll do no such thing! You may be able to do what you like with that woman you work for, I doubt if she has any more breeding than a servant girl herself. Master Hugo never did have any taste when it came to women, but in this house a servant knows her place.'

'It seems to me it must be a *hiding*-place,' Eliza retorted, 'and a very good one too. It doesn't look as though there's been a servant around the house for months – *years* even. As for Miss Alice, she's the sister of a rector and her father was something very important in a cathedral, a Bishop, or a Pope or something and I'm her lady's maid, not a kitchen slavey. I'm only doing this here because I don't want *her* going hungry, she's not used to it. But I'm not staying in this kitchen listening to you saying things about her. I'll leave *you* to get on with the cooking and tell Miss Alice why!'

'Oh, no you won't!' As Eliza wiped her hands on her apron, Miss Grimm moved to block the kitchen doorway. 'You'll stay here and do whatever needs doing. You've got far too much spirit for a girl in service, but you're loyal to your mistress and there's no fault in that. If what you say is true she's got a better background than others he's brought to Helynn.'

'Captain Trevelyan's brought women to the house before, and you think she's like *them*?'

'One night, when he'd been drinking, he boasted that there was always a woman to warm his bed in India and it's something he's got used to, but if you think I'm being disloyal to my employer by telling you this, then you can think again. I owe Hugo Trevelyan nothing. I was taken on by Mr Albert, Hugo's father, and the late Mrs Trevelyan, bless her soul. It was Master Hugo's ways that put her in an early grave and turned the mind of his father, him and the death of Miss Isabella, their daughter – although she was nearly as wild as her brother.'

Eliza's show of spirit seemed to have tapped an unexpected well of humanity within the severe exterior of the housekeeper and she continued, 'I'll be glad when Master Hugo returns to India and the house gets back to normality again, or as normal as it can ever be with poor Mr Albert the way he is. Fortunately, there are only a few days left before he goes and I doubt whether we'll ever see him again. He's already milked the estate so dry we'll have even more of a struggle keeping things going than we have had these last few years.'

Eliza listened to Miss Grimm in increasing alarm. It was quite evident that Helynn Manor and its occupants were in as penurious a state as it appeared to be, but it was what had been said about Captain Hugo Trevelyan that she found particularly disturbing.

'Miss Alice would *never* have come to Helynn had she known all this about him. The only reason she agreed to come here was she felt beholden to Captain Trevelyan because he probably saved her life when the pony pulling the trap she was in bolted. He managed to stop it before it reached a sharp bend in the lane where it would have certainly overturned. She's led a very sheltered life and is nothing like any of the women you've been talking about. Do you think she's in real danger? What can I do?'

'You can do nothing right now, it will be dark very soon with no moon tonight. Get on with the cooking and feed them all, but when you go upstairs and help your mistress to dress for dinner warn her about Master Hugo. He will be alright while we are about, but when the meal is over and we are sent away he will begin drinking heavily, no doubt trying to persuade your mistress to join him. The best thing she can do is leave him on some pretext, go to her room and lock herself in. There are strong bolts and it's a stout door.'

Giving Eliza an appraising look, she added, 'The trouble is *you* are a pretty young girl, Eliza, and I've seen by the way Master Hugo looks at you that he is fully aware of that. If he can't have your mistress then he'll come after you and the doors of the servants' rooms are flimsier than the others. You'll need to be on your guard.'

Eliza went cold at her words, it was as though time had gone into reverse and she was back at the home of Lady Calnan, fearing the unwelcome advances of her employer's husband.

Was history about to repeat itself and take away the happy life she had enjoyed during the three years since she had been cast ashore as a shipwrecked convict on the Cornish coast?

When dinner was almost ready to be served Eliza left the now almost friendly Helynn housekeeper in charge of the kitchen and went in search of Alice.

She was in the sitting room and seemed relieved to see Eliza, readily agreeing to her suggestion that she should accompany her to her room and help her dress for dinner.

Once in the room, Alice said, 'I was so relieved to see you, Eliza, Captain Trevelyan took me for a walk around the garden and made some amorous and highly improper advances. I was quite upset but when I insisted we return to the house he took me to the sitting room and tried hard to persuade me to drink with him. I declined, but it certainly never influenced *his* drinking. He had a great deal and I fear he will be quite drunk – dangerously so – by the time we have finished dinner.'

'You are probably right.' Eliza told Alice what the Helynn housekeeper had said about Captain Trevelyan; his women, his habits, and her suggestion of what Alice should do when he began to drink heavily.

Alice was horrified. 'This is *terrifying*, Eliza, I realise now how stupid I was to come to Helynn knowing so little about him, but he seemed such a *gentleman*. He fooled Reverend David too, he would never have allowed me to come here had there been even the slightest hint of Captain Hugo's true character. Oh dear, I wish we were able to harness up the pony and trap and return to

Trethevy right away, but it would be utter folly to attempt it now, in the dark, but we will leave first thing in the morning. In the meantime there is no question of you sleeping in a servant's room. You will sleep in this room and we will bolt the door against him. It is always possible, of course, that Captain Trevelyan's father can do something about him, but he still has not put in an appearance and I find that most disturbing.'

'He has something seriously wrong with him,' Eliza explained, 'Miss Grimm said his mind had been turned by the goings on of Captain Trevelyan. I don't know exactly what she means by that, but it doesn't sound as though he is in any state to do anything.'

'That is certainly not reassuring,' Alice agreed, unhappily, 'but if he does not join us for dinner I will demand to be taken to him.'

Alice was aware that although she spoke with her usual authority, it was no more than empty bravado. She was in a very difficult situation – and probably a most dangerous one. There was no possibility of her and Eliza leaving that night, with or without the goodwill of Captain Trevelyan.

Aware that Eliza knew this too, Alice added, 'If Captain Trevelyan refuses to take me to him you and I will come up here, bolt the door and leave Helynn at the first opportunity in the morning.'

As Alice finished talking, her glance went to the bedroom door which was now closed – and she gave a gasp of dismay.

'The door, Eliza … look at the door. There *are* no bolts, somebody has removed them! We have no way of keeping *anyone* out. What is going on, Eliza? What is happening to us?'

Chapter Six

*M*ISS GRIMM BROUGHT Albert Trevelyan to dinner that evening and seated him at the head of the long dining-table, in a high-backed Carvers' chair which reminded Alice of the Bishop's throne in her father's cathedral.

The reason he had not put in an appearance earlier was immediately apparent. Seemingly unaware of anyone in the room, his vacant expression was that of a man whose mind was far away from all things temporal.

Following the instructions given to her by Miss Grimm, Eliza placed a soup plate in front of the master of the house without saying anything and the ancient butler carefully ladled soup out for him.

The aroma rising from the soup succeeded in bringing Albert Trevelyan back to the world occupied by the others in the room and, looking around him, he seemed to be seeing them for the first time, although his mind was still pathetically muddled.

Frowning at Hugo, he shifted his glance to Alice and his expression underwent an amazing transformation. Showing uninhibited joy, he cried, 'Isabella! Nobody told me you were here. What a delight it is to have you home!'

Turning his attention to the butler, he said, 'Jenkins, why did *you* not tell me?'

The deaf butler never heard him properly and, before he

could reply, Hugo cast a brief glance in Alice's direction before saying, 'Isabella arrived unexpectedly this afternoon, Father, and you were sleeping. We thought we would keep it as a surprise for you.'

'I have no need of any of *your* surprises.' Raising his voice he shouted, 'Jenkins, fetch some of that French wine from the cold room, half-a-dozen bottles. It's high time we had something to celebrate at Helynn.'

'I'm not certain we have six cases of champagne there, sir.'

'I said bottles, you fool and of course we have them!' Albert Trevelyan bawled, irritably, 'Go and fetch them – and be quick about it.'

When the aged butler hurried from the room in a short-paced shuffle, Albert Trevelyan beamed at Alice. 'Make a start on your soup, my dear, you must be tired after your long journey. We can leave talk of what you have been up to until after the meal, you must be hungry after travelling all that way.'

Still beaming, the master of the house began spooning soup into his mouth with a liberality which ensured that his patterned silk waistcoat was not excluded from the first course.

While his father was so engaged, Hugo leaned across the table towards Alice and said softly, 'Don't worry about anything my father says. He thinks you are Isabella but that was a rare moment of near-rationality, sadly it will not last. By the time dinner is over he will have forgotten you are here, let alone who he thinks you are.'

Alice found it upsetting to be mistaken for Albert Trevelyan's dead daughter but she resigned herself to accepting the incident as yet one more bizarre happening in her disastrous visit to Helynn Manor. But she soon had more serious concerns.

When the champagne arrived the ancient butler was carrying only five bottles and not six but, true to Hugo's prediction, Albert Trevelyan had already forgotten why they had been brought to the dinner table and he did not query Hugo's explanation that they were celebrating his own homecoming.

Hugo wasted no time in getting the 'celebration' underway and by the time the meal came to an end there were only two full bottles of champagne remaining.

By this time the son of the house had become loud-voiced and not only leered openly at Alice across the table, but was also beginning to make thinly-veiled insinuations about how the evening's 'celebrations' should progress.

When the three diners moved to the sitting-room, the East India Company cavalry officer continued his heavy drinking but by now had moved on to brandy.

Suddenly, Albert Trevelyan rose to his feet and left the room without a word of explanation. Taking advantage of his departure, Hugo rose from the armchair in which he was seated and moved unsteadily across the room to sit down heavily upon the settee occupied by Alice.

'You have hardly touched your drink, Alice, is there something you would prefer. A port, perhaps, or a gin?' His voice was slurred and, although Alice had met with few drunken men in her lifetime, she realised Hugo had already drunk far more than was good for him – or for her.

'No thank you, I am not used to strong drink and I had a glass of champagne with my dinner.'

'It was only the one glass, as I recall, Alice, and we are celebrating your visit to Helynn and an opportunity to really get to know each other. What will you have to drink?'

'I am quite content with what I have, thank you – and I think we can talk more easily if we are facing each other across the room.'

'Come now, Alice, surely you are not going to behave all prim and proper with me, after all, I *did* save your life.'

'For which I have expressed my gratitude, as has my brother.'

'Expressed with words only, Alice, surely I deserve something more than that? I think …'

Before Hugo was able to give Alice the benefit of his thoughts the door opened and Albert Trevelyan returned to the room carrying two pistols and closely pursued by Miss Grimm.

Leaping unsteadily to his feet, Hugo demanded, 'Father! What are you doing with those pistols? Be careful!' He hastily pushed aside one of the weapons that was pointed in his direction. 'Are they loaded?'

'Of course they're loaded, you don't go on guard with an unloaded weapon!'

'On guard? What are you on guard for – and against whom?'

'I don't expect *you* to understand, you have never put family before self. Had you looked after your sister the way a brother should I wouldn't have to sit up night after night in the hallway making certain Kendall never again comes near her, but I can't stay here talking to you, I have a father's duty to perform. You can sleep well tonight, Isabella, there will be no Kendall coming anywhere near you.'

With this, Albert Trevelyan turned and left the room.

Hugo made as if to follow him, but he found his way barred by a determined Miss Grimm. 'Leave him, he'll come to no harm seated in the hall in the darkness.'

'He's a totally confused old man with two loaded pistols, anything could happen. If one were to be fired accidentally….'

'Nothing will happen. He has the pistols with him most of the time "in case Kendall comes to the house", but within half-an-hour or so he will fall asleep. I'll gather up the guns then wake him and lead him up to his bedroom, by which time he will have forgotten all about Isabella and Kendall and will be grumbling because I have let him fall asleep downstairs and not made certain he was safely tucked up in bed.'

'I think I will take Eliza to help me and go up to bed too,' Alice said, welcoming the unexpected opportunity to escape the unwelcome attentions of the son of the house.

'You can't go to bed yet,' Hugo protested, 'We have much to talk about and the evening is still young!'

'There is also a great deal of washing-up to be done and the kitchen put to rights ...' This from Miss Grimm. '... Your servant girl will be busy for an hour or so yet.'

'As I have said before, Eliza is my personal maid, not a kitchen servant,' Alice retorted. 'Please tell her she is needed upstairs in my room – or do I need to go to the kitchen and tell her myself?'

Before the housekeeper could reply, Alice turned to Hugo Trevelyan. 'Thank you for your hospitality, Hugo, I will see you in the morning, before I return to Trethevy.'

Leaving Hugo still protesting, Alice pushed past the indignant housekeeper and hurried upstairs, taking with her the lighted candle in a holder that had been the sole light in the passageway outside the sitting-room.

Chapter Seven

*I*T WAS ANOTHER ten minutes before Eliza came to her employer's bedroom and Alice was greatly relieved to see her, saying, 'I feared that every sound I heard was Captain Trevelyan coming up to the room. He is drinking very heavily and was quite angry when I left him to come upstairs. I do not trust him, he is certainly no gentleman and I am seriously concerned lest the bolts were deliberately removed from the door. Do you think we should move some of the furniture against it?'

'I can do better than that!' reaching into the large pocket of the kitchen apron she was wearing, Eliza pulled out a sharpening-steel. 'I took this from the kitchen, it will serve in place of the top bolt and we can use the poker from the fireplace for the bottom one. It's a very stout door and with these in place we'll have nothing to fear from Captain Trevelyan.'

'You are an absolute wonder, Eliza. I would never have thought of replacing the missing bolts in such a fashion. You don't know how very relieved I am. What would I do without you?'

Pleased by Alice's praise, Eliza said, 'Lieutenant Jory says I'm "resourceful".'

It was a word that had made her feel important at the time and she had carefully stored it in her memory, but quoting the source of such praise proved to be a mistake.

'I do not think I want to hear anything about Lieutenant

Kendall, Eliza, he would seem to be no better than Captain Trevelyan. Perhaps all so-called "gentlemen" are the same.'

'You don't really believe that,' Eliza protested, 'and you can't believe anything Captain Trevelyan says, especially if it's about someone he thinks means something to you.'

'It is not only the captain who has spoken of how badly Isabella Trevelyan was treated by him, Captain Trevelyan's father and Miss Grimm have also mentioned his name. *They* have no reason to lie about him.'

As Alice was talking she was forcing the poker firmly into the bolt fittings at the bottom of the bedroom door frame. Eliza had already performed the same task at the top of the door with the sharpening steel and the door was now secured as efficiently as if the original bolts were in place.

Greatly relieved, Alice relaxed a little and asked Eliza, 'Did you see Mr Trevelyan in the hallway when you came upstairs?'

'I came up the servants' staircase,' Eliza replied, 'Miss Grimm warned me to keep away from the hallway because Mr Trevelyan is on guard there. She says he is really quite harmless but not always responsible for his actions and there *could* be a nasty accident.'

'This visit to Helynn has turned out to be an absolute nightmare, I will be greatly relieved to be away from it, Eliza. We will leave for Trethevy as soon as possible in the morning.'

'At least we will be able to sleep soundly knowing that no one can get into the room,' Eliza replied, 'and hopefully Captain Trevelyan will get himself so drunk he'll forget all about you.'

Hugo Trevelyan did become *very* drunk but, far from forgetting about Alice, he became more obsessive about her with every drink and eventually determined to do something about it.

The two women were just dozing off, Alice in the bed and Eliza on a chaise-longue, when they heard a sound from the passageway outside the bedroom, as though someone had fallen against a piece of furniture.

A faint sliver of yellow light appeared in the narrow gap between door and floor and in the darkness of the bedroom they both held their breath in fearful anticipation of what was about to happen. They heard the sound of the door handle being turned and the door was forced against the makeshift bolts, then pushed again … and again.

After a lengthy pause, there came a knock on the door and Hugo Trevelyan's soft but drink-affected voice called, 'Alice, what have you done with the door? Open it, I wish to talk with you.'

Both women remained silent in the darkness and Hugo's plea was repeated, this time louder than before. He knocked again, the sound reflecting his growing anger.

His attempt to provoke a response continued for some minutes before the patience of the drunken son of the house was finally exhausted. After hammering on the door with both fists, he charged at it, using his shoulder as a battering ram.

Both women inside the room were terrified and Eliza rose from the chaise-longue to check that the makeshift bolts were holding firm.

They were and Eliza whispered to Alice 'The poker and the steel haven't budged. He's not going to be able to get in at us.'

Hugo Trevelyan realised it too and, making no attempt to keep his voice down now, he shouted, 'You are a stupid and ungrateful little nobody, Alice, and you will end your days as a dried-up spinster. I should never have bothered to save your life.'

His outburst was followed by moments of unintelligible mumbling before he banged on the door for the last time, shouting, 'Very well, we'll see if your maid has more life in her than her mistress. You can stay cowering in your room imagining how much *she* is enjoying me … Damn!'

The oath came as the sliver of light disappeared from beneath the door and the women realised Hugo had dropped the candle. Fortunately, it had gone out.

After muttering about getting another drink first, he could be heard crashing his way along the dark passageway in the direction of the main staircase and both women breathed huge sighs of relief.

'Thank the Lord you had the brainwave about the makeshift bolts, Eliza, I shudder to think what would have happened had he …'

Alice never completed the sentence. There was the sound of a shot from the direction of the main staircase and they heard Hugo shout furiously, 'You bloody old fool! You could have killed me. Give me the other gun before you do it again.'

'Come near me and I won't miss again. I'll teach you to come here in my house after Isabella.'

This time it was Albert Trevelyan's voice, followed by that of Miss Grimm, then everyone seemed to be talking at once, although it was not possible for the two women in the bedroom to discern what was being said.

'Do you want me to go out and find out what has happened?' Eliza asked tremulously, hoping Alice would not say 'Yes'.

'No, if Captain Hugo has been shot it is no more than he deserves. If he has not, *you* would be the one in danger. Miss Grimm is there with them, she can sort things out, but I doubt if we will be able to sleep now, not after all that excitement. See if you can find a light for the candle, Eliza. We will pack our things and leave Helynn at first light. Captain Trevelyan will be in a drunken sleep by then, although we might have trouble sneaking past his father if he remains in the hall. *I* don't want to be shot!'

'We don't need to go out of the house that way. We'll use the servants' staircase and leave through the kitchen, it's closer to the stables anyway, but do you think you can harness the pony to the trap? I've seen both old Percy and Tristram do it quite a few times, but I'm not sure I could do everything by myself.'

'It should pose no problem. When I was a young girl I would sometimes help the servants to harness the horse to our dogcart. It was a long time ago, but I feel certain we will be able to manage it between us. We *have* to, Eliza, I do not intend remaining in Helynn manor for one minute more than is absolutely necessary. I feel I have been a guest in a lunatic asylum!'

Chapter Eight

ALICE AND ELIZA left Helynn Manor via the kitchen door the next morning when dawn was ushering in the new day, brushing away the last scattering of stars from the waking sky.

Harnessing the pony to the trap took longer than they would have wished but after only a few initial errors it was done and they led pony and trap from the stables, keeping on grass as much as possible until they felt they were out of hearing of those in the house.

Once in the trap they hurriedly left Helynn behind, driving the pony at a sharp trot, relying upon memory of the previous day's journey to guide them back to Trethevy. Although neither woman spoke their thoughts aloud, they were constantly in fear of hearing the sound of Captain Hugo Trevelyan coming in pursuit of them.

Much to the relief of both women, their memories served them well and they chose the correct roads and lanes, helped by the occasional granite signpost erected at major highway junctions.

They arrived at the rectory mid-morning, to find Tristram alone there. Reverend David had taken Percy with him intending to visit the poorhouse after the service, where the oldest resident, a friend of Percy, was dying.

In her mistress's room as Eliza was unpacking clothes, Alice said, 'It is such a relief to be home again safely, Eliza, it was the most dreadful night I have ever experienced in the whole of my life. Quite unbelievable!'

Putting unwanted thoughts aside of the nightmares she still occasionally had about some of the nights spent in prison and on the hulk in her 'other life', Eliza replied, 'Are you going to tell Reverend David about what happened there?'

'No,' Alice replied firmly. 'Certainly not immediately. He would only fuss about it. I will say that Captain Hugo's father was unwell and we felt we were giving them unnecessary extra work. It will mean leaving a great deal unsaid, but I will not be telling an untruth.'

Eliza accepted that it was the best way to deal with the matter, but she asked, 'What will you tell him of the rumours we heard about Lieutenant Jory?'

Alice had been brushing her hair but, lowering the brush to the dressing table, she said unhappily, 'I don't know. He will have to be told something to explain why I am no longer welcoming Lieutenant Jory to the rectory – and I really do feel I could not face him again. He has behaved in a deceitful manner that I find truly hurtful. He allowed me to become very fond of him. Perhaps I read too much into his attentions to me but he must have realised my feelings towards him, and actually encouraged them at a time when he would have been courting poor Isabella Trevelyan. It is quite unforgivable.'

'I think you should listen to *his* side of the story, Miss Alice, I wouldn't take the word of *anyone* at Helynn about *anything*, there wasn't one of them right in the head!'

Giving her maid a fleeting wan smile, Alice said, 'I agree with your assessment of the occupants of Helynn, Eliza, it must be one of the most bizarre households in the land, but they *all* had the same story to tell about Lieutenant Jory and poor Isabella Trevelyan. I found that quite as upsetting as anything else that happened during our visit to Helynn.'

Eliza still refused to believe what had been said at Helynn about Jory Kendall, but she knew Alice was genuinely upset by what she had been told and did not pursue the matter. Nevertheless, her mistress's change of attitude towards the naval lieutenant might affect her and Tristram.

'If Lieutenant Jory is no longer welcome at Trethevy does it mean Tristram and me won't be able to go to the Camelford fair? Reverend David said he could stay here for the nights both before and afterwards if he was going to take us to the fair and bring us back again in his carriage. Will he not be coming now?'

Alice was aware that although Eliza was careful not to reveal her true feelings towards Tristram to her employers, she was very much in love with him in her quiet but intense manner and it was a romance which met with the approval of both Alice and her brother.

'The arrangement has been made and we will not change it. When is the fair?'

'This week, on Saturday.'

'So soon? It would be difficult to change anything now, even if I wished to, but I will need to find somewhere to go for that weekend, I really do not wish to meet with him again.'

'Perhaps … perhaps me and Tristram ought to change our minds about going to the fair if it's going to make things difficult for you.'

'No. You and Tristram have both been looking forward to Camelford fair for months, you must go. I will think of something. Now, if you have finished unpacking, I think I will have a little rest. You must do the same too, neither of us had any sleep last night. Check that all is tidy for Reverend David's return, then take a rest in your room. You were a tower of strength at Helynn in very difficult circumstances, I *do* appreciate it, thank you.'

*

Reverend Kilpeck did not return with Percy until that evening. Tintagel poorhouse's oldest resident had died during the afternoon and David had spent some time discussing with the churchwardens a funeral befitting a centenarian who had long been the oldest inhabitant of the parish.

By the time the two men reached Trethevy Alice and Eliza were up and about and, after expressing surprise that Alice had returned from Helynn after such a short visit and hearing the story she and Eliza had agreed together for their unexpected return, David said, 'I have some news for you too, both good and bad.'

'Tell me the good news first,' Alice replied, 'I am not in the mood for bad news right away.'

'After you left yesterday we had a visit from Dean Fitzjohn and his daughter Ursula ...' – Edgar Fitzjohn, Dean of Windsor, was the distant relative who had been instrumental in appointing David to the living of Trethevy – '... It seems he was at University with Reverend Wallis, vicar of Bodmin and both he and Ursula are holidaying with him for a couple of weeks. They came here yesterday evening and were most disappointed you were not here, but their host, Reverend Wallis, would like us to have dinner with him on Tuesday, at Bodmin vicarage.'

Showing the pleasure he felt at having received such an invitation, David beamed at Alice. 'Bodmin is one of the most important and lucrative livings in Cornwall and Reverend Wallis is an important churchman. He could be a considerable influence in my future, I accepted the invitation, of course, trusting you would be home by then. I hope you approve?'

'I am absolutely delighted, Ursula and I were childhood friends, as you know, how is she?'

Alice was grateful for the opportunity to move away from the subject of Hugo Trevelyan and her visit to Helynn, but she was taken aback by the enthusiasm with which David answered her question.

'Ursula has grown into a beautiful girl, very beautiful, she is intelligent too and well-informed on Church affairs. I found her most enjoyable company.'

Aware that David had been attracted to a girl for possibly the first time, Alice was thrilled for him. 'What a pity I wasn't at home when they called, but I look forward to meeting with Ursula again after all these years.'

'Well, you will have your opportunity on Tuesday, I said you would be very disappointed at missing her – at missing both of them – but as I was quite certain you would be home by then, I agreed we would both spend the whole day with them, remaining until after dinner. It will be the first time we have been away from the Trethevy rectory together for a long time.'

'I look forward to that very much, David. Very much indeed.'

She meant it, not only for the prospect of a day out with her brother. David had never before shown such enthusiasm at meeting a girl. Indeed, he had rarely shown enthusiasm for *any-thing* outside his calling. She thought that Ursula, who had always been a plain, rather serious girl, must have grown into someone rather special to have this effect upon him, but David was talking again.

'Now, you must prepare yourself for the bad news. I am afraid this is not good. Eval Moyle has returned from America and is back on his farm.'

Chapter Nine

'*I* THOUGHT THERE was a warrant out for Eval Moyle's arrest?' Eliza had been thinking about the news given to her by Alice the day before. Today was a Saint's day and a local holiday and she was returning to the rectory with her employer after an early morning service, conducted by Reverend David at the tiny Trethevy church. She had thought they had seen the last of the vindictive preacher when he left for America in a hurry after the Truro 'riots' and was unhappy to know he had come back into their lives.

'The warrant was cancelled with all the others, when it was realised there was no case to answer in respect of the riot charges. Even had it not been, I am not sure it would still be valid after all these years. No doubt Moyle went into the matter before returning to Cornwall. We will just have to hope America has changed the man he once was.'

Eliza had her doubts about Moyle being a changed man, but there was nothing that could be done about him and she had other matters to think about. The fair at Camelford was only a few days away now, and that afternoon she would be walking out with Tristram. She had no doubt their visit to the fair would be the main topic of conversation.

She was wrong.

They certainly spoke of the fair, wondering what would be

there to enjoy. Neither had been to any of the country fairs before, but old Percy had and when telling them about his experiences he had been fulsome about the delights they would discover.

'What are you most looking forward to seeing?' Eliza put the question to Tristram as they followed a path that led along the cliff-top towards the nearby tiny fishing village of Boscastle, nestling in a coastal valley.

'I don't know, the wrestling and boxing might be fun.'

'Fun for you, perhaps, I don't see anything enjoyable about two grown men doing their best to kill one another!'

'We don't *have* to watch them,' Tristram replied hurriedly. 'There'll be lots of other things to see. Old Percy said the last fair he was at had all sorts of animals like he'd never seen before and there'll most likely be a dancing bear, a Punch and Judy, jugglers – and even someone able to swallow a poker!'

'Ugh! I don't think I'd like to do that.'

'You won't have to but there's going to be lots of things you'll enjoy eating.'

'Now that's something I *can* look forward to,' Eliza said, happily. 'Eating something I haven't had to prepare and cook myself. It's going to be worth going all that way just for that.'

'It's going to be worth it for me to spend the whole day with you.'

It was said so seriously that Eliza looked at him in surprise, but she replied, 'I'll enjoy being with you for the day too.'

'Will you? I mean, *really* enjoy it?'

'Of course, I wouldn't be going with you otherwise.'

At that moment their arms brushed against each other and it seemed somehow right that they should link hands, hers small and light, his strong and calloused from hours spent splitting logs with an axe the previous day.

'I'm glad,' he said happily, adding, 'We do like being together, don't we?'

'Of course we do, we're together now, aren't we?'

'I wish we could be *really* together, Eliza.'

'What do you mean, *really* together?'

Eliza thought she *knew* what he meant. It was something other couples did when they had been walking out together for far less time than she and Tristram, but she had always put off thinking about it. Mainly, as she had to admit to herself, because she did not know what her reaction would be to him. They had been coming out like this whenever possible for some three years, but for the most part it had been along the open cliff top, or other places where they might be seen by others. They had kissed frequently and recently she felt his kisses were becoming more demanding. She had felt a strong urge to respond to them, but remembered the promise she had made to Alice about her behaviour when she was with Tristram. Besides, should she become pregnant it would reflect badly on her employers, Reverend David in particular. It would also bring to an end the happy life she had so unexpectedly been able to enjoy for the past three years.

'You must know what I'm talking about, Eliza.'

'I might, but why don't you say it right out so I can be sure?'

She was playing for time, not only in order to put her own confused thoughts in order but also in the hope that he might be too embarrassed to say what it was he wanted them to do together.

Taking her by surprise, he said, 'All right then.' Releasing her hand and taking her arm, he brought her to a halt, 'Why don't we get married?'

'Get married ? Us? You and me?'

'That's right, you and me.'

'But you hardly know anything about me?

'We've worked in the same household for three years and been walking out for much of that time, what don't I know about you?'

Eliza's thoughts were in turmoil. There was so *much* Tristram did not know about her – but did it really matter? Tristram wanted to marry her for what she was now, not for what society, the law, had once declared her to be – a convicted thief, sentenced to transportation.

'You haven't given me an answer, Eliza.'

Tristram felt a sense of disappointment that bordered on despair. He had been mentally building up to this moment for weeks and had decided he would propose to her at Camelford fair, the first whole day they would ever have spent together. But, walking along the cliff-top, holding her hand, his feelings had overcome him and he could delay the proposal no longer.

He had not *seriously* considered that she would refuse him. In truth, in his mind it had never been a question of whether or not they *should* get married, more a question of when it would be.

'Why do you want to marry me?' She needed to ask the question twice before he responded.

'Why? Why *do* people get married?'

'Because they love each other and want to be together, always.'

'Well, I want *us* to be together always.'

'What for, just so you can do things to me, have your children and someone to look after you in your old age? Is that why you want us to be married?'

'Yes … No! Not just for that.'

Tristram was confused, aware this was going all wrong.

'Then what else?'

'Because … well, because you're *special*.'

'That's getting better, but you still haven't said how you *feel* about me. The way two people should feel about each other if they are going to get married.'

'You must know how I feel about you, Eliza. I wouldn't have asked you to marry me otherwise.'

'But you *haven't* asked me, you've just *suggested* we should get married. You could have been talking about buying a pig, a horse, or a dog. Anything!'

Bewildered, Tristram said, 'It's nothing like buying a pig, or any other animal, Eliza. I want you to marry me because I love you, you must know that.'

'I *didn't* know it, Tristram, and I'm no good at guessing.'

Suddenly gripping his arm in both her hands, she added, happily, 'But I know it now, and that's what I wanted to hear you say.'

'So you *will* marry me?'

Eliza was far more excited than she dared to show him, but she still needed time to think of the implications of marrying Tristram and what she would need to tell him of her past – and she did not believe she could keep such an important secret from the man to whom she was married.

'I'll let you know on the day of the fair.'

When he looked bewildered, she explained, 'I know what it is *I* want, Tristram, but I need to talk to Miss Alice and Reverend David and … oh, there are lots and lots of things I need to think about, but you can kiss me now if you want to. I mean, *really* kiss me so I tingle all over….'

Chapter Ten

*L*IEUTENANT JORY KENDALL arrived at the Trethevy rectory early in the evening of the day before the Camelford fair. He brought with him a huge bunch of roses, picked from the Kendalls' rose garden by his mother and sent with her best wishes to Alice, together with an invitation to spend a few days with the family at the Kendalls' mansion at her earliest convenience.

It should have been an exciting moment for Alice. Not only would it signal recognition by the Kendall family that she existed, but be an acknowledgement by them that she occupied a special place in their younger son's life.

But Alice was not at home. She was spending a few days at the Bodmin vicarage with her childhood friend. Ursula would be returning to Windsor with her father in a few days time and their Bodmin host had invited Alice to his vicarage in order that she might spend the last few days of Ursula's holiday with her.

It was a perfect excuse for Alice not to meet up with Jory during his visit but Eliza was strongly critical of her decision, so much so that Alice felt a need to remind her that she was her *ladies* maid and not her *nurse* maid. Nevertheless it did not stop Eliza from using subtler means of letting her employer know she felt she was wrong.

In truth, Alice was not happy to be avoiding Jory. Despite all she had learned at Helynn about his unforgivable conduct towards the late Isabella Trevelyan, she found herself thinking of him quite as much, perhaps even more than before, despite a determination to convince herself she had eliminated him from her life.

Nevertheless, she tried hard to dismiss him from her thoughts and she left for Bodmin having reminded Eliza about the way she was to behave at the fair. Then she set off in the pony trap to see her friend. Tristram was driving her there and Eliza did not doubt that he would receive a similar warning along the way.

Jory had arrived at Trethevy in one of his family's carriages, emblazoned with the Kendall family's crest on both doors. The groom driving the splendid vehicle had shared Tristram's room overnight and now he and the Trethevy employee were together on the driving seat, while Eliza sat inside, with Jory.

Eliza felt very important as they bowled along the narrow lanes on the way to Camelford, slower vehicles and pedestrians giving way to them, unaccustomed to such grandeur on the rural back roads.

Jory seemed wrapped in thought for some time after their early morning departure from the rectory and when he did speak it was quite apparent what he had been thinking about.

'It was very disappointing that Miss Alice was not at the rectory for my visit, Eliza. It is a long time since I last saw her and I had been greatly looking forward to our meeting.'

'I expect Miss Alice is disappointed too, sir,' Eliza lied, 'but it is many years since she saw her best friend and as she's someone Reverend David seems quite smitten with they might well have important things to talk about.'

'Even so, she could have written a note to me, explaining matters.' Jory was upset, he had been looking forward to spending time with Alice. 'Is there something I should know about,

Eliza? You went with her to Captain Trevelyan's home, is there anything more than a friendship between them?'

'Oh no, sir, I can assure you of that. There is nothing between Captain Trevelyan and Miss Alice and there never will be!'

Eliza realised she had been too emphatic and Jory was aware of it too.

'How can you be so certain, Eliza? Did something happen at Trevelyan's home I should perhaps know about? Was he less than gentlemanly towards Miss Alice?'

Alice found herself in a difficult situation. She liked Lieutenant Jory very much and would be delighted if she could heal the breach between them, but a loyal maid did not talk about her mistress's private life. On the other hand she was probably the only person able to bring them back together, although she would need to be careful what she said to him.

'Nothing happened between them, sir, and I should know, I slept in Miss Alice's room that night although that was only because the house wasn't really in a state to have visitors, but it seems you are known to the Trevelyan family.'

'I doubt it, Eliza, to the best of my knowledge I have never met any of them.'

'Well they certainly *believe* you have, sir, they had a great deal to say linking you with Captain Trevelyan's sister, a Miss Isabella. I believe she died some time ago.'

'They think I had something to do with an Isabella Trevelyan? That is quite absurd. I have never even heard the name, but why on earth should Captain Trevelyan lie about such a thing – unless his intention was to discredit me in Miss Alice's eyes? If that is the reason it is thoroughly despicable.'

'It wasn't only Captain Trevelyan who spoke about it, sir. His father and their housekeeper seemed to know you too.'

'That is sheer nonsense. I would take it up with Trevelyan right away if I could, but someone I spoke to recently mentioned that he will be returning to India very soon and is probably already in London. But that will not stop me from calling on his father and demanding an explanation from him.'

'You would be wasting your time, sir.'

Eliza told him of the senior Trevelyan's behaviour and his mental state. Although it had not been her intention, as she talked Jory gained a fairly accurate idea about some of the things which had occurred during Alice's visit to the Trevelyan home and he was appalled.

'It sounds very much as though mental instability runs in the family, Eliza, your visit to them with Miss Alice must have been a great trial. I intend getting to the bottom of this ridiculous story that I was somehow involved with the unfortunate daughter of the family, but I am very disappointed that Miss Alice should have given credence to such infamous lies about me.'

'She didn't *want* to, sir, I'm sure of that, and she wouldn't have, either, if such stories only came from Captain Trevelyan. It was because the same things were said by his father and the house-keeper too. They were so convincing it would have been difficult for anyone *not* to believe what they said.'

'Well, thank you for telling me, Eliza. I can assure you that *whatever* was said, I know nothing of Isabella Trevelyan and am quite certain I never met her, but I *will* find out what this is all about and put things right between Miss Alice and myself.'

'That would make me happy, sir, and Miss Alice too, I'm sure.'

Camelford fair was all, and more, than Tristram had promised Eliza it would be. As the Kendall carriage neared the small market town which unevenly straddled the River Camel, it passed a great many men, women and children heading in the same direction.

Most of those they met with on the road stood politely to one side as the carriage passed by, but shortly before entering the town it was almost forced to a halt by a large group of marching men carrying banners and lustily singing a Methodist hymn.

When they were eventually clear of the group, Eliza asked, 'Who were they, did they belong to the fair?'

Jory smiled, 'I doubt it, the banners were proclaiming the evils of drink and encouraging men to join the temperance movement. They must intend holding a rally at the fair. It could cause trouble. A great many men, and some women too, see fair day as an opportunity to get very drunk. It is a good day for the publicans, their premises stay open for as long as there are drinking men left with money in their pockets and if the temperance men are too vociferous it is not unknown for publicans to offer free beer to their customers to chase them away from their premises.'

At that moment Tristram's face appeared at the open window as he precariously hung down from the roof of the carriage and called, 'Did you see who was leading the temperance men?'

When both occupants answered in the negative, he shouted, 'It was Eval Moyle. I'd say he's on his way to make trouble at the fair.'

When Tristram disappeared from view, Jory said, 'With any luck Moyle will get himself arrested again. The Camelford mayor has brought a police sergeant and two constables from London to deal with any trouble at the fair. They won't put up with any nonsense from Moyle.'

'It's a pity he didn't stay in America,' Eliza said, 'but perhaps he caused trouble there too.'

'I don't think so,' Jory replied, 'I have heard that he is in fact very happy there and has come home to persuade his brother to sell their farm and return to America with him. It is said that with the proceeds from the farm he intends building a chapel there.'

'I hope he succeeds in selling it quickly and goes away again,' Eliza said. 'He gives me the shivers.'

'Hopefully he will be far too busy saving sinners to trouble you or Tristram,' Jory said, optimistically, 'and here we are at the fair now. I will show you and Tristram where my recruiting booth is and we will meet up there at the end of the day for the journey back to Trethevy.'

Chapter Eleven

*T*HE FAIR WAS every bit as exciting as Tristram had predicted and it seemed to her that every man, woman and child in North Cornwall must be there.

The young couple walked around the fair for more than an hour, taking everything in before they began spending the money they had, which had been supplemented by a generous gift of ten shillings each from Alice Kilpeck, in recognition of their 'loyal service' to Reverend Kilpeck and herself over the last three years.

They first visited the 'menagerie', which contained a couple of lions and a skeletal tiger, confined in cages in which they paced back and forth ceaselessly, the tiger baring yellow teeth in a ferocious snarl when prodded by a farmer's walking stick. The farmer, who had declared the animal to be 'No more'n a oversize farm cat', complained bitterly to the menagerie owner when, much to the delight of the watching crowd, the animal seized the offending stick and happily began chewing it into small pieces.

When Tristram and Eliza left the large marquee the farmer was demanding that the menagerie owner reimburse him for the value of his walking stick, while the animal owner was threatening to sue the farmer if his 'valuable' animal became ill through eating it.

Next they saw a dancing brown bear wearing a studded collar to which was attached a short chain, secured to a heavy stake driven into the ground. Its owner turned the handle of a hurdy-gurdy while the unhappy bear shuffled clumsily, swaying from side to side.

The sight upset Eliza who said the bear looked 'sad'.

She cheered up when Tristram took her to watch a marionette show which included dancing puppet cats and dogs as well as the gaudily dressed dolls.

At midday, Tristram treated Eliza to boiled-roast goose at one of the many refreshment booths. It was a delicious meal in which the bird had first been boiled and then roasted over an open fire until browned. It was the first time Eliza had tasted the delicacy and she enthused about it.

While they were eating, Tristram became suddenly serious and asked, 'You haven't forgotten your promise to me, Eliza?'

'Promise?' Feigning puzzlement, she said, 'What promise?'

'You *have* forgotten! You promised me …'

Seeing her mischievous smile, he said accusingly, 'You're teasing me, Eliza, that was *cruel*.'

'Yes, it was,' She agreed, 'but I don't want to tell you right here and now and have you do something silly in front of all these people.'

He looked bewildered for a few moments, then, as enlightenment came to him he looked at her with increasing delight, 'You mean…? Does that mean the answer is "Yes"? You *will* marry me?'

'It means I'll give you my answer before the day is out, but somewhere a little more private than in the midst of so many people.'

Tristram was confident from her enigmatic reply that he knew what her answer was going to be and, grinning happily, he took her extended hand and allowed her to lead him to where a group of red-faced and perspiring bandsmen were doing their best to drown out the voices of perhaps a hundred Primitive Methodists who were singing hymns at the tops of their voices in a counter-bid to swamp the sound of the brass instruments and their rendering of more popular songs of the day.

Jory Kendall's recruiting booth was nearby and the contest between brass band and Methodists was amusing him. After telling the young Trethevy couple that he had already signed on a satisfactory number of potential coast guards, mainly ex-royal navy sailors, he commented on the musical battle taking place between singers and band.

'At least this is a peaceful contest. I don't think the gathering of the temperance campaigners will pass off as peacefully. They are a target for the hard-drinking men at the fair, mostly miners and more and more of them seem to be arriving by the minute. The London police have reinforcements from local and special con-stables, but they will be hard put to contain the miners if fighting begins. I suggest you both keep well clear of them.'

Fighting did break out between the two groups, but the London police sergeant was experienced in such brawls and suc-ceeded in containing it before it got out of hand.

He was aware that if he arrested any of the drunken miners and locked them up, their colleagues would undoubtedly combine to break them free. Instead, he and his men arrested them in a firm, no-nonsense manner and ejected them from the fair, with a warning that if they returned and caused trouble they would be taken before the special magistrates' court which was at that moment sitting in the town, and conveyed *immediately* to Bodmin gaol to serve out what would undoubtedly be a harsh sentence.

His tactics worked and serious trouble between drinkers and abstainers was avoided.

However, there were other law-breakers in the festive crowd who were not so easily deterred and Eliza and Tristram found themselves caught up in their activities as darkness fell over the fair.

The young couple had briefly parted company, Eliza pausing to examine the goods on a stall exhibiting bonnets, gloves and hand-kerchiefs, while Tristram, ostensibly seeking a folding gardeners' knife to take back for Old Percy, had actually returned to a stall where, among the cheap jewellery offered for sale was a small silver heart, suspended on a delicate silver chain.

Eliza had admired it and he intended buying it as a present to seal their betrothal when, as he fervently hoped, she would consent to marry him. In addition to the money given to him by Alice he had more, saved from his pay especially for this purpose.

Returning to where he had left Alice, they had just come within sight of each other when a woman with a revealing low-cut bodice, stumbled and fell against Tristram as she attempted to hurry past. When he held out his arm to prevent her from falling to the ground, she said, in an accent that was not Cornish, 'I'm sorry, young sir, it's not like me to be so clumsy.' Laughing up at him, she added, 'It must be the gin my friend has been giving me, I'm not used to it!'

The fumes from her breath tended to confirm her statement and, smiling at her, Tristram said, 'That's alright, m'dear, no harm done and it's what fair day is all about.'

At that moment Eliza, who had hurried through the crowd, pushing people out of her way, reached them and, grabbing the woman as she turned away from Tristram, she cried, 'Oh no you don't! I saw your hand go into his pocket and take his purse.'

Trying to free herself from Eliza's grip the woman said, 'What d'you mean? I've done nothing of the bleedin' sort. Search me if you don't believe me.'

'She won't find anything if she does,' the voice was that of one of the London policeman who appeared on the scene with a firm grip on the collar of a nondescript, weasel-featured little man. In his other hand he held a purse, and he added, '… because I have the purse here.'

While the constable was talking, an increasingly dismayed Tristram had been fumbling in the pockets of his fustian jacket and now he exclaimed, 'That's my purse. She must have taken it when she fell against me and passed it to him, though I didn't see her do it!'

'She did it alright, I saw her.' This from Eliza.

'She's lying,' the woman pickpocket cried, 'I've never seen the purse before – or him, neither.' She indicated the weasel-faced man.

'I've never seen her, either,' said the man in question, 'and that purse you're holding belongs to me.'

'Then you'll be able to tell me how much is in it,' said the constable, giving the man a non-too-gentle shaking as he was speaking.

'What do you think is in it?' retorted the woman's accomplice. 'It's money, of course, but before you ask me how much is there, I don't know. I've been spending on me dinner and more pints of ale than I remember.'

'How about you, lad,' the policeman addressed Tristram, 'Can you tell me how much is in it?'

'Not exactly,' Tristram confessed, 'but you'll find a silver heart and chain in there, I've just bought it for Eliza and this woman must have seen me count my money out when I was paying for it.'

Handing the purse to Tristram, the constable said, 'Open it up and show us, lad.'

Tristram opened the purse and drew out the necklace.

'You still say it's yours?' The constable asked triumphantly, addressing the man he was holding and giving him a teeth-rattling shaking once again.

'I'm not saying nothing,' said his prisoner, sulkily.

At that moment the London police sergeant put in an appearance. Greeting the prisoner he said, cheerfully, 'Hello, Archie, you been up to your old tricks again?'

Recognising defeat, the prisoner's shoulders sagged and,

downcast, he said, 'Ain't it just my luck to run into you? I thought I'd seen the last of you when I left London.'

'Well you thought wrong, Archie, we're getting everywhere these days.'

Turning to the woman, the sergeant said, 'It's a pleasure to be meeting up with you again too, Maudie, especially as you seem to have teamed up with Archie. You've earned your pay today, constable. Maudie Huggins is one of the most skilful dips in the business. Them as knows say she can take a ring off a woman's finger without her even knowing it!'

'That's all in the past,' the woman protested in a whining voice. 'I'm an honest woman now and,' indicating her accomplice, she added, 'I've never seen him in all my life – but I've seen *her*!'

Pointing a finger at Eliza, who had released her hold on her when the sergeant arrived, Maudie said, 'She was on the same hulk as me at Woolwich, where they sent me for a year because they had no more room in Newgate.'

Jerking a thumb at Tristram, she added, 'It was him calling her Eliza that jogged my memory. We all felt sorry for her on the hulk 'cos she was no more than thirteen and had been sentenced to be transported.'

Sceptical, the sergeant said, 'Is that right? Tell us, Maudie, when was this?'

'I don't know, two or three years ago, I suppose.'

'Then what's she doing here now? Did they turn her around as soon as she reached Australia and send her back again because she was so young?'

'How should I know that, but I saw her being taken off the hulk to start the journey there.'

'Perhaps she flew back here just for the summer, like a swallow.' Sniffing the air close to her face, the sergeant said, 'You've been drinking too much gin, Maudie, you'd do well to leave it alone, you've started imagining things.'

'Of course she has,' Tristram said, indignantly, 'Eliza and me work for Reverend Kilpeck at Trethevy. We've both been there for years.'

'I might have been drinking,' Maudie said, angrily, 'but drink ain't affected me eyesight, or me memory. She's the one you should be nicking, not me.'

'Well, you'll have plenty of time to feel hard done by, Maudie, you and Archie are going straight before the magistrate and you'll no doubt be going back to the prison hulk, but this time you'll end up going to Australia yourself.'

After searching Archie and recovering a surprising number of purses, the sergeant handed back Tristram's purse to its rightful owner, saying, 'We've already had reports of purses being taken and of someone answering Maudie's description being involved, we won't need yours. Thanks for your help, young man, and you too, young lady. We'll deal with this pair now.'

With this the sergeant and constable handcuffed Maudie to Archie and marched them away.

To Tristram it had been an exciting incident and one he would relate with relish over the days and weeks ahead. His elation was not diminished even when he saw Eval Moyle standing at the front of the crowd who had gathered about them and realised he must have witnessed the whole incident and heard what had been said.

Eliza did not share his elation. Pale and shaken, she felt physically sick and, suddenly concerned, Tristram led her away to buy her a drink that he said would 'perk her up.'

Chapter Twelve

*T*HE DRINK HELPED but it was still a very subdued Eliza who asked, 'Why did you spend your money on buying such a lovely necklace for me, Tristram?'

'Because you are special and because I think we are going to look back on today as being special too. It was going to be a surprise for when you say you'll marry me. I hope you will and that it'll help you forget all about what happened back there.'

When Eliza made no immediate reply, Tristram showed his concern by saying, 'You mustn't let anything that pickpocket said upset you, Eliza. She just made up the story to take attention away from herself. Anyway, she'd had so much to drink I doubt if she'd have recognised her own mother if she saw her. The police sergeant knew that because he'd had dealings with her before, in London.'

Tristram's words failed to have their intended result. Indeed, they actually made Eliza feel even worse and, arriving at a sudden decision, she said, 'Can we leave the fair and go somewhere quiet for a while.'

'Of course we can, then perhaps you'll feel well enough to give me an answer, Eliza. It's far more important than anything else that's happened today. We'll take a walk along by the river.'

They walked in silence to the river that ran through the small town and headed downstream along the river bank for a short distance, until noise from the fair became less obtrusive. Here, in the bright moonlight, they came upon a spot where a giant elm tree had been felled close to the path and Eliza suggested they should seat themselves on the stump which had been left protruding from the ground.

When they were seated, side by side, Tristram said eagerly, 'Are you ready to give me an answer now, Eliza?'

'I'm ready, but I have something to tell you first. When it's said you might not *want* to marry me.'

He began to protest, but Eliza silenced him, firmly. 'Please, Tristram, let me tell you what needs to be said before you say anything more.'

'If that's what you really want, but nothing you can say will make me change my mind.'

'Not even if I were to tell you that everything that woman said about me is true? That she *did* see me on a prison hulk and that I *was* sentenced to transportation?'

Her bald statement left Tristram speechless for a great many moments. When he had recovered sufficiently, he said in a strangled voice, 'You're having a joke with me, Eliza, it *can't* be true, you've been working at the rectory since you were fourteen.'

'I was only *thirteen* when I was sentenced to seven years transportation for stealing three guineas from the husband of my employer.'

Tristram found it difficult to take in what Eliza was telling him, but eventually he said, '*Did* you take the money?'

'Yes, but I didn't steal it. There were about fifteen guinea pieces on his bedside table but I only took what was due to me in wages. If it hadn't been for the way he was behaving towards me I wouldn't have needed to try to get away from the house, but if I hadn't gone right away I'd have been in even worse trouble, although it wouldn't have been with the law. I'd have probably found myself expecting his baby.'

Belatedly accepting that Eliza was not playing a joke on him, Tristram queried, 'Didn't you tell that to the judge, or whoever it was who tried you?'

'I told it to the constable who arrested me. Lady Calnan, my employer, knew too, but no one mentioned it in court.'

Still finding it difficult to fully accept her story, Tristram asked, 'But if you were sentenced to be transported how did you escape – and you must have done, or you'd be on the other side of the world now?'

'You remember the great storm three years ago when I was found down at the cove below Trethevy?'

Eliza told Tristram how when the ship taking her to Australia foundered on the rocks of Lundy Island she had escaped with the ship's boatswain and others in one of the ship's boats, only to have it swamped by giant waves in the Bristol channel when the last action of the selfless boatswain had been to tie her to the broken-off mast before the boat sank beneath them.

Washed up unconscious in the cove below Trethevy, it had been assumed by everyone that she was the sole survivor of the *Balladeer*, a ship wrecked on the Lye rock, at the entrance to Bossiney Haven, one of a number of ships lost in the storms of that tempestuous night.

When she eventually recovered consciousness, in the Trethevy rectory, Eliza had encouraged their assumption, grasping the unexpected opportunity to begin a new life as Eliza *Smith* and not Eliza Brooks.

Eliza's confession was too much for Tristram to take in immediately and he remained silent for a long time before saying, in a choked voice, 'You've lived with this ever since Miss Alice found you among the rocks and had you taken to Trethevy rectory?'

'Yes and for months I lived in constant fear that someone was going to come along and say, "You're not Eliza Smith, sole survivor of the *Balladeer* but Eliza Brooks, convicted thief who's under sentence of seven years transportation." Then, as time went by, all that had happened in the past gradually began to fade and I really began to believe I *was* Eliza Smith, trusted personal maid to Miss Alice and her brother, Reverend David Kilpeck. I never dreamed my past would come back to haunt me today, of all days. It was going to be the happiest day of my life ...'

Eliza's voice broke and her whole body shook as she took great gulps of air in a vain attempt to maintain control of herself. 'I ... I'm sorry, Tristram, truly I am.'

Pushing down against the tree stump she tried to rise to her feet, but Tristram was too quick for her. Pulling her back, he said, gruffly, 'No, come here.' His arms went about her and suddenly she broke down and began to weep uncontrollably, her head against his shoulder.

Eliza cried for a long time and, even when the tears ceased, great sobs racked her body for many minutes and she felt she might have fallen to pieces had Tristram not been holding her so tightly to him.

When the sobs became less violent and were occurring with less frequency she raised her head to look up at him, but the moonlight was not bright enough for her to see his expression.

'Thank you, Tristram. Thank you so very much. I don't know what I would have done had you not been here with me. Thrown myself in the river, probably.'

'Now that's silly talk, and you know it. Anyway, I *am* here with you and always will be, if that's what you want.'

'You mean you still want to marry me, even after what I've told you about me?'

'Nothing has changed as far as I'm concerned. You're still the same girl I fell in love with and want to marry, and none of the bad things you've been through would have happened if everyone had known you as well as I do. If I'd been about then you'd never have gone through what you have. I would have seen to that.'

'I wish you had been, but I'm glad I've got you now, I really am.'

'Does that mean you *will* marry me?'

'Only if you're really sure it's what you want.'

'You know it is, Eliza. Besides, I think you need me around to take care of you.'

'I think I do, too, but you won't ever say anything to anyone about what I've told you, or that my real name is Eliza Brooks and not Eliza Smith?'

'Of course I won't. Anyway, it won't be *either* Smith or Brooks once we're married, it'll be Rowe, *Mrs* Eliza Rowe.'

'Then the sooner we can change it the better. I *do* want to marry you, Tristram and I'll be the best wife to you that any man has ever had, I promise.'

By the time they returned to the fair, things were beginning to quieten down. Jory Kendall's recruitment tent had already closed and he was in the beer tent with two of the coast guards who had been helping. They had enjoyed a successful day and their happy mood was boosted by the news that Tristram and Eliza had to tell them.

It was an excuse to call for another round of drinks, this time including the newly-engaged couple, and Eliza tried very hard for Tristram's sake to shake off the frightening shock given to her by Maudie Huggins. Yet, try as she might she felt sick deep in the pit of her stomach because, after all these years, the past she had tried so hard to forget had come back to haunt her with its grim memories.

Chapter Thirteen

O N THE RIDE back to Trethevy, Tristram felt hurt that once again he was obliged to ride on the outside of the coach, beside the coachman, while Eliza sat inside with Jory Kendall. He felt the young naval officer might have allowed him to sit with her, in view of their recent betrothal and the celebrations they had all so recently enjoyed together at the fair.

However, Jory wanted an opportunity to talk over his own problems with Eliza, although he did not broach the subject he wished to discuss immediately.

Unaware of her encounter with Maudie Huggins and Archie, he said, 'I have no need to ask whether you and Tristram enjoyed the fair, but did it come up to your expectations?'

'Yes.' She was tempted to say something about the pick-pocketing incident, but felt it wiser not to mention anything about it. Instead, she remarked, 'There didn't seem to be any trouble between the teetotallers and miners.'

'No, well nothing to speak of. In fact before we left I saw Moyle chatting to the police sergeant from London and they seemed to be getting along well together. Perhaps he has come back from America a changed man.'

'I doubt it, but hopefully he won't be here for very long. Tristram says the same as you said, that he and his brother are selling up their farm and going to America together to build a chapel where Eval can preach.'

'I wish them luck, but I went to Moyle's farm some years back, when his boat was caught smuggling. It is a most pleasant place, but it hasn't been farmed well by the two brothers.'

'I don't know anything about it, I've tried to keep well away from anything to do with Eval Moyle, even though I knew he wasn't there.'

Changing the subject completely, Jory said, 'I think Miss Alice is going to be very surprised when she hears that you and Tristram intend to be married.'

'Not all that surprised,' Eliza replied, 'We've been walking out for quite a while now and I'm sure she knows how much we both mean to one another. It will come as more of a shock to Reverend David. He is so wrapped up in his church and the parish that he doesn't know much of what's happening at the rectory.'

'At the moment I feel very much the same way,' Jory said, seizing upon the opening she had given to him, 'Especially where Miss Alice is concerned. I have no chance of convincing her I had nothing to do with any one of the Trevelyan family unless I speak to her and am able to satisfy her that their insinuations, whatever they may be, are unfounded. It is very sad the Trevelyan daughter died and quite understandable that the family should grieve for her loss, but if she were alive she would be able to verify the fact that we were not even acquainted. Do you know what illness caused her death?'

'It wasn't an illness, sir. She committed suicide. That's what seems to have made the family particularly bitter.'

'You mean the family believe *I* was somehow responsible for the poor girl killing herself? Good Lord, it gets worse and worse!'

'If you wish, sir, I'll tell Miss Alice that you're very upset at not seeing anything of her lately, that we spoke about the Trevelyans and you are quite certain you have never even met *any* of the family, far less had an affair with Captain Trevelyan's late sister.'

'Thank you, Eliza. I would write her a letter, but this is some-

thing I need to *talk* about with her. Unfortunately, if she is determined to avoid me there is little I can do except find the proof
that I am completely innocent of any wrongdoing against the
Trevelyan family. It is a damnable situation. Fortunately, now I
am land-based I should be able to make the necessary inquiries.
Had I still been at sea the situation would have been irre-
deemable, but so as not to make a complete fool of myself, are
you absolutely certain Miss Alice and this Captain Trevelyan do
not have some sort of understanding?'

'Absolutely certain, sir.' Eliza had already told Jory she had
spent the night at Helynn manor in Alice's room, now, after a
momentary hesitation she told him the whole story of the night
she and her employer had spent at Helynn.

Jory was outraged. 'It's fortunate you never told me this before,
Eliza, I would have gone after Captain Trevelyan and called him
out, even if I had to go to London to find him.'

Eliza thought it was a good thing that she had not told Jory
Kendall the full story of the stay at Helynn before today. Hugo
Trevelyan was an army officer, a very *experienced* army officer. No
doubt he would have proved far more proficient with a pistol
than a naval man.

When he was less angry, Jory asked, 'I am not surprised I have
never met any of the Trevelyans socially. From all you have told
me about them, it is quite apparent there *is* a problem with mental
instability in the family. No doubt that is the true reason the
daughter of the family committed suicide. Was there *anyone* in the
household who appeared in any way normal?'

'Yes, Miss Grimm, the housekeeper. She is stern and short-tem-
pered, but that's hardly surprising. She's been responsible for
running the household for many years. Without her I don't know
what would happen to Helynn and Mr Trevelyan.'

'Thank you for telling me about this, Eliza, I am disappointed
that Miss Alice did not feel able to discuss the Trevelyans' accu-

sations with me, but now I understand the reasons for her apparent change in attitude towards me I intend to do something about it. I return home tomorrow but will go to Helynn the following day to find out exactly *why* they think I had something to do with the death of their daughter.'

Jory said nothing more to Eliza about the Trevelyan family but he remained deep in thought for the remainder of the journey and, after wondering whether she had been right to tell him about the visit she and Miss Alice had made to Helynn, she returned to her own unhappy thoughts about her encounter with Maudie Huggins at the Camelford fair.

Alice Kilpeck returned to the rectory early the next afternoon, brought back in the Bodmin vicar's light carriage driven by his groom. She arrived only hours after Jory had left on his journey home and was greeted by her brother who immediately gave her the news that Tristram had proposed to Eliza at the fair and been accepted.

He, Eliza and Tristram had discussed their wedding and it had been decided that, subject to Alice's approval, it should take place in the Spring of 1844, giving the young couple some eight or nine months to make their preparations for life together.

The betrothal came as no surprise to Alice, who had seen it coming almost from the day Tristram first came to work at the rectory, far longer than had the young couple themselves.

Upstairs, as Eliza was helping her employer to change out of her travelling clothes, Alice congratulated her and asked, 'Have you and Tristram given any thought to where you will live once you are married?'

'No. Although it was about a week ago when he first asked me if I would marry him I only said "yes" when we were at the fair, yesterday. We have hardly had any time to ourselves to talk about it since then. My mind is still in a whirl.'

Eliza could not explain that the distressing encounter with Maudie had pushed marriage to Tristram into second place in her mind. Lying awake in the darkness of her room, it had loomed much larger than happier thoughts of life with the man she was to marry.

'I have seen this coming for a long time but I hope you will both stay on with us here at the rectory after you are married?'

The question took Eliza by surprise. She had never even considered that by marrying Tristram she might not continue working at the rectory. 'Of course! I wouldn't want to work anywhere else. I've been happy working here, and still am.'

'Splendid! Then we will have to think of somewhere for you both to live together. Your present room is far too small for you both and the space above the stable is not suitable for a newly-married couple. I have one or two ideas – but we have plenty of time to think about them.'

Abruptly changing the subject to one that had been occupying *her* mind, Alice said, 'You have not told me anything about the fair, did you see much of Lieutenant Jory while you were there?'

It was a casually put question, but Eliza felt the reply meant a great deal to her employer. 'He brought a coach with the family crest on the doors to take us to the fair and it looked so impressive that everyone on the road made way for us. It made me feel very important. The fair itself was noisy, but it was a lot of fun.'

Eliza went on to tell Alice about many of the things they had seen there before giving her information about the man she believed she really wanted her to talk about.

'Me and Tristram saw Lieutenant Jory once or twice while we were there, but for most of the time he was busy talking to men who wanted to become coast guards. Then, when things had quietened down and he'd finished for the day, Tristram and me went to him and told him we were going to be married. Lieutenant Jory and some of the men who were with him wished us "good luck", then made us sit down and have a drink with them before Lieutenant Jory brought us back here.'

'Did he seem upset because I was not here when he arrived?' Alice did her best to appear to be taking no more than a polite interest, but did not quite succeed.

Eliza nodded, 'He thought it was because you've fallen for Captain Trevelyan, so don't want anything more to do with him. He was particularly upset because he'd brought a lovely bunch of roses picked by his mother especially for you. They came with an invitation from her for you to pay a visit to the family home. You'll see some of the roses in the living room. They smelled so lovely I was going to put some here, in your bedroom, but I felt you might not like me to do that.'

Her nonchalant manner disappearing, Alice said, 'His mother sent me an invitation to visit … and some roses? Jory must have told her about me and made her think I meant something to him otherwise she would not have done that! Why has he not said anything to *me* about the way he really feels?'

'I think he might have, had you been here.' Eliza sounded more unsympathetic than she really was. She *wanted* Alice and Jory Kendall to get together, but felt that Alice had behaved very foolishly by becoming infatuated, however briefly, with Captain Hugo Trevelyan.

Vigorously brushing imaginary dust from Alice's outdoor clothes, Eliza said, 'I think Reverend David must have told him about your being rescued from the runaway pony and trap, and of us going to Helynn with Captain Trevelyan because he asked a lot of questions about him, and about our stay there.'

'He had no right to ask you anything, especially as he told *me* nothing about his association with Isabella Trevelyan.'

'I don't think there is anything to tell. I *did* mention that the family and Miss Grimm spoke of him having known Isabella Trevelyan and he swore that he never knew her, or even *of* her, but he's a clever man and realised that might just be the reason you don't want to see him – that, and your feelings for Captain Trevelyan.'

'I have *no* feelings for Captain Trevelyan, at least, certainly not *fond* ones.'

Hastily, Eliza said, 'I think I was able to convince him there was nothing between you and Captain Trevelyan, but he made me say more than I perhaps should have about what the family and Miss Grimm had said about him. Before he left here this morning he said he was going to Helynn manor tomorrow to sort out why it is they think he knew Isabella Trevelyan when he didn't.'

'He must not go to Helynn, you know that, Eliza. Captain Hugo's father was sitting up all night with a gun, waiting for Lieutenant Jory to come to the house. If he goes there he is likely to be shot, and if he learns that it was Captain Hugo who first told me about he and Isabella there could be serious trouble between them too!'

'Well, there's no danger that he and Captain Trevelyan will meet because Lieutenant Jory knows he's on his way back to India, he said so, but you're right about Mr Trevelyan. He's mad enough to shoot anyone.'

'Then Lieutenant Jory has to be stopped from going to Helynn. If he goes there and gets himself hurt, or even worse, I'll never be able to forgive myself. If I had not been foolish enough to agree to go to Helynn with Captain Trevelyan, without really knowing anything about him or his family, he would not be putting himself in such danger. Find Tristram and tell him I want him to ride to Lieutenant Jory's home and take a letter to him from me. Hurry!'

Hastily hanging up the outdoor coat she had been brushing, Eliza had just reached the bedroom door when Alice called, 'No ... wait!'

When Eliza stopped and turned to face her employer, Alice said, 'Have Tristram make the pony and trap ready, then come back here and help me dress again.'

Adopting a determined attitude that Eliza recognised as a sign that she was not to be argued with, Alice declared, 'I will go to the Kendall home myself, tell Lieutenant Jory face-to-face of the danger he would be in by going to Helynn manor then ask him to explain why the Trevelyans should believe he was somehow involved with Isabella.'

'You have only just come in from a long journey, Miss Alice, wouldn't it be better if you sent a note by Tristram telling him of the danger of going to Helynn and asking him to come here to talk to you instead?'

'No, Eliza, Lieutenant Jory is not a man who would be deterred from doing something because it is dangerous. He would be just as likely to decide to call in at Helynn on the way here anyway. Hurry now, it is going to take us four or five hours and I would like to be at Jory's home before it is dark.'

Chapter Fourteen

ACCOMPANIED BY ELIZA and with Tristram taking the reins of the pony, Alice left Trethevy in the trap with the protests of her brother ringing in her ears. He had protested that such a journey should be undertaken by him, but it was Sunday and there were services to conduct. As it was he would need to walk to Tintagel to take the last of them and he complained that if it rained, he was likely to get very wet on his way to and from the church.

The route to Lostwithiel took the trio past a field that was part of the Moyle farm and here Eval Moyle was re-building a length of free-stone wall that had been in need of repair for many years.

The wall was alongside the lane and as they approached Moyle ceased work and stood watching them, one hand resting on the stonework. When they drew closer Alice braced herself to ignore the insults she expected him to direct at them as they passed.

None came, although he looked directly at them and kept watching until they passed out of sight along the winding lane.

'I have been dreading meeting him ever since I heard he had returned from America,' Alice commented, 'and the very sight of him frightened me, but perhaps going away has mellowed him, although there was a smugness about him, almost as though for some reason he felt superior. Perhaps it is because he has seen something of the world now and we haven't.'

'I don't believe he's changed very much,' Tristram said. 'He led a temperance parade to the fair yesterday and had there not been a strong force of constables to keep order they would have clashed with the miners. I think that was probably his intention, although I must say he seemed friendly enough with the sergeant from the London police when I saw them chatting together later.'

Recalling what had gone on at the fair and Eliza's revelation about her past, he suddenly fell silent.

Knowing nothing of his thoughts, Alice commented, 'Well, he should be returning to America as soon as he has sold his farm. Hopefully it will be soon, then we can all forget about Eval Moyle for ever.'

Talk of the fair made Eliza unhappy and, in common with Tristram, it was the encounter with Maudie and not marriage that were uppermost in her thoughts. The unease she had experienced since then intensified and she felt it was somehow connected with Eval Moyle, yet she could not see how he could be involved with the incident in any way at all.

There were a great many hills between Trethevy and Lostwithiel and the journey took longer than the five hours estimated by Alice. The setting sun was balancing on the far horizon when they eventually reached the top of the hill above the town.

Looking down upon Lostwithiel with its jumble of houses and the ancient castle that together had once constituted one of the most important administrative centres in Cornwall, Alice realised she did not know where the Kendall home was situated. She did not even know the name of the house!

Fortunately, the family were very well known in the area having been established there for centuries and a passing farm-hand directed them off the main road to where Pendower Manor, the home of the baronial family, was hidden among trees in the middle of an extensive estate.

It was fortunate they had asked before reaching the small town itself because the road into the town was extremely steep and the already tired pony would otherwise have had to turn around and take them back up the precipitous and winding lane.

Pendower Manor was everything that Helynn had not been. The house was extremely impressive with a number of substantial outbuildings and the whole surrounded by well-tended gardens.

The great wooden door at the pillared entrance to the house was opened by a footman who first asked her name and, when she said she had called to speak to Lieutenant Jory Kendall, invited Alice to take a seat in the impressive marble-floored hall while he informed Lady Kendall of her presence.

Seated in the hall, Alice felt suddenly very nervous. It was not only the thought of meeting with Jory again and trying to explain why she had so assiduously avoided him recently, but also the opulence of her surroundings. Baron Kendall was quite obviously a man of considerable wealth and importance.

She realised, depressingly, that there was a huge gulf between Jory's social standing and her own as the orphaned sister of an insignificant cleric in a small, unimportant and impoverished Cornish parish. Alice suddenly felt that the dream she had once entertained of one day becoming Jory's wife was no more than that … a dream. His parents would be seeking a wife for their son from among aristocratic families similar to their own.

Her depressing thoughts were interrupted by the arrival of Lady Kendall who was accompanied by an attractive and well-dressed young woman who bore such a close family resemblance that Alice knew immediately she must be a sister to Jory.

Lady Kendell greeted her warmly, saying, 'My dear, what a wonderful surprise! When Jory returned to Pendower and said he had not seen you during his visit to your home, I thought we were never going to meet you – but where are my manners?'

Waving her companion forward, she said, 'This is Lowena, Jory's sister, she too has heard a great deal about you from Jory.'

Lowena Kendall greeted the visitor to Pendower with a smile that emphasised her youthful beauty and Alice guessed correctly that she was the baby of the family. She had such an open expression that Alice took to her immediately.

The greetings over, Alice said, 'I really must apologise for this intrusion, but I came here to speak to Jory on a most urgent matter concerning his safety.'

'Oh dear! I am afraid Jory is not in the house. A coast guard messenger arrived this morning to say his presence was required immediately at Falmouth. He remained at Pendower until Jory's return when they both left to board a steam launch awaiting them at Fowey.'

Alice's spirits fell at the realisation that her arduous dash across the width of Cornwall had been in vain. Aware of how she must be feeling, Lady Kennedy said kindly, 'Come into the sitting room, my dear, we will order some refreshment for you and you can tell us what this is all about.'

'I have left my personal maid and a servant with the pony and trap, I wonder whether they might be taken care of? It has been a long journey for them too. They are the young couple who announced their betrothal after being taken to Camelford fair by Jory yesterday. But before I forget I must thank you for the beautiful roses you sent with Jory. Their scent fills my brother David's rather gloomy rectory.'

'I am glad they brought you pleasure, my dear, and I will send someone to bring your servants in immediately. Jory has told us all about them. He has a very high regard for the young girl who I believe had a quite remarkable rescue from a shipwreck a few years ago. He also told Lowena and I how she saved him from taking a beating from one of these dissenting ministers. I look forward to meeting them both later. In the meantime Lowena will take you to the sitting-room while I organise sustenance for you.'

Chapter Fifteen

O N THE WAY to the sitting-room, Lowena took Alice's arm and said, 'I am so happy to meet with you at last. Jory has talked so much about you. He has never ever spoken about anyone else in quite the same way. It is very exciting, especially as he is my absolutely *favourite* brother and we have always been close to one another.'

Lowena's enthusiasm made Alice feel guilty. Then, angrily, she told herself *she* had nothing to feel guilty about. Her reason for being here was because of Jory's involvement with Isabella Trevelyan. Yet if Jory and his sister were so close, would Lowena not have known about the association and been less enthusiastic about meeting *her* now? She had also declared that Jory had never spoken about anyone else in quite the same way.

Alice found it very confusing, and not a little embarrassing.

When they reached the sitting-room Lowena continued to talk of Jory in an enthusiastic and uninhibited manner until Lady Kendall entered the room closely followed by two maids. One carried a tray on which were the various items for making tea, the other maid's tray bore plates on which were a variety of cakes and biscuits.

When tea and cakes had been passed around, Lady Kendall smiled at Alice and said, 'Now, tell me about this concern for Jory's well-being which has brought you all this way in such haste.'

'Actually, I feel rather foolish having come here to warn Jory about a danger that is no longer imminent now he has been called away by the coast guard. I could have written to tell him about it.'

'You were not to know that and if the danger still exists I will send someone to Falmouth to warn him, but I would like to hear about it first.'

Hesitantly at first, but growing in confidence as she spoke, Alice told the story of being invited to Helynn Manor by Captain Trevelyan, stressing that when she went there she took Eliza with her, as both companion and personal maid, but found it such an eccentric, indeed, *alarming* household, that she and Eliza left after a stay of only one night. However, while there she became aware that the family and their servants, such as they were, bore such a deep and unreasonable hatred for Jory that Albert Trevelyan, the head of the household armed himself and kept guard in the hallway at night, lest Jory should try to come to the house to visit his long-dead daughter.

Alice ended her explanation by saying, 'It seems that on the journey back from Camelford Fair, Eliza told Jory about our visit to Helynn Manor and of their obsession with him. When he left the rectory this morning Jory told Eliza he intended going to Helynn tomorrow to find out what it was they thought he had done. Unfortunately, Albert Trevelyan is incapable of holding a reasonable conversation with anyone and would have shot Jory at the mere mention of his name.'

Lady Kendall realised there was a great deal Alice had not told her about the visit to Helynn and her reason for going there in the first place, but she did not doubt that had Jory gone to Helynn to speak with its owner, he would have been in very real danger.

'You were absolutely right to come here to warn Jory, my dear, and I know he will appreciate your making such a journey because of concern for him. It is unfortunate that he has been called away before hearing about the dangers of visiting to

Helynn directly from you, but I will write a note telling of your warning and have it delivered to him right away. It is always possible he might have decided to go to Helynn before returning home. But, tell me, why should this man have such an obsessive hatred for Jory, what exactly is he supposed to have done to the Trevelyan family?'

Alice related what she and Eliza had been told by the various members of the household about Jory's alleged affair with Isabella Trevelyan and of her ultimate death, allegedly as a direct result of his actions towards her.

When Alice finished speaking, Lady Kendall said indignantly, 'Such behaviour is quite out of character for Jory! I would like to know when all this is alleged to have taken place? He was out of the country in Far Eastern waters for three years and on his return was virtually a cripple. When he was fit enough he secured a post with the coast guard and stayed with them until taking command of *Vixen*, by which time he had met with you, Alice. I hope you will not feel too embarrassed when I say there has been no other girl in his life during that time. I really think the Trevelyan family have made a grave mistake in implicating Jory in anything to do with the daughter of the family.'

'That *is* what I thought when Captain Trevelyan first intimated that Jory was in some way responsible for the death of his sister, but when I visited Helynn and the same thing was said by Captain Trevelyan's father and the family's housekeeper, Miss Grimm, I began to believe there *must* be some truth in what they were saying.'

'Did they actually say it was *Jory* who was involved? They called him by his first name?' The question came from Lowena.

Alice thought about it before replying. '*Captain* Trevelyan actually said it was Jory, the others referred to him as "Lieutenant Kendall" … although one of them – I think it might have been Miss Grimm – confirmed that he came from Lostwithiel.'

'This *Captain* Trevelyan, the member of the family who invited you to his family home. Is he a particular friend of yours?' Once again the questioner was Lowena and she succeeded in embarrassing Alice.

'No,' she confessed. Then, telling both Kendall women how they had first met, added, 'He came to the rectory and later stayed there at my brother's invitation. When he invited David and I to pay a visit to his family at Helynn, I felt it would be churlish to refuse in view of the fact that he had saved my life. David was unfortunately unable to go because of Church commitments, but as Captain Trevelyan had behaved like a perfect gentleman during all the time he had been at the rectory and I thought I would be a guest of his family, my brother approved of my acceptance of the invitation. I ensured that Eliza came with me, of course, and in view of the situation we discovered at Helynn it was most fortunate I did so. She stayed in my room for the whole of that one night I was there. I was going to say she *slept* in my room, but I am afraid that neither of us was able to sleep. As it was we left the house via the kitchen door as soon as there was light enough for us to harness the pony to the trap.'

'You don't mean this Captain Trevelyan made improper advances?' Lady Kendall was horrified.

'I never gave him an opportunity,' Alice declared, 'but he certainly did not behave as a gentleman should and was drinking very heavily indeed. I realised I had been extremely foolish to accept the invitation to visit his home and was very glad I had Eliza with me. It is not a normal household.'

'It *certainly* is not,' Lowena said emphatically.

'You know the family?' Her mother asked in surprise.

'I know *of* them, Mother, and I believe I know for whom Jory has been mistaken, although I don't think *he* is in any way responsible for the Trevelyan girl's death, either.'

'You *know* who is the cause of all this trouble?' Lady Kendall demanded. 'Who is he?'

'The person who is really responsible for all this is Isabella Trevelyan, but as that unhappy girl is no longer alive the only other person who can prove that poor Jory is in no way involved is cousin Jeremy.'

'Jeremy?' Lady Kendall was startled but then her expression changed and she said, 'Of course, I remember now! There *was* a scandal with some girl, but it was kept very quiet.'

Turning to Alice, she explained, 'It all happened when Jory was in China, so he most certainly was *not* involved. But if my memory serves me well the name of the girl involved was never mentioned.'

'Not to *everyone* in the family, perhaps,' Lowena said, 'but Jeremy and I have always been very close and he confided in me. He was actually very fond of the girl, but it is fortunate that the relationship with her went no further than it did. Isabella Trevelyan was trouble, and it would seem she still is, even though she is no longer with us.'

'Well Jeremy is not at home at the moment so he is unable to tell us exactly what it is the Trevelyan family think Jory has done, and why.'

Lowena shook her head. 'Jeremy is very like Jory, Mother, he would never say anything to blacken the reputation of any woman, especially as she is dead now. I would not normally betray *his* trust either, but in view of what is being said about Jory and the trouble I believe it has caused between he and Alice I think I am justified in speaking about it, especially as Jeremy regards Jory as his hero.'

Alice felt uncomfortable that Lowena had realised all was not well between her and Jory, but she said nothing and Lowena continued, directing her story mainly at her.

'Jeremy is a few years younger than Jory, and his home has

always been in the old dower house, no more than half-a-mile from Pendower. He joined the navy as a boy but, because his father was in the House of Lords, he gained quite rapid promotion and as a young and impressionable lieutenant found himself in the Admiralty, in London. It was here he met with Isabella Trevelyan who was a few years older than Jeremy, and he became utterly besotted with her.'

The latter remark brought forth a murmur of disapproval from Lady Kendall, but Alice said nothing and Lowena continued her story.

'I think Isabella was flattered at first, especially as Jeremy was able to introduce her to London "society", but when she began to make the acquaintance of some of the men on the fringe of the Royal Court, she jilted Jeremy and before very long was mistress of the younger son of a Scots duke, a notorious roué. However, when she discovered she was expecting his child, he discarded her, as did the so-called friends she had made during the time she was with him. By then Jeremy had been sent to sea and with no one to turn to and ashamed to return to her home in Cornwall she committed suicide.'

'What a dreadfully tragic tale – although the girl brought it upon herself, of course,' Lady Kendall said, 'but the Trevelyan family can hardly blame a Kendall for what happened, certainly not our Jory.'

'I think the Trevelyans must have been given a deliberately false story by friends of her lover about what happened to Isabella. The family would no doubt have known about Jeremy, but she would have kept her association with the son of the Scots nobleman from them.'

While Lowena was speaking, Lady Kendall had been watching Alice closely and was aware she was upset by the story, but perhaps even more dismayed because of how it had affected her own relationship with Jory. Now she said, 'How dreadful it must be for you to have people believing such things about Jory, and with so many of them telling you the same story, how could you not accept it as the truth? Jory is a lucky man, a lesser woman would have left him to his fate – even if it resulted in him being shot! We are all most grateful to you for coming here to warn him.'

Feeling thoroughly miserable, Alice said, 'I feel ashamed now for ever doubting him, I should have known better.'

'My dear, you were in a quite impossible situation with people on all sides telling you Jory had done something quite dreadful and not having him there to tell you otherwise. Had he not been to sea for so long you would have seen far more of each other and you would have learned that he is the most honourable of men. As his mother I admit to being biased in his favour, dreadfully biased, but I believe him to be incapable of deceit, as I am quite sure Lowena will agree.'

'Well, perhaps he is not quite the paragon of virtue you depict him to be, Mother, but I will agree that he is a special brother and I love him very much.'

Lady Kendall was still watching Alice closely and she thought her to be close to tears. 'It is a great relief to all of us to have things resolved, in our own minds, at least, but I am so pleased to see you, Alice, that I have quite forgotten the long journey you have had. Lowena will take you to freshen up before dinner and you will spend the night with us, of course.'

When Alice protested that she had not told David she would be away from the rectory overnight, Lady Kendall said, 'He will realise you could not possibly make the return journey from Trethevy in a single day, your pony would drop dead before you were halfway home! Besides, now we have you here I have no intention of allowing you to leave us so soon. You must spend a few days at Pendower, in order that we might all become better acquainted. We will send your pony and trap home with your groom tomorrow to let your brother know what is happening, and find a room for your maid. It will be a great pleasure to have you here with us.'

Chapter Sixteen

ALICE WAS MADE to feel very welcome at Pendower Manor, quickly becoming firm friends with the lovely Lowena. She also took an immediate liking to Lord Kendall, the head of the family, who returned home two days after Alice's arrival, having been at the House of Lords in London.

A rather abstracted and reserved man, he did not seem in the least surprised to find her staying in the house and Lowena said it was because her brothers had always been in the habit of frequently inviting their friends, both male and female, to come and stay at Pendower and he had become resigned to having them about the place. Lady Kendall had an easy-going nature too and it was apparent to Alice that Jory belonged to a loving, understanding and caring family.

Jory replied to his mother's letter by return. He was delighted that Alice was a welcome guest at his family home and grateful to her for the warning she had for him. He was intrigued by the reason for her visit and declared he would try very hard to return home before Alice left, so he might learn the full story of what it was Jeremy had done to make the Trevelyans believe it was a Kendall who had been the cause of Isabella's tragic suicide.

Unfortunately, on the fifth day of Alice's stay, Lady Kendall received another letter from him in which he said he would be unable to return to Pendower as he had hoped because he had been summoned to the Admiralty in London for a meeting about proposed changes in the Coast Guard Service. He also hinted of a promotion in the offing for him.

Reluctantly, Alice felt that as Jory was not likely to return to Cornwall in the immediate future, she should return to the Trethevy rectory and her brother. David had been without her or Eliza for almost a week. He was not the most practical of men and she felt he needed to have someone at the rectory to take care of him.

It was agreed Alice should return on the following day, having been given Jory's London postal address. As she and Lowena were walking together in Pendower's beautifully kept gardens, shortly after the decision had been made, Lowena said wistfully, 'I wish you did not have to return to Trethevy so soon, Alice. I understand your reasons for leaving us but what will happen to David when you eventually marry? Will he be able to cope in the house without you, and with only a female servant for company, will his parishioners not talk about him?'

'They most certainly would,' Alice agreed. 'A parish priest is always a favourite subject for gossip but David needs to have someone living in the rectory to take care of him. He could employ an elderly housekeeper, of course, but actually, there are the first signs of a romance between him and the friend I was staying with when Jory last came to Trethevy. Her father is Dean of Windsor, and that puts such a great distance between them that courting is not going to be easy.'

'I am sure that if they are serious about each other they will find a solution,' Lowena said, sympathetically, 'and, as you say, if you leave the rectory perhaps your brother could bring in a much older woman to take care of him, if only as a temporary solution.'

'Perhaps,' Alice agreed, 'but it is not a problem that needs to concern anyone in the immediate future. I have received no offer of marriage from anyone yet.'

Astonished, Lowena said, 'You mean Jory has not actually proposed to you? He talks so much about you when he is home that Mother and I felt quite certain you had already agreed to marry him!'

'To be perfectly honest, although we have always been very comfortable in each other's company on the occasions we have met, he has never actually said *anything* about his feelings for me.'

'Well! That is taking being honourable too far! I never took my brother for a such a laggard. *I* know how he feels about you and so does Mother. In fact the whole family knows.'

'I think Eliza is aware of his feelings too.' Alice gave her companion a weak smile, 'It seems I am the only one not to know, and I have behaved so badly towards him recently I would not blame him if he decided to change his mind.'

'I know Jory better than that, Alice. Quite frankly I think the thought that you might have taken an interest in another man has given him just the jolt he needed. When he next comes home I will tell him you have charmed every man who has come to Pendower during your stay here and that unless he makes his feelings clear very soon he will find he is last in line of those asking for your hand in marriage.'

Alice laughed, 'It makes me very happy to know that I meet with *your* approval, Lowena, but I think we must wait for Jory to decide what he wants to do – and when.'

'Nonsense!' Lowena declared. 'He is my last brother to marry and I enjoy being a bridesmaid. It is *time* he married and you are absolutely right for each other. Mother likes you very much and Father thinks you will make Jory "a good wife" – and that is the first time Father has actually approved of any of the women his sons have eventually married. Besides, I want you as my friend, so he *has* to marry you.'

'Thank you. You have all been so very kind to me while I have been staying here I feel I am part of your family already and you and I are certainly friends. I hope we always will be, but I think it is for *me* to convince Jory that he wants to marry me, and I can promise you that if he really *does* I will give him every possible encouragement.'

As Alice was driven away from Pendower Manor, Lady Kendall and Lowena stood outside the main entrance waving until the carriage passed from view. Inside, Alice sat back in her seat and said to Eliza who was seated opposite to her, 'I feel quite emotional about leaving Pendower, the family made me so very welcome it was as though I had known them for years.'

'It is a very happy household, Miss Alice. Most of the servants have been working there for many years and wouldn't want to work anywhere else. They know they'll be looked after when their working days are over too. A lot of cottages dotted about the estate are kept 'specially for them and Lord and Lady Kendall see they want for nothing. It's easy to see why Lieutenant Jory is such a nice man.'

'You always have been a champion of Lieutenant Jory, Eliza, even when *I* doubted him, but you are right, he *is* a good man and Lowena in particular thinks the world of him.'

Settling back in her seat happily, Eliza said, 'I am glad you and Lieutenant Jory are friends again, Miss Alice, and that Captain Trevelyan has gone back to India. I had the shivers whenever he looked at me. He was a thoroughly bad man. Worse even than Eval Moyle.'

It was a comparison that was destined to undergo revision all too soon.

Chapter Seventeen

AS THE KENDALL carriage neared Trethevy Eliza found herself becoming excited at the thought of seeing Tristram again. It was something she had never experienced before and it gave her a warm feeling. It was a realisation that she belonged to someone, and had someone who belonged to her.

Suddenly, the carriage slowed and the groom hauled his pair of horses to a halt. Looking out of the carriage window at Alice's request, Eliza found herself looking at Eval Moyle. He was standing in the centre of the lane close to an open field gate and looking up to talk to the groom.

They had been brought to a halt because Moyle's brother, accompanied by a dog, was driving a small flock of sheep along the lane in the opposite direction to that being taken by the carriage.

Pulling her head back quickly, Eliza said, 'It's Eval Moyle and his brother. They're putting sheep in the field just here.'

'At least it is not a bull,' Alice commented, adding, 'Did Eval Moyle see you?'

'I don't know.'

'Well, we will keep quiet until we move on again to avoid any possible nastiness from him.'

The two women maintained a silence inside the carriage, but Eval Moyle had seen the crest on the door of the vehicle and, not recognising it, they heard him say to the coachman, 'I haven't seen you before, you'll not be from these parts.'

'No, this is Lord Kendall's carriage, I'm bringing their guest and her maid back to the rectory at Trethevy.'

'Are you now?' Moyle replied, with unexpected interest. 'Well, I won't keep you waiting any longer than can be helped, there'll be folk happy to see them back in Trethevy, I don't doubt.'

Listening from inside the carriage, Alice whispered to Eliza, 'Is that really Eval Moyle, I cannot believe what we are hearing?'

'I think that listening to him behaving so politely worries me even more than when he's being himself.' Eliza replied.

The two women remained silent then until they heard Eval Moyle's voice once more, 'That's all the sheep in now, so you be sure and get them two women to the rectory, safe and sound.'

The next moment the coachman flicked his reins over the horses' backs and the carriage jolted into motion. As they passed by Eval Moyle there was a smile on his face and Alice said, 'That is certainly not like the Moyle we know of old.'

'Do you think he might have turned a bull loose in the church-yard again?'

'He knows better than to do that. Besides, the bad-tempered bull was sold off soon after he went to America, but his behaviour has made me feel uneasy. I hope Reverend David is alright. He has always felt a need to prove himself against Moyle.'

David Kilpeck was well, but he was greatly relieved to see Alice and his first words were, 'Thank the Good Lord you are back home, I have never been so hungry in all my life. I might have accepted it had it been Lent, that *is* a time of fasting, but not when one should be fattening oneself to face winter! The only saving grace is that it brought home to me, albeit in a small way, just how much Our Lord must have suffered from fasting day and night for forty days in the wilderness. For me, a week was far too long. Of course, I *had* food, but, unfortunately, most of it was inedible when cooked by Nellie, the young kitchen-maid found for me by Percy. She is no cook, bless her. When I tried to voice my feelings as kindly as I might, she brought me a meal prepared by her mother and I realised then that poor Nellie's lack of cooking skills is inherited! However, now you are back all is well with my world once more.'

With this, he kissed his sister on the cheek and beamed at her happily before saying, 'You will be delighted to know I have had a wonderful letter from Windsor – from Ursula. You and I have been invited to spend a week or two with her and Dean Fitzjohn. She and her father paid a visit to Trethevy before leaving Bodmin to return home. They thought our little church absolutely charming and Dean Fitzjohn is most impressed with what we have achieved there. He said we have worked wonders.'

Suddenly self-conscious, David shifted his weight from foot to foot nervously before saying, 'I was also able to have a chat with Ursula when we were left alone for a while. We … we came to a tentative arrangement. She said she would speak to her father, but feels he would have no objection to marriage with me – after a suitably lengthy engagement, of course, and she is confident Dean Fitzjohn will recommend me for a more lucrative living when one becomes vacant.'

'David! I am delighted for you, and for Ursula too. She is a lovely person and I know you will be so happy together. Oh, what wonderful news! But why did you take so long before telling me about it? It is the most important thing that has ever happened.'

Alice flung her arms about her brother and hugged him and he said, happily, 'I am so glad you approve, Alice. I was worried about how you would react to the news, although I was hoping that perhaps you and Lieutenant Jory … Were you able to spend some time with him? When Tristram returned to the rectory he said he had been called away to the Admiralty in London. Did he return to Cornwall before you left the Kendall's home?'

'Unfortunately, no, but Lord and Lady Kendall and Jory's sister Lowena – especially Lowena – made me feel very welcome at Pendower Manor, which is a truly magnificent house, David. Before I left, Lowena and I had a long walk around the gardens and she told me that Lord and Lady Kendall both approve of me.'

'That too is exciting news, Alice, when do you think you and Jory might be married? I expect they will want you to marry in their family church, but I hope I will be allowed to have some part in the ceremony.'

'You are being rather presumptuous, David, Jory has not yet asked me to marry him, and he is the one I would be marrying, not his family, no matter how much we may think of one another.'

'Of course, but in great families like the Kendalls parental approval for a marriage is always of great importance.'

'Well, we will have to see what transpires when Jory returns from London, but the Kendalls are a truly lovely family and ter-ribly proud of Jory. They believe that while he is in London he is going to be promoted to the rank of commander.'

'More splendid news! Actually, while you were away I met with Reverend Tyacke, the vicar of St Petrock, in Padstow, where they have seen a great deal of Jory. He also spoke highly of him and said he was extremely well thought of in the coast guard and fishing communities. He predicted he will go far in the service. But mention of London reminds me, we had a visit here yesterday from two London policemen.'

'What on earth for, why should London policemen come to call on us here, at Trethevy?'

'One of them was the sergeant who was hired with a couple of London constables by the magistrates at Camelford to come to Cornwall and ensure there was no trouble at the fair. It seems they arrested a woman who was seen by Eliza to steal Tristram's purse and pass it to an accomplice. I believe the policemen want to speak to her about it.'

'Neither Eliza nor Tristram has said anything to me about it, I find that most surprising.'

'Not really, Alice, they both had far more important things to think about.'

While they were speaking, Eliza had entered the room from the kitchen carrying a tray on which was tea she had made for them and she heard much of their conversation.

Hurriedly putting down the tray, she queried, 'Why should policemen want to come here? Tristram and me told them all we knew and they gave Tristram back the purse the woman took from him. I can't tell 'em any more than I already have.'

'Well, I haven't seen them since, although I believe they were going to Bodmin to talk to the two people involved in the theft who were both sent to the gaol there by the Camelford magistrate. The policemen have probably learned they are wanted for a great many more crimes.'

After relating brief details to Alice and her brother of what had occurred at the Camelford fair, Eliza returned to the kitchen deeply troubled that London policemen should have called at the rectory asking for her.

Chapter Eighteen

SERGEANT GRUBB AND a constable from London's Metropolitan Police Force called at Trethevy again early the next morning, soon after David had left to take an early morning communion service at Tintagel. Eliza opened the door to them and realised straightway that their visit had nothing to do with the pick-pocketing incident at Camelford fair.

Both men were wearing the top hats and high-buttoned jackets adopted as uniform by the London police and, to her utter dismay, Eliza recognised the constable accompanying the sergeant immediately. It was the policeman who had arrested her on the charge of stealing three guineas from Sir Robert Calnan, and who had been in court to see her sentenced to transportation for a period of seven years. It was this man who spoke to her now.

'Hello, Eliza, I never expected to see you again, especially when it was reported you'd died in a shipwreck on your way to Australia. I thought at the time it had probably been a merciful release for you, but here you are again, large as life and you've hardly changed at all. I'd know you anywhere, for all that you're more than three years older and a lot prettier.'

The leer he gave her was lost on Eliza. She felt as though everything about her was revolving and would have fallen had not Sergeant Grubb stepped forward and caught her. She recovered quickly, but the whole of her body was shaking uncontrollably and he continued to support her.

He was still holding her when Alice came from inside the house to see who was at the door. At the same time Tristram appeared from the stables, where he had been cleaning out the stall recently vacated by the Kilpeck's pony.

'What do you think you are doing with my maid?'

Alice's question was interrupted by a distraught Tristram, who cried, 'Leave her alone, she's done nothing wrong.' He would have pushed past the constable to go to Eliza, but the policeman barred his way, saying, 'No you don't. Who are you, anyway?'

'I work here at the rectory – and I'm going to marry Eliza.'

'Then you're going to have to wait a long time for her. She was sentenced to seven years transportation three years ago and still has the full sentence to serve.'

Alice listened to the exchange in speechless disbelief, and Tristram repeated, 'I tell you she's done nothing wrong.'

'The judge thought otherwise,' the London constable retorted, 'and I should know, I was the one who arrested her and was in the Old Bailey when she was sentenced.'

'Then you're the one who "forgot" to tell the judge that the only money she took was what was owed her for wages, and that she left behind much more money than she'd taken, as proof she weren't no thief. You knew full well why she needed to take the money and run away but you didn't bother to tell the judge that either.'

The sergeant looked sharply at the constable, but it was to Tristram he spoke, 'None of them things matter any more, young man, she's an escaped felon and will be taken before a judge in London. The best you can hope for is that she's not given a longer sentence for escaping – although in view of the circumstances of her escape I'd say she'll most likely be treated mercifully.'

'Mercifully? To serve a sentence for something she hasn't done?'

Tristram was very close to tears and a desperately confused Alice said, 'Tell them they have made a mistake, Eliza. Tell them they must have confused you with someone else.'

Still shaking and tearful now, because of Tristram's distress, Eliza shook her head, 'It *is* true, Miss Alice … at least, what they're saying about me going to court and being sent away for seven years, but I didn't steal any money. I only took what was owed me in wages from Sir Robert's bedside cabinet, I left behind all the other money he had on there. Lady Calnan knew that.'

Pointing to the constable who had admitted having arrested her at that time, she cried, '*He* knew it too, but he never told it to the judge. He knew I wasn't no thief, and I'm *not*, Miss Alice.'

'I know that, Eliza. Try not to be too upset and we'll have all this settled in no time.'

Gathering her wits about her with some difficulty, she said to the sergeant, 'Can you leave Eliza here at the rectory while everything is sorted out – and it will be, you know?'

'I'm sorry, Miss, I've travelled all the way here with Constable Wicks to identify her as Eliza Brooks – although you know her as Eliza Smith. She's a prisoner who was sentenced to seven years transportation, and who is unlawfully at large. She'll be taken to Bow Street police station in London to appear before a magistrate, then lodged in Newgate prison until arrangements can be made to take her before a judge. He'll no doubt confirm her conviction and order that her sentence be carried out.'

'But you heard what she had to say about it, Sergeant, she is no thief, as I will testify. She has worked here at the rectory for more than three years, ever since I found her half-dead down at the cove when she was no more than a child, having miraculously survived a horrific shipwreck. Surely you can show some compassion for her.'

'I can *feel* compassion for her, Miss, and I do, but she is a convicted felon and as such my duty is to arrest her and let the law take its course.'

'Please! Will you wait until I contact my brother, Reverend Kilpeck? He is taking a Communion service at Tintagel church but will be home before too long. He will tell you ...'

Alice was distraught, but Grubb interrupted her, 'He'll be able to say nothing to prevent me performing my duty, Miss Kilpeck. Brooks – or Smith, as you know her, will be taken by Constable Wicks and myself to Padstow to catch the steamer to Bristol. From there we'll be travelling on a train to London.'

His face showing the anguish he felt, Tristram said, 'I'll come to London to see you in prison, Eliza, I promise you, and I'll do everything I can to stop them sending you away.'

Remembering the degradation of Newgate, Eliza said tearfully, 'I don't *want* you to come and see me there, Tristram. I want you to remember me as you know me here. That's how I want you both to remember me.'

'We won't need to *remember* you, Eliza, we'll have you here with us,' Alice said, determinedly. 'Don't give up hope. Reverend David and I will do absolutely everything in our power to have you released. You'll be back here with us at Trethevy and this nightmare will be over before you know it.'

Recovering from the initial shock of the arrest of the maid she trusted implicitly and for whom she had great affection, Alice was being positive for her sake, but she felt entirely helpless in the present situation and at the moment had no idea how she or David were going to be able to do anything at all about it.

The two London policemen drove off in the hired light carriage with their handcuffed prisoner squatting on the floor of the vehicle behind them, and the constable roughly warding off Tristram who ran beside the carriage as it set off, trying to reach in and grasp one of Eliza's fettered hands.

Standing at the garden gate and watching Tristram's touching but impotent actions, Alice saw Eval Moyle farther along the lane, watching what was going on. There was no apparent reason for him to be there and remembering his manner when he had stopped the carriage in which she and Eliza were returning to the rectory from their visit to Pendower, Alice thought he had undoubtedly been far more helpful to the London policemen in their enquiries than was absolutely necessary.

When a thoroughly dejected Tristram returned to the rectory, Alice gave him no time to dwell upon the misery he was so obviously feeling about the arrest of Eliza.

Giving him one of her sternest looks, she said, 'You quite obviously knew all about the problems Eliza had before she came to Trethevy, so I think you owe Reverend David and I an explanation. I will not dwell upon the disappointment I feel that neither you nor Eliza had enough trust in us to tell us about them, instead I want you to come into the rectory and tell me everything Eliza has said to you about her arrest, trial and the shipwreck which brought her to us, and how it is that the police have caught up with her after all this time. I want to know *everything*, you understand? We are going to have to act with great speed if we are to help her.'

Book Three

Chapter One

*H*ER ARREST HAD an air of unreality about it for Eliza, coming as it had after more than three happy years at the Trethevy rectory and with the prospect of life opening out still more once she was married to Tristram. Feeling numb inside, gone was the bright, resourceful girl who had found her true potential working for the Trethevy rector and his sister.

It was as though the past three years had never happened and she had reverted to being an unhappy waif with no more control over her life than she had enjoyed during her previous existence in London.

When nature and the rough state of the North Cornwall lanes brought back some feeling to her body, she said to Sergeant Grubb, 'I need to piddle.'

'Can't you wait until we reach Padstow?' Sergeant Grubb turned his head to look at her.

'I doubt if I'll be able to hold on to it until we reach the end of this bit of lane. If I don't go soon I'll wet me'self and that won't be pleasant for any of us.'

'Alright.' The sergeant said, resignedly.

Constable Wicks had the reins and the sergeant said to him, 'Pull in to the next gateway and she can go in the field.'

Guiding the horse off the road at a gateway only a short distance along the lane, Wicks said, 'I could do with going myself. You stay here and I'll take her.'

The way Wicks had looked at Eliza when she had opened the door to them at the rectory had not been lost upon the sergeant and he said, 'No you won't. *I'll* take her. You can go once I've brought her back – if that's still what you want.'

Helping Eliza from the carriage, Sergeant Grubb opened the gate for her to enter the field and led her alongside the hedgerow for a short distance before saying, 'Here's as good a place as anywhere.'

'Can't you take these handcuffs off, they're going to make it awkward for me?'

'You'll manage. I'll look away while you're going but you can keep talking so I know you're not getting up to anything you shouldn't.'

'I don't feel very much like talking, what do you want me to say?'

'Well, for a start you can tell me all about the money you took from your employer in London and why you did it. Then, if you still haven't done, you can tell me how it is you came to escape from the ship that was taking you to Australia, when everyone else on board was drowned.'

'Alright, if that's what you want, but you can turn away while I'm piddling.'

Sergeant Grubb did as he was told and, speaking to his back, Eliza gave him a shortened version of her arrest and subsequent conviction in the London court. Then, in response to a question from him she explained why she felt she had to leave Lady Calnan's household so hurriedly in order to escape the attentions of her husband.

'Why didn't you tell all this to the judge when you came to court?' The sergeant queried.

'I told Constable Wicks when he arrested me but he reminded me that I'd been a workhouse girl when I was put into service and he asked me what else I had expected to happen? He said I ought to have been grateful enough to Sir Robert to give him what he wanted in exchange for being allowed to work in a fine house with good food and a roof over my head. He said I should have thought myself lucky to be doing it in bed with a titled gent and not in a back alley with some worthless street hooligan who'd probably been with half the poxed-up whores in Shoreditch.'

'He said that to you when you were ... how old? No more than thirteen?'

'That's right, so if *he* wouldn't take any notice of me I knew it would be no good telling it to a judge who was probably friends with Sir Robert anyway.'

'What about this ship you were being transported on, how is it that *you* escaped when everyone else was drowned?

Eliza sighed, 'It's a long story, far too long to tell you now, and I've finished piddling, so unless you've changed your mind and are going to let me go back to Trethevy we might as well get on with what you have to do. I got used to the idea of being transported once – though I didn't even really know what it meant then – so I suppose I can get used to it again. I've had three lovely years working for Miss Alice, which is probably more than I've ever deserved, I can always remember that when I'm unhappy. I dread having to go back to a hulk again, but I suppose I'll get used to that too, in time.'

Eliza was very close to tears and Sergeant Grubb said, gruffly, 'Like I said to your employer, I feel sorry for you, girl, but I'm paid to arrest those who break the law and however you look at it that's what you've done. Mind you, there are different ways of doing this job and if you've been telling me the truth then I'll be having words with Constable Wicks about the way *he* does it.'

Back at the entrance to the field, Wicks was leaning on the gate, puffing on a briar pipe and when they reached him he said with a smirk, 'I hope you kept a close eye on her all the time, Sergeant?'

'I did what needed to be done, no more, and no less, and you are on duty, Constable, so you can put out that pipe right now.'

Grumbling, Wicks said, 'I was only making sure you'd remembered what Mr Moyle told us, she can take people in.'

'Moyle? Eval Moyle?' Eliza said incredulously, 'You've been talking to him about me? He hates Reverend Kilpeck and Alice and he hates me because I work for them. Moyle is a bully, a violent man, and a liar. You won't hear him say anything good about anyone. You ask Lieutenant Kendall, he was threatened by Moyle.'

'Are you speaking of Lieutenant Kendall the coast guard officer? How do you know him?'

'He and Miss Alice will likely be getting married sometime soon. He's been coming to the rectory for more than three years and me and Miss Alice were staying at his home where his father Lord Kendall lives until yesterday. It was Lieutenant Kendall who took me and Tristram to Camelford fair in his father's carriage.'

'You move in high circles for a workhouse girl,' Constable Wicks said, scornfully, 'but he'll drop you like a hot potato when he knows what sort of young woman you really are.'

'Lieutenant Kendall knows *exactly* what sort of person I really am,' Eliza retorted, 'and if he'd been at the rectory when you came there he wouldn't have let you take me off, I'll tell you that. He'll be *Commander* Kendall soon and he's in London at the Admiralty right now. As for Eval Moyle ... I bet he didn't tell you that he had to run off to America because the Truro magistrate put out a warrant for his arrest when he started a riot there.'

As she was talking Alice realised that so many things were falling into place. Moyle had been at Camelford Fair. He must have overheard what Maudie Huggins had said about her and told the London police sergeant about the storm when so many ships had foundered in the waters around Cornwall – including the ship carrying the convict women to Australia – and how she had been found among rocks in the cove where another ship had been wrecked and everyone believed her to have been the sole survivor from *this* vessel.

Even as all the facts dropped into place, Police Constable Wicks put her present predicament into perspective when he remarked sneeringly, 'Whatever *you* think about Mr Moyle, he wasn't wrong about you, was he? You are an escaped convict who's been living a lie for more than three years.'

'I was only a convict because you never told the whole truth about me to the judge. You may not have actually lied about me, but if you'd told him about what Sir Robert Calnan did – and that I'd only taken what he owed me from his money I would never have been on a convict ship. I might never even have gone before a judge. You're just as bad as Moyle but in a different way, that's all.'

Constable Wicks tried to shrug off her accusation with a dismissive smile in the direction of his companion, but the London police sergeant had climbed into the driving seat of the carriage and was looking straight ahead impassively.

Chapter Two

*T*HE LAST GESTURE of kindness made towards Eliza before she was thrown into the legal system of England's capital city came from the wife of Padstow's constable.

Shut up in the small fishing port's lock-up, Eliza's story was told to the woman by her husband, and the kindly Cornishwoman took her food, soap, towel and a blanket. Then she stayed talking to her for more than an hour, trying to give what comfort she could to the dejected young prisoner.

When the woman had gone Eliza was left to her own thoughts which grew ever gloomier with the passing of the hours. When darkness fell she cried herself into a fitful sleep that was frequently disturbed by a rat, or a mouse – it was too dark inside the lock-up to identify the inquisitive rodent – which scurried back and forth among the beams in the low-ceilinged and windowless room.

Soon after dawn the sympathetic constable's wife brought Eliza a cooked breakfast, explaining that the London policemen would soon be along to collect her because the steamer travelling between Hayle and Bristol was due to pass by the mouth of the river estuary at eight o'clock and only prospective passengers waiting in a boat out in the bay would be picked up.

'It'll be another twelve hours before it reaches Bristol, and there's no telling when your next meal will be coming, m'dear.

Them two policers being men, and from Lunnon at that, will satisfy their own bellies but I doubt if they'll give much thought for anyone else. You get this down you and I'll know you'll be alright for the rest of the day. My Bob's the constable here and he's told me your story and why you're being taken up to that wicked city. You'd think that after what you went through when you were shipwrecked, they'd have better things to do than come all this way just to arrest you. There's many around here who deserve to be going, but some seem to get away with any-thing they like. Now you take that young Winnie from Trevone ...'

Eliza ate her breakfast in silence while the constable's kindly wife related the story of 'Winnie' who, it seemed, frequented the bars down by the harbour, picking up foreign sailors and as well as satisfying their 'lustrous' needs, also succeeded in relieving many of them of their purses as well.

'I can see *you* ain't that kind of maid,' said the woman as she took the empty plate from Eliza and made her way from the lock-up, 'and I shall tell they two Lunnon policers they ought to be ashamed of themselves coming all the way down here to Cornwall just to take a young girl away to a wicked place where I'm told most of the women are like that Winnie, 'specially as my Bob tells me you've spent the last three years taking good care of a preacher and his sister. It's a pity they folk up Lunnon way don't have better things to do.'

With this observation, the constable's wife left the tiny cell and went on her way, grumbling to herself about the shortcomings of 'they folk from Lunnon.'

No more than ten minutes after the woman's departure Sergeant Grubb and Constable Wicks came to the lock-up and she was handcuffed and taken through the streets of Padstow, a subject of great interest to those who were abroad at this early hour. Boarding a waiting boat, she and the two London policemen were then rowed out of the estuary to await the Bristol bound steamer.

Once on board the vessel, Eliza shared a cabin with her escort and, in spite of the Padstow woman's gloomy prediction, was given a meal at noon which proved to be her last meal of the day.

Soon after eight o'clock that evening the steamer berthed at a dock in the very heart of Bristol, where it was surrounded by the noise and bustle of one of the country's busiest ports.

It was the first city Eliza had been to since leaving London and she found the activity going on about her intimidating, but there was little time to observe it in detail before she was bustled inside a closed police van and driven through the streets to the police headquarters, only a short distance from the docks.

Here she was locked in a large, communal cell which had only dank straw strewn on the floor on which to sleep with no bedding and a couple of wooden buckets to serve as toilets for a number of women, mainly thieves and drunkards, with whom she would be sharing the cell.

There was little sleep for Eliza that night. Not only were many of the women noisy and fractious, but their numbers were frequently supplemented throughout the night hours by a number of complaining prostitutes who had been arrested in the busy port, most having frequented the many dockside bars and inns that catered for sailors from all over the world.

The next morning, Eliza was taken from the cell by the two London policemen and without breakfast and having had no time to wash or otherwise tidy herself, she was driven to the railway station in the same police van that had conveyed her from the police station the previous evening. Here she and her escort boarded a London bound train.

Four hours later, thoroughly depressed by the sight of row

upon row of London houses backing on to the railway line, all of which seemed dirty and dreary in comparison to Cornwall, the train arrived at its destination and she was taken in a Hackney carriage to Bow Street police station.

Here Sergeant Grubb managed to obtain a bowl of soup and a hunk of bread for her but she barely had time to finish it before she was hustled before a stony-faced magistrate. After listening to the charges against her and speaking only to ask confirmation of her name, he remanded her in custody to Newgate, 'In order that further enquiries might be made.'

She was escorted to the prison handcuffed to Sergeant Grubb and on the way asked him how long she was likely to remain in Newgate.

'I shouldn't think it'll be too long,' was the reply. 'They'll need to find the record of your conviction and sentence and have Constable Wicks formally identify you as being Eliza Brooks. Then I'll give evidence about the manner of your escape from the ship taking you to Australia and your subsequent arrest, then you'll be sent back to the Old Bailey for a judge to decide on whether you'll be sent to Australia again for seven years, or whether he'll add to it because you escaped from custody.'

'It wasn't exactly an "escape",' Eliza pointed out, close to tears, 'I was got off the ship by the Mate. If anyone helped me "escape" it was him but you can't do anything to him because he was drowned, and if it wasn't for him so would I be. But perhaps it would have been better if I had been.'

'Now don't get thinking like that, girl. I know things look bad for you now, but while there's life there's hope, and I believe there are a lot of women sent to Australia who settle down and eventually make a good life there for themselves.'

'I had made a good life for myself, in Cornwall and would have settled down to a good life with a kind husband! Anyway, what you're saying ain't what I heard before, when I was on the hulk waiting for a ship to take me out there. According to the women who knew all about transportation it's hell on the ship going out there and even worse once you've arrived.'

'Well, as you know yourself, you can't believe everything people tell you, especially the sort of women who are in prison.'

'You mean the sort of women like *me*?'

Sergeant Grubb found he had no answer to Eliza's embittered question and he remained silent.

That night, at home with his wife, soon after his young daughter had gone to bed, Sergeant Grubb spoke to his wife about Eliza, commenting that he felt very sorry for the predicament she was in, having spent the last three years making a good and honest life for herself.

During all the years they had been married, Sergeant Grubb's wife had never known him to be so visibly moved over any of those he had arrested in the course of his duties.

'She sounds as though she is a nice girl who has been really hard done by. Isn't there anything you can do to help her?'

'I can tell the court how she has spent the past three years and how highly she is praised by everyone who knows her, but that won't alter the fact that she is under sentence of seven years transportation. The best she can hope for is that the sentence won't be increased and I can't guarantee that.'

'It sounds very hard to me,' his wife said. 'It's a pity she hasn't got someone to speak up for her. I hate to think of a young girl like our Mary suffering in that way with no father, or anyone else, to speak up for her.'

'So do I,' Sergeant Grubb said unhappily. 'It kept me awake last night worrying about it, but I can't think of anything I can possibly do to help her.'

Eliza's plight kept him awake again that night. Lying in bed beside his sleeping wife, he went over the case in his mind, trying desperately hard to think of any way he might possibly be able to help her.

Chapter Three

NEWGATE PRISON HAD not changed. It was still the place of Eliza's nightmares and memories came flooding back as soon as the first iron-barred door slammed shut behind her and the smell of the place hit home in full force. It was the stench of unwashed bodies, primitive sanitation and the indefinable odour of human misery.

She had been travelling for two days without a wash or an opportunity to tidy herself to any degree, but her dress and personal appearance were still far superior to any of the women with whom she would be sharing a large, straw-strewn communal cell, and because of this she attracted unwanted attention.

A few of the women crowded around her, eyeing her up and down and one of them quipped, 'Well look at this, they're treating us as ladies at last and have brought in a maid to look after our every need. I think we'll start off by having tea and biscuits, ducks, and mind you use the best china, we're expecting guests.'

Her words brought forth a mixture of jeers and coarse laughter and one prisoner, big-busted and grossly overweight said, 'I like those clothes you're wearing, dearie, some of my men get a thrill out of seeing women wearing clothes like that. I've often wondered what they'd do if *I* was to dress myself up as a housemaid.'

Another of the women, carrying only marginally less weight than the one who had spoken to Eliza now said, 'You try putting on what she's wearing and your blokes will see more of you than they'll enjoy seeing, because more than half of you'll be hanging out.'

Her comment provoked more laughter and the first speaker turned on her angrily, 'Are you saying I'm fat?'

'It don't matter whether I'm saying it or not, you *are* fat. Fat as a pregnant old sow.'

'Why you…!' The insulted woman launched her considerable weight at her insulter and they both fell to the floor scattering straw about them as they screamed obscenities, at the same time yanking out hair and throwing wild blows at each other.

The communal cell erupted in noise as the women convicts encouraged one or other of the combatants, the sound quickly spreading to other cells, some of whose occupants could see what was happening, others merely using it as an excuse to make a noise.

It was not long before warders had gathered in sufficient numbers to enter the cell safely with batons flailing and the participants were seized and dragged off to one of the prison's 'cold holes' where they would remain for a few days in order to cool off.

The incident had unnerved Eliza, but at least her clothes were safe for the moment. One of the prisoners who had watched the antics of the two fighting women with quiet contempt now approached and asked Eliza, 'Are you all right?'

When Eliza nodded, the woman said, 'My name's Grace, what's yours?'

When she was told, Grace said, 'We're well rid of those two, they're women of the worst type, selling themselves for the price of a gin in the alleyways behind the dockland ale-houses. One of them had the cheek to ask me if I would take her on when she got out. I told her, someone like her would frighten *my* gentlemen away! Now you're very different, Eliza, a girl like you could make a great deal of money in my establishment in Covent Garden, especially dressed up in a neat and clean maid's uniform. You have the looks and the bearing that attracts men. With a little tuition from some of my girls you'd soon be attracting your own regulars. What are you in here for?'

Eliza had quickly realised this woman was a brothel keeper, but she was obviously of a class above the other occupants of the communal women's cell who appeared to leave her alone. It would be as well to remain on a friendly footing with her if it were at all possible.

'I was sentenced to seven years transportation for stealing from my employer, even though I only took what was owing to me in wages. That was three years ago, but the ship taking me was wrecked in a storm. Luckily – or so I thought at the time – I survived. I've spent the time since then working as a ladies' maid, in Cornwall.'

'What a *fascinating* story, my dear, but that means of course you will be sent off to complete your sentence.'

Eliza was aware the woman was disappointed that she would not be able to recruit her to entertain the men who frequented her 'establishment' but, anxious to keep her as an ally, she asked, 'How long will you be in here?'

'Only until one of my many influential men friends hears of my predicament and pays the fine imposed on me by one of the few magistrates in the area who is not one of my regular visitors.'

Looking speculatively at Eliza, Grace said, 'I don't suppose you have any influential friends able to make life easier for you while you are in here?'

Eliza shook her head, 'All the friends I made are in Cornwall and that's a long way from Newgate.'

'I wouldn't know, my dear, I have never found it necessary to venture away from London and because of that I am familiar with all aspects of city life … even what goes on here, in this ghastly prison. I know the head warder and his little whims very well. If I explained them to you and informed him that you were willing to be nice to him, life in here could be far more pleasant for you – indeed, for both of us. What do you say?'

Despite her wish to keep this woman on her side, Eliza was unwilling to pay the price Grace was asking for her friendship. 'It's because I wouldn't be nice to the husband of my employer that I was sentenced to transportation in the first place. I'm not likely to change the way I think just to make things a bit more comfortable here, in prison.'

Looking at Eliza disdainfully, Grace said, 'Then more fool you. Every time you sit down you are sitting on a fortune, why not use it and make life easier for yourself?'

Angry now, Eliza threw caution to the wind, 'If you are so good at giving good advice, what are you doing in here with all the rest of the women like me who've broken the law?'

'I am here simply because I failed to pay enough to the police-men on the beat to close their eyes when they saw men coming to my house at all times of the day and night. One of them became greedy when I failed to pay what he asked and so he would stand right outside the door, watching the world go by. He frightened off those gentlemen to whom discretion is most important, with the result that my income fell off so alarmingly I had less to pay to those policemen who were more amenable. One of them reported me to his superior officers in a fit of pique and my estab-lishment was raided. But why am I telling this to you? You have the chance to make things easier for both of us, my dear. If you are foolish enough to turn down such an opportunity then I am afraid you must accept the consequences.'

*

Eliza had very little sleep that night in Newgate prison. The communal cell was extremely crowded and included among their number were women who should have been committed to an asylum. One of these was a young woman who alternated between pleas to The Lord to take her, and shrieks of loud insane laughter.

Then, just as Eliza was dozing off in the early hours of the morning there was a stealthy movement before she felt the hands of someone searching her body, seeking anything that might prove to be of value.

Lashing out with her fist, she struck the unseen would-be robber in the face and had the satisfaction of hearing a grunt of pain, then the woman was gone but Eliza found she was unable to sleep for the remainder of the night.

In the morning one of a group of gipsy women who had been arrested under the Vagrancy Act sported a bruised eye and, confronting her, Eliza warned that if the actions of the previous night were repeated, this time she would ensure she had something heavy in her hand when she struck out.

Eliza hoped this would be the end of the incident but later, when a cauldron of soup was brought in as the main meal of the day, she found great difficulty pushing her way through the gipsies in order to reach the cauldron. She eventually succeeded, only to have the bowl of soup 'accidently' knocked from her hand as she returned with it to a place in the corner of the cell.

Eliza faced the prospect of going to bed hungry that night but, unexpectedly, Grace came and sat down on the straw beside her and produced bread and cheese. Handing it to her, she said, 'Don't ask where it came from, just accept that it's from "an admirer". See sense and not only will there be more to come but you might even be given a cell to yourself.'

Wolfing down bread and cheese quickly in case Grace should decide to take it back, Eliza said, 'I'm grateful for the food, but I told you, I'm in here because I refused to give a man what he wanted from me. Besides, before I was arrested again I had agreed to marry someone in Cornwall, a good man who would look after me properly.'

'That was in Cornwall,' Grace retorted, 'but you're never likely to meet up with him again. You're in Newgate now and have upset that lot over there.' She indicated the gipsies, 'So if you stay here things can only get worse. When are you expecting to be taken before the judge?'

'I don't know, nobody has told me.'

'Well think about what I've said. It's entirely up to you whether you appear before him looking clean and tidy, creating a good impression, or stand in the dock dirty and unkempt, looking like one of them.' Once again she jerked her head in the direction of the gipsies.

That night the hopelessness of her situation flooded over Eliza as never before and she cried silently for many of the hours of darkness. Fortunately, no one tried to rob her but, just in case, she kept a firm grip on the only thing of value that she possessed, the silver heart necklace that Tristram had bought for her at Camelford fair.

The thought of Tristram made her tears flow even faster and by morning, tired and defeated, she was in such a despondent frame of mind she was almost ready to agree to any proposal Grace might put to her, but the self-confessed brothel keeper seemed to be avoiding her.

Then, early that afternoon, Eliza received a surprise visit from the governor of the prison – and with him was Commander The Honourable Jory Kendall in full naval uniform!

Chapter Four

*E*VENTS MOVED FAST for Eliza following the arrival of Jory Kendall. Feeling as though she was in a dream from which she feared she would all too soon wake up, she was led from the crowded communal cell and taken to a small, single cell which, while by no means luxurious, was vastly superior to the one she had just left, even having a wooden sleeping bench on which she would be able to sit during the day.

Here, showing considerable deference to the now-senior naval officer, the governor said he would leave them alone for a while, telling Jory he should call for one of the warders should he wish to leave the prison before the governor's return.

When he had gone, a tearful Eliza stammered her thanks to Jory for coming to find her in the prison, asking, 'Has Miss Alice written to you and asked you to come here to try to make things more comfortable for me?'

Jory had been shocked by the tired and dishevelled appearance of Eliza but, trying not to allow his feelings to show, he replied, 'No, although I have no doubt an urgent letter from her is on its way, but I had a visit from Sergeant Grubb, the policeman we both met at Camelford fair, and who arrested and brought you here from Trethevy. He is a kindly man, Eliza. Although he had no alternative but to carry out his duty to arrest you and bring you here, he is not happy about the circumstances of your conviction. Despite the knowledge that his career would be at risk should his superiors learn of it, he came to see me at the Admiralty and informed me of your arrest, and told me the story behind it.'

'How did he know where to find you? When you last met you were both in Cornwall.'

'He said you told him on the journey from Cornwall that I was here in London. But to get back to the *reason* for you being here, why did you never tell Miss Alice about your past? She would have realised, as Sergeant Grubb obviously does, that your conviction was an appalling miscarriage of justice and would have judged you solely on your loyalty and service to her.'

'We neither of us knew anything about each other when she found me among the rocks after the storm. Had I told her before she really got to know me, she and Reverend Kilpeck would have felt obliged to report me to the magistrates and they would have arrested me and sent me back here. Instead, I had the chance to make a new life for myself and prove to everyone that I'm honest. Besides, I loved working for Miss Alice and was so happy at Trethevy I didn't want to risk losing everything. I was even happier when I got to know Tristram and he said he wanted to marry me. I thought that once we were married I would be taking his name so no one would ever know I'd once been Eliza *Brooks*. Now it's all gone wrong and I'm back in prison, waiting to be transported once more. I'll never see Tristram ever again and it was wrong to let him fall in love with me. But I did tell him all about me after that woman at the fair said who I was. I should have told Miss Alice and Reverend Kilpeck then too, but I was afraid they wouldn't want me working for them any more. Will you tell her I didn't mean for this ever to happen and that I could never have found someone nicer than her to work for?'

Jory thought he had never seen anyone quite as unhappy as

Eliza was right now. He felt he wanted to hug her and tell her that everything was going to be all right, but he could do neither. All he was able to do was tell her there was still hope.

'You must not give up, Eliza. I believe in you and I don't have the slightest doubt that Miss Alice, Reverend Kilpeck and Tristram do too, just as Sergeant Grubb does. So if all goes as well as I hope it will, you'll be able to tell her yourself.'

'What do you mean? What can you do? The judge sentenced me to transportation and nothing can change that. Even Sergeant Grubb said so.'

'Well, that is what he believed, but I intend *trying* to do something about it. First, I need you to tell me exactly what happened all those years ago to make the judge believe you were guilty of stealing that money. Tell me everything you can possibly remember about it and I'll see if there is anything that *can* be done. In the meantime, while I am trying you will be staying here, in this cell alone and I'll give the prison governor enough money to ensure you are given everything you need. Now, take your time and tell me what happened to you....'

Later, having listened to Eliza's account of all that had contributed to her arrest and conviction and promising he would do all he could for her, Jory was leaving the prison when he passed the communal cell where Eliza had been held prior to his visit. There was another quarrel going on and the noise and language was more foul than on any mess-deck occupied by sailors on a man-of-war.

He realised these were the type of women Eliza would be incarcerated with on board a transport taking her to far-off Australia. Jory had known a number of officers and men who had served on board the transports and was aware that by the time they had arrived at their destinations they had become little more than floating brothels where convicted women had no rights and had been forced to accept they were there to be used by whoever wanted them.

Jory determined that Eliza would not be subjected to such a fate. He would leave no stone unturned in his efforts to prove her innocence and succeed in having the conviction against her quashed.

Jory had intended putting off finding Lady Calnan until the following day but after his visit to Newgate he decided to begin making enquiries about her straightaway.

Back at the Admiralty he informed his colleagues of what he was doing and was told by a fellow officer that Lady Calnan had been involved in a much publicised divorce the previous year. He also knew that she was almoner in St Bartholomew's Hospital and Jory decided he would try to speak to her there.

The smart young naval commander in full naval uniform attracted a great deal of attention at the hospital and the staff were eager to be helpful. A messenger was sent off to inform Lady Calnan he was there and she immediately invited him to her impressive office.

Lady Calnan was a woman of middle age, with an aristocratic bearing, but she looked very tired and Jory felt that she was probably a dedicated woman who threw herself wholeheartedly into the work she was doing, caring for the welfare of the poorest of the hospital's patients and their families. He felt optimistic that she might prove sympathetic to his self-imposed quest.

Reading from the visiting card Jory had given to him, the messenger introduced him rather grandly to Lady Calnan as 'Commander the Honourable Jory Kendall' and, standing up to greet him, she said, 'I am pleased to meet with you, Commander, but what is a handsome young naval officer doing calling on an elderly woman like me?'

Waving him to a seat on the opposite side of the desk, she

added, 'Are you perhaps here on behalf of the family of one of your ratings?'

'No, Lady Calnan, it is a far more personal matter, and one I sincerely hope is not going to cause you any embarrassment.'

'I am intrigued, Commander Kendall, it has been many years since anyone succeeded in embarrassing me. Do go on.'

'It concerns someone you employed more than three years ago, a young housemaid named Eliza Brooks, I don't know if you remember her?'

The expression on the almoner's face changed immediately, 'Of course I remember her. Indeed, I doubt whether I will ever be able to forget the poor, unfortunate child. She was found guilty of stealing three guineas from my then husband, and sentenced to transportation. She *never* stole money from him, Commander, but took only what was owed her from a large sum of money he had placed on a bedside table, leaving the remainder there. It was not the action of a thief. Furthermore, if Robert had not tried to take advantage of her she would never have taken anything and would probably still be working for me. It was a case that should never have been taken to court especially since, as I understand it, the ship on which she was being transported was wrecked in a storm and she and all the other unfortunate women on board died. It is a tragedy I will have on my conscience to the end of my days.'

Suddenly, Lady Calnan's eyes misted up and she said, 'There, I am showing emotions in front of a complete stranger so you *have* succeeded in embarrassing me, Commander Kendall.'

'For which I apologise, Lady Calnan, but I am also able to offer you an opportunity to ease your conscience once and for all. Eliza did *not* die when the ship carrying her to Australia foundered.'

The almoner looked at him in disbelief. 'But it was reported in the newspapers at the time. There was a dreadful storm and a number of ships foundered. The vessel on which she was being transported was wrecked. I believe it was on the rocks of Lundy Island. Everyone on board perished.'

'Everyone except Eliza. She was saved by a brave ship's mate who, although he himself was lost, succeeded in tying Eliza to the broken mast of a ship's boat and she was washed up on the beach in a Cornish cove. Although *close* to death, she was saved by the sister of a rector in charge of a small, coastal parish. Here, assuming another name, she has been working for the past three years as a personal maid. A very trusted and loyal maid.'

'Is this true, Commander? Are you absolutely certain? If so, you have brought me news that will give me great joy and peace of mind, but why are you here to tell me of this now? What is *your* connection with Eliza?'

'I was in charge of Cornish coast guards at the time of the storm and actually helped in the rescue of Eliza. I have met her many times since then because I hope to marry the rector's sister for whom she has been working. Both I and Alice, her employer, have a great affection for the girl, partly because of the manner in which she came into our lives, but also for the many ways in which she has proved her loyalty time and time again, towards both of us. I recently took Eliza and the young man she hopes to marry to a fair being held in Cornwall and while there she was instrumental in arresting a couple who were picking the pockets of those attending the fair. Unfortunately Eliza was recognised by the woman pickpocket and as a result she has been re-arrested. At this very moment she is in Newgate prison, from where she will undoubtedly be transported to serve the sentence imposed upon her more than three years ago – unless it can be proven she has been victim of a miscarriage of justice.'

'As indeed she was!' Lady Calnan said, emphatically. 'A *grave* miscarriage of justice, but how can I help?'

'I discussed the case at some length late last night with an uncle who is a Judge of the Queen's Bench. He has agreed that if I can provide him with firm evidence that a miscarriage of justice has occurred, he will take immediate steps to right the wrong and Eliza will be pardoned and freed. Would you be willing to sign a written statement declaring what you have just told me, that she took only what was owed to her and left a much larger sum – and also the reason why she took the money in the first place?'

Jory thought she might draw the line at saying anything against the man who had been her husband at the time, even though they were now divorced but he was delighted when she said, 'It was not the first time my husband had interfered with the maids nor, unfortunately, the last. I will happily, *most* happily, sign a statement to that effect and also give Eliza the character reference she should have had at the time of her trial. There is a resident lawyer in the hospital, we will call him to my office now and you can take my statement away with you. You will go with my everlasting gratitude and a sum of money which I hope may compensate Eliza in a small way for my failure to give her support when it was so desperately needed.'

Chapter Five

*T*RISTRAM AND PERCY were clearing an overgrown corner of the rectory garden where it was intended to plant a shrubbery, supervised by a rather lack-lustre Alice when they heard the sound of horses and a wheeled vehicle making its way along the lane.

It was twelve days since Eliza's arrest and despite sending three letters to Jory, giving him details of the arrest and, in the last letter, actually *begging* him to find out details of what was happening to her, she had heard nothing.

In desperation she had written to Lady Kendall too, asking whether Jory was in fact still at the Admiralty in London, informing her of the reason she wanted to know.

She had received an extremely sympathetic reply from Lowena, saying her mother and father were taking a holiday on the Continent and expressing deep concern for Eliza, whom she described as being a 'lovely young girl' who had been highly praised by Jory.

Lowena promised *she* would write to him and that she was confident he would do everything in his power to help Eliza.

In the meantime, Alice was having problems with Tristram. At his request, when he had begun working at Trethevy she had kept the bulk of his earnings for safekeeping in the rectory and now she had refused to hand it over to him when he announced that he intended going to London to learn what was happening to Eliza.

Instead, she had promised that when news was received from Jory she would take him to London, at the expense of Reverend Kilpeck and herself, to do whatever was possible to make life more comfortable for Eliza.

Tristram had not been happy with her decision and Percy, concerned about what might happen to a young countryman in a big city like London, had warned her that Tristram was seriously contemplating leaving Trethevy and making his way to the capital, with or without money.

Now, listening to the vehicle in the lane and grateful for the opportunity to straighten up and ease his aching back, Percy said, 'That don't sound like no farm wagon to me.'

'How can you tell?' Alice asked.

'Because a farm wagon creaks and groans like my old bones,' Percy replied, 'and whatever's coming along don't. It's squeaking and rattling like a carriage that ain't used to such lanes as we've got hereabouts.'

Whilst doubting whether the old man had sufficient knowledge of vehicles to differentiate between them merely by their sound, Alice was sufficiently intrigued to walk towards the gate to see what might be passing.

To her surprise it was a carriage drawn by two horses and as it came to a halt in front of the gate, she recognised the Kendalls' groom who had brought her back to Trethevy after her visit to Pendower.

Tristram recognised both coach and groom too and believing, as Alice did, that it must be Jory with news of Eliza, he threw down the shovel with which he had been working and hurried to the gate to join her.

It *was* Jory and as the groom jumped down from the carriage and opened the door he stepped out and gave Alice a happy smile. Opening the gate to go and meet him, Alice asked eagerly, 'You have news of…?'

She stopped and looked in amazed delight as Jory turned and helped an uncertain but very smartly dressed Eliza from the carriage.

'Eliza! What has happened? How is it…?' Suddenly lost for words, Alice rushed towards the young girl and the next moment was hugging her close. Both women were tearful, but, remembering Tristram, Alice stepped aside and the next moment Eliza was being held close by her future husband.

'It seems there is a hug for everyone but me,' Jory said, ruefully.

Pulling away from Tristram, but finding his hand and holding it painfully tightly, Eliza said, 'Commander Jory deserves the biggest hug of all! He's proved that I never stole money from Sir Robert Calnan, and made them give me a written pardon to say I'd never done nothing wrong. He bought me these new clothes too, and says I can wear them for when I get married, but I've washed and ironed my maid's clothes, Miss Alice, and I've got 'em with me.'

'Oh Eliza, it's so wonderful to see you back here and to know you have not changed one iota.'

The statement called for another hug from Alice and, when it ended, Eliza said, 'I am so happy you're pleased to see me again. Like I told Commander Jory, I was afraid you might not want to have me at Trethevy again, after the lies I told you about myself.'

'Eliza, I really don't think I could manage without you now, and as for what you told me about yourself after you recovered from the shipwreck … I fully realise you could have done nothing else. You did not know me then and I might well have turned you over to the magistrate. I honestly believe that had I found myself in your situation I would have done exactly the same. Come, we will all go into the house and enjoy a cup of tea. Percy as well, as it is a very special occasion, then *Commander* Jory can tell us all how he was able to perform this wonderful miracle.'

It took a long while for the full story to be told and, halfway through the telling Reverend David returned to the house and it had to be re-told.

Jory disclosed that once his uncle was in possession of all the facts, he used his considerable influence to have a full pardon issued for Eliza and even managed to have a small amount of compensation paid to her from the public purse.

Once she had been freed, Jory had bought her new clothes, then travelled with her to his parents' home where, as she proudly stated, Lowena treated her more like a lady than a servant, and as soon as was possible, Jory brought her back to Trethevy.

When all the explanations had been made and some of the excitement had died down, Tristram and Eliza were allowed to go off together for a while and Jory said he would like to take Alice for a short ride in the Kendall carriage. He would not say why, but he was unusually insistent and eventually a puzzled Alice agreed.

After a whispered conversation between Jory and the groom, Alice was handed into the carriage and, with Jory seated opposite to her, the carriage set off.

They had not travelled very far when the groom cautiously guided the carriage on to a track that was very badly rutted and, looking out through the glass of the carriage window, Alice said, 'Where are we going? This track leads to Eval Moyle's farm.'

'That's right.'

Jory's curt reply was accompanied by no explanation and Alice said, 'Why are we coming here? If you have any score to settle with Moyle you are too late. He and his brother left yesterday to go to America.'

'I know.'

Once again there was no explanation and Alice said, 'But if the Moyles have left, why *are* we coming here?'

'Have you ever been to the Moyle farm before?'

'No, there was no reason why I should, and a great many reasons why I should not! Have you?'

'Yes, a long time ago, when a boat that was part-owned by Moyle was confiscated by the coast guards for smuggling and Moyle's part in it was being investigated. There was insufficient evidence to implicate him but the boat was never returned. I was surprised that a man like Moyle should live in such a beautiful spot as this, but you'll see it for yourself, we are almost there now.'

Moments later the carriage halted in a small, sheltered valley, hidden from the road by a number of tall elm trees Here, in front of a rambling and decidedly tumbledown house, a stream gathered speed over and between rocks on its way down to the sea, which could be seen beyond a thick carpet of gorse that followed the course of the stream.

Helping a still-puzzled Alice from the carriage, Jory said, 'Here we are, this was the home of the Moyle family, what do you think of it?'

'Well, the house is in keeping with a man like Moyle, but its position is not. As you said before we reached here, it is beautiful, really beautiful, and that view is magnificent. But why have you brought me here?'

'Because it is important to me that you like it. You see, as soon as I knew the Moyles had put it up for sale, I asked my solicitor to buy it for me, keeping it a strict secret that it was *I* who wanted it, of course. As a result I purchased it for what is really a bargain price.'

'You have bought it ... but why? The house is in a dreadful state. You could not possibly live in it.'

'That's why I have an architect coming from London next week to look at the spot and design a house, a mansion, to be built in its place.'

Stunned by the news of Jory's purchase and the plans he had for the Moyle farm, it was only now that a ridiculous explanation came to Alice of why he might have brought her here.

'It is all very exciting, Jory, but why is it so important that you should bring me here to see it today, of all days?'

'Because this has been a very happy day for so many of us, Alice, and I needed you to see it because I hope you will come here often before the architect arrives, so you can decide what you want, and where.'

'What *I* want? It is to be *your* house, Jory.'

'Well, that is another reason I wanted you to see it all before the plans for the house were drawn up and approved. I don't think I could live here alone, Alice, and if you are going to share it with me then it is important that you should have the house exactly as you wish it to be. Not only that, I wanted us to always be able to remember it was here that I asked you to marry me. So, will you, Alice Kilpeck?'

For a few moments, Alice found it difficult to breathe, let alone talk, but when her breath returned, she said, 'When you arrived with Eliza you complained that everyone was being hugged except you. Before I give you my answer I think we should remedy that....'